The Shoe Tree

DORIS OBERSTEIN

This is a work of fiction. Names, characters, organizations, places, events, and incidents are either products of the author's imagination or are used fictitiously.

For MOM and DAD

I wish you were here to share my life-long dream.

PREFACE

I've been influenced by Thornton Wilder's 1928 Pulitzer Prize winning novel, *The Bridge of San Luis Rey*. He based many of his chapters upon the lives of five interrelated characters who died in the collapse of an ancient bridge in Peru. Wilder explores the timeless question: "Is there a direction and meaning in lives beyond the individual's own will?" My interpretation presents another view of how everyday people cope with events in their lives.

"We all go through the world trapped in our story, our own point of view."

~Richard Linklater

Chapter 1

It was Liz's turn at the wheel, but hours of driving during the night and the monotony of the car's headlights on the desolate, featureless road had lulled her into a trance. Afraid of nodding off and perhaps losing control of the car, she blinked hard and dug her fingernails into her palm, forcing herself to focus. Her mind kept wandering. *Here I am, five months pregnant; and we're driving across the country to visit Dwayne's parents. What was I thinking when I agreed to this fiasco of a trip? Am I crazy?*

As if on cue, the baby gave her a small flurry of kicks. She patted her small roundness to let the baby know she understood and would take care of everything. She glanced at Dwayne, hoping he'd offer to spell her, but he seemed to be sound asleep. She smiled and blew him a juicy kiss. Nothing short of a bomb would rouse him; he was extremely tired after driving for too many hours. But in her condition, she also deserved the rest.

He must have sensed her need because he opened his eyes and yawned. "Pull over, hon, I'll take over for a while."

As the sun projected its first shafts of light, Dwayne pulled into the deserted rest area off the highway. The colorful panorama of turquoise and cerise clouds reflecting the brilliant sunrise was lost on him because he had only one thing on his mind; something he'd eaten had given him severe cramps. He rushed into the dimly lit men's restroom. Just as he unzipped his jeans, an obese man with a hooded sweatshirt and dark sunglasses barged into the stall, almost breaking the door hinges.

"O.K., sucker, gimme your wallet!" the intruder snarled. His breath smelled of liquor. The knife in his hand shook.

Afraid of angering the armed stranger, Dwayne swallowed hard and willed himself to remain calm. "Wait a damn minute!

You're asking the wrong guy. I'm down to my last few bucks." He took out his wallet and handed over thirty-one dollars. Without another word, the robber snatched the money and ran.

Hours later, his composure regained, Dwayne rolled past an enormous stand of Joshua trees. He saluted them, recalling a childhood story of a group of Mormons who wanted to relocate out of Utah more than a century ago. As they traveled, they kept asking their leader how they'd know where they should settle. His response, 'We'll get a sign,' temporarily satisfied them. When they came upon the tall Joshua tree which looked like a man with his arms raised, they accepted this as their sign. They settled in Nevada.

It was early morning. The intense heat formed patterns of a liquid mirage on the highway up ahead, making Dwayne feel light-headed – almost as seasick as if he were sailing in a storm. He didn't want to pull over and wake Liz. Negative thoughts bombarded him like rubber bullets. Needing to stay awake, wanting to hear his voice while sorting his thoughts, he began to speak softly. "What more can happen to me? My firm's out of business. Who'll hire an architect in this crappy economy? I'm thirty-five and I'm exhausted from job hunting – any kind of job. Liz was laid off several months ago when her bank closed and now she's pregnant. Even her part-time gig as an editor has dried up. Nada available for either one of us in New York. Our savings are almost gone and our credit card is nearly maxed out."

He couldn't believe that he was crying and talking to himself. "I have to admit that I'm desperate. Boy! I. Am. Such. A. Loser! Just as Pa predicted."

He drove faster, white knuckles gripping the steering wheel, feeling as if he were running fast in a violent nightmare. His blue eyes turned steely gray as he recalled the mugging in the restroom last night. He wanted to scream but controlled his voice to keep it soft, afraid of waking Liz. "That son-of-a-bitch mugged me in the men's room at the damned pit-stop. That bastard took my last few bucks. Wow, I need to get it together before Liz wakes up, because she doesn't need my negativity."

2

He continued to take deep yoga breaths. "Isn't this a stupid time to start a family? What were we thinking? Where will I get the money to support us?"

The speeding car raised a sandy cloud which left a gritty feeling on his teeth. It reminded him of his childhood and family trips in desert areas like this in the ancient Ford. The fine grains of sand penetrated every possible opening in this old car, even before he shut off the air conditioning to save on gas mileage and opened the windows, letting hot air blow into the car. Attempting to keep awake, he slowed down as he rolled his head from side to side; his wet thick blond hair blowing back and forth over his sweaty forehead like a shiny waterfall.

His thoughts traveled faster than the car. "Maybe I should cash in my insurance policy. Hey! Now that's an idea! I'm worth more dead than I am alive." He sat up a little taller. He gulped. "Am I crazy? Things may be hopeless, but how could I do such a thing to Liz and our baby?"

Desperate to change his frame of mind, he stuck his head out the window and swallowed the dusty hot air. It only added to his discomfort by making him thirsty. "I doubt that it went below 100 last night, after a high of 114 degrees during the day, but that's Nevada for you. They say dry heat isn't so bad. Are they kidding? Hot is hot! And I always hated this stupid intolerable temperature." He turned on the radio. "Boy, do I need to relax."

"Hey! Turn that down, Dwayne!" Liz moaned without lifting her head.

"Sorry. I thought it was soft enough. Go back to sleep, Liz."

She sat up. "Oh! It's morning! I can't believe I slept so long. Did you stop to nap?"

"You slept for both of us."

She playfully cuffed his shoulder. "Guess I haven't been much help with the driving. Are we in Nevada?"

"Yep. Right in the middle of nowhere."

"Want me to take over?"

"I'm okay."

3

"You must be tired after driving all night. I'm sorry. I should have stayed awake to keep you company after..."

Dwayne bit his lip and shook his head. He didn't want to rehash what had happened at the rest area.

A minute later, Liz broke the silence. "Let's stop to stretch and have breakfast."

His mood changed as fast as the heat lightning flashes he'd experienced all night. He snickered. "I knew the minute you woke up, you'd think of food. That's my girl, growing bigger every day." When he reached across to pat her stomach he experienced the sudden thump. "Whoa! I've never felt the baby kick before. Bet he'll be a fantastic football player."

They'd had this conversation many times while looking up possible names. Several months earlier, they decided they didn't want to know the baby's sex in advance. Now she smiled. "Or, a brilliant female soccer star. Hey! I'm starving. Please pull over."

"You've got it. We can picnic under that tree up ahead. It's the only one on this almost barren strip. Look at that. There's something strange about it."

"Maybe strange isn't the right word but it seems to fit, what with the splashes of color. I love the tiny, puffy clouds above it. Doesn't this scene look like a pointillist painting?"

As they neared the tree, they realized why it looked odd from the distance. There were dozens of pairs of colorful sneakers, shoes and boots tied together by their laces, hanging haphazardly from the jagged, leathery-looking branches. An unexpected breeze caused a few of the smaller shoes to move. It seemed surreal. This enormous fir tree had grown wild, with two old gnarled trunks fused around each other, as if hugging for strength to withstand the desert heat and nightly winds.

Liz stared as they walked in a circle around the tree, holding hands. "I'll bet if these shoes and sneakers could talk, they'd have many tales to tell. I feel such energy here."

"This is tailor-made for you. You've been complaining about not being inspired by any interesting new subjects to write about these days."

"Yes! Maybe I'll write something like… like *The Bridge of San Luis Rey*. I remember that it was required reading in high school."

"Yep! I read it too. There were many people who died when a rope bridge in South America collapsed and …"

"Each chapter described the life of a different person who died in the accident. I think the idea of many plots will be great for my book. I visualize writing a new chapter with new characters and a new episode for every pair of shoes or whatever. I'll just jot…"

Dwayne took a picnic basket and a blanket from the car. "Wait a second, Liz; let's eat first. I'm tired after driving all night."

"Fine. Do you want a peanut butter and jelly sandwich? Or, jelly with peanut butter?"

"That's it? Things are that bad? Why didn't you tell me?"

"Would that have helped? We needed to use our money for gas."

"That's why I turned off the air conditioner a while back. It sucks up too much precious gas. Well, I'm not hungry after all. This is your breakfast, and then you'll have the rest for your lunch."

"Absolutely not! I insist you have this. Don't play the martyr. We're sharing!"

He sighed deeply as he leaned against the tree. "I've made a real mess of our lives, haven't I? Everything bad that could possibly happen has dogged us. The Peter Principle and Murphy's Law combined in full force. And the robbery last night was the final straw. I was stupid to agree to take this trip across the country so you could meet my folks."

"Hey! Some of it's my fault, too. I haven't sold any of my stories lately. So much for freelancing. Lord knows I've been upset, but have I complained? We'll have a big dinner with your family tonight." She tapped his arm. "Have you given any more thought to joining your Dad's clothing business? Sounds good to me. We've reached bottom, so I'm willing to relocate out here to change our luck."

"Hold it! You promised not to bring that up! I always hated it here. I wouldn't raise our kid in this rotten desert." He'd never spoken so sharply before. He ran his fingers through his hair as his face changed as quickly as a kaleidoscope. "Sorry I got lost last night. In the darkness, the roads seemed unfamiliar and this new highway has thrown me. No signs, no exits. There's plenty of equipment, but no workers. I don't even know how we got on it."

"We're headed in the right direction, anyway. I know it'll be all right." They ate their sandwiches silently, gazing up at the tree.

He waved his arm in a circle. "You know what? All these shoes on this tree remind me of the Dr. Seuss book about the hat salesman who wore all his hats, as high as a giraffe's head."

"Well, Dwayne, aren't you the literate one! Promise me you'll read that book to our baby. This tree is kind of mysterious! I can't wait to find someone who can explain it, an anomaly growing right in the middle of God's country."

"You'll make it into a fabulous story, Liz. You're such a creative writer!"

"I wish my agent had as much confidence in me as you have…" His head bobbed. She noticed that he couldn't seem to keep his eyes open. "You're really tired, aren't you? Why don't you nap awhile?" She pointed to their dusty old car. "I'll guard the treasure."

He didn't laugh with her. "Forget the guard duty! I'd like to know where we are. If you see a car on this deserted road, flag it down and wake me."

She watched him fall into a deep sleep. He had driven too many hours and she felt that he needed to rest. Softly rubbing her belly, she mused about this turn of events. Reliving her past life, she concluded that years before she met Dwayne, she had sold her soul. Suddenly, she became disappointed in herself. After graduate school, she'd been unemployed and hungry so she settled for second best because it became a no brainer; she'd met an older man who promised her a comfortable lifestyle. He made unilateral decisions for them both, but she was willing to accept his parameters and she assumed the codependent role. Life seemed good and she felt secure.

Then everything changed. He had changed. Despite his new negative and disinterested attitude, she developed a more active social life. Some of her short stories were published and she found a part-time job as an editor. Although her family never liked her partner and tried to give her advice, it was too late to be implemented. Finally, their fragile cocoon burst. They parted. She had no choice but to become independent. Facing an uncertain future, she experienced an epiphany when she realized that she was living alone for the first time in thirty years and actually enjoyed her own company. She moved forward, amazed at her resilience. No one was going to deter her growth, her freedom. No one was going to hurt her again. She had become her own person. Because she liked herself and enjoyed her new single life, people were drawn to her and she found herself in a large circle of friends.

She met Dwayne at a party and immediately fell in love. He seemed to be everything she'd ever wanted in a soulmate. In retrospect, she thought, it was his infectious laugh that she heard across the room that drew her to him. She smiled at his sleeping form and blew him a kiss.

Just a short time later, Dwayne woke with an excruciating pain in his chest. Frightened, he wondered if this was the sign of a heart attack. Or was this indigestion? Clenching his teeth, he grabbed his shirt in his fist and thought, I'm a wreck. My nerves can't stand all this damned pressure. It's probably just another panic attack like I've had recently.

Eyes wide with fear, Liz touched his shoulder. "Are you all right?"

His pain subsided. He breathed deeply. Gazing at her, he thought how adorable she looked with her long hair pinned up in a colorful plastic clip which looked like butterfly wings. Dark curly tendrils fell unevenly around her beautiful face and down her neck, giving her a childlike appearance. How did he ever deserve her?

7

He forced himself to smile and drawled like a Westerner, "Sorry, Ma'am. Didn't mean ta scare ya none. That were just a bad dream – but now I'm rarin' to git goin'. Didn't mean ta sleep this long."

She didn't smile back. "Don't try to cover up. Are you really alright?"

Satisfied that he was, they gathered their things, took a last look at the tree, and drove away. They were both quiet, lost in their own thoughts, afraid to voice growing fears. Dwayne had no idea of where they were; was afraid the car might run out of gas; worse than that, there was no power left in the cell phone and the car charger had broken during the trip. Searching for a distraction, he reminded himself of the old dream he had of designing an open ranch house with a kitchen and a fireplace in the center, much like Hestia, the Greek Goddess, had envisioned.

He almost jumped and tried not to panic when Liz broke the silence. She asked, "This is odd, isn't it? Not even one car driving by. I feel like we're in *The Twilight Zone.*"

Anxious to remain positive, he kept it light. He nodded. "Good simile. I loved that show. Rod Serling, right?"

"You were always too good at Trivial Pursuit. Remind me to throw that game away." Then her tone became serious. "Tell me the truth; we're running out of gas, aren't we?"

"Hey! None of that! I know we'll make it…"

She pursed her lips. "Cars don't run on a promise."

"This one will! If only this damned road had signs. I haven't seen an exit, and we have no idea of where we are. But when the sun rose this morning, I was relieved to know that we were travelling north."

"Well, at least we see telephone poles and wires on this highway, so we'll reach civilization eventually."

He noticed she looked pale and attempted to change the mood. "Or, maybe I can climb a pole to hook into a telephone line." They were running out of inane conversation and became silent again.

Minutes later, driving around a bend, he saw an exit and several buildings.

"Civilization," whispered Liz, inadvertently patting her belly to reassure the baby. "We made it!"

But Dwayne was the one who now felt totally reassured. His spirits soared when he pulled into the gas station. "Yes! Look, Liz! They accept credit cards, and there's a diner across the street."

Working hard to control his nerves, he called out to the skinny attendant in a dirty tattered jumpsuit who sauntered out from the dilapidated garage, "Hey! I'm happy to make it here. Fill her up! Regular, of course. Can you can give me directions to Durhamville?"

"Yessir. It's a few hours at best. When ya drive outta here, look yonder to the left to go north, if that's where you're heading. Follow this ole road apiece, and ya'll see signs for it. Don't know how ya got past the barriers to git on the incomplete new highway in the first place."

Holding back her tears, Liz wanted to hug that kid. This was the first inkling they had that they were heading in the right direction and their ordeal would be over.

Gas tank filled, oil checked, they were anxiously looking forward to a hot lunch and some coffee to jump-start their foggy brains with caffeine. They entered the nostalgic, fifties-looking diner. A woman who appeared to be about that same vintage, jumped up, smoothing her tight uniform over her square, buxom body. "Welcome, folks! Sit anywhere ya please. I'm Joan, the proprietor, chief cook and waitress." She recited the limited menu in a heavy monotone, which resonated from her immense chest as if she were talking in an echo chamber.

After lunch, when Liz asked her about the exotic tree they'd just visited, Joan plopped down on a chair, joining them like an old friend. "Ah, the shoe tree! I swear they built the new highway to make it more convenient for everyone," she chuckled. "It all started a few years ago. The story goes: a young couple stopped to rest at that ole tree; had a terrific fight. The guy tied her shoes together, threw them up onto a high branch and drove away, leaving the gal barefoot and stranded. Ten minutes later, he turned around, but someone passing by picked her up and dropped her here, 'cause I'm the onliest place around. She was crying her eyes out when her boyfriend came looking for her. They made up and left her shoes on the tree as a memento of their first big fight."

Liz couldn't wait. "So now, whenever people drive by, they add their shoes for luck or whatever."

Joan laughed. "Say, who's telling this story, anyways? Our tree's become loaded and famous. I'm so close, that folks stop by here to grab a bite, telling me why they tossed their own shoes or boots onto it. Seems like a bleeding hearts club meets here! Every story is different. Some real happy stuff; some of it sad, but usually with feel-good endings. You name it. One thing I've learned; there ain't no such thing as a new yarn, and I've heard 'em all. But I remember one different angle that's worth telling – a teenaged kid came in here, looking down and out. He drove an ole jalopy, said he had no money to speak of, and certainly, no future. A while later, he came back real excited, babbling about climbing the shoe tree to change his run-down boots for a better pair and danged if he didn't find the biggest wads of big bills rolled up in the toes. Some danged ole fool must of forgotten where he stashed his savings. 'So, what the hell,' I told him. 'Keep it! The owner's long gone.' He left here excited, positive his luck had changed."

"What a great beginning for a novel," said Liz. "I'll call it *The Shoe Tree*. I know what you're going to say, most people would think of the wooden shoe trees that goes into shoes." She laughed at her simple title, but it seemed to fit. "I wish we could talk more now, but Dwayne's folks are expecting us. May I call you to hear more stories?"

Joan reached for Liz's hand. "From the looks of things, you'll have plenty 'a time to conjure up your own tales. But call anyways. I'll be happy to help you. There's bound to be more people coming by when the highway officially opens. Can't happen soon enough to help my business. Send me a copy when it's finished, with your autograph, will you?"

Liz hugged her. "Thanks for giving us so much of your time. I feel as if we've known each other forever; maybe in another life."

"You know, I do believe things are sorta ordained. I've always liked Shirley MacLaine's philosophy that we've lived many lives. I'd like to think we'll meet again. Betcha I'll have some real good stories for you, so for sure keep in touch."

Energized by the experience, grinning idiotically, Dwayne surprised Liz when he turned back onto the highway.

"Hey! Aren't you going in the wrong direction?"

He admitted, "You'll see why in a minute. Maybe Dad was right – he's been sounding a lot differently lately – I'll take him up on the offer to join the family clothing business. We really don't have any choice, do we? We've needed a fresh start. My folks are thrilled to know they're going to be grandparents and the bonus is our kid will grow up with relatives close by."

She didn't respond.

He thought back to how his life completely opened up when he attended college in New York. He'd been a country boy but he dramatically changed as he watched, listened and learned from the new relationships he forged. He was a quick study, socially and intellectually as he absorbed knowledge from his professors and from his peers, even to the extent of working hard to drop his mid-western patois. The only times he reverted back to his accent was when he became upset or overtired, something that rarely happened.

Deeply tanned, his boyishly handsome face was framed by blondish-white hair and his years of farm work had toned his lean, muscular body. As a teenager, he'd always been involved with girlfriends, but the sophisticated girls he met in graduate studies were a challenge that he quickly overcame with his perpetual positive attitude and sense of humor.

But he was no match for Liz who beguiled him the moment he met her. Her reaction was as powerful as his as they left the noisy gathering to walk and talk for hours. They were attracted to each other that first night and made it a permanent relationship.

He stopped daydreaming as he parked next to the shoe tree and opened his duffle bag. When he found what he wanted, he tied a pair of his leather sailing shoes together and tried to heave them up to a high branch. It wasn't as easy as he imagined – they almost fell back right on him the first couple of times – but he wound up and threw them uphanded.

"What're you doing?" Liz screeched. "You loved those Docksiders."

He came back to the car and hugged her. "I still do. But I won't need sailing shoes in the desert."

Chapter 2

Several hours later, as they approached Dwayne's childhood home, Liz's heart sank. It looked like a deserted building in an old western town, with weathered flaking shingles crying for paint and a few gutters haphazardly hanging, ready to fall with the next strong wind. The landscaping, devoid of flowers, was scruffy, lacking any xeriscape design with cactus that she'd anticipated. They'd driven at least a mile past the nearest farm.

Dwayne drew in a long breath, holding it an inordinate amount of time while taking it all in. "Well, here's the old homestead. It's changed a lot since I left."

Liz couldn't face him. She sensed his ambivalent feelings, although she knew he wouldn't verbalize them; he was going to make the best effort to put their lives together. So be it. She'd do whatever she could to make the transition go smoothly.

The dusty screen door burst open as a thick-bodied grey-haired woman ran to the car, arms wide open to greet her son. "Just look at you, Dwayney." Her voice rose in a high scratchy pitch when she said his name.

Her body stiff with pain from days of traveling, Liz strove to control her negative emotions. After profuse hugs from his mother, Dwayne extricated himself from her arms to help Liz out of the car. The hot sun burned on their faces.

"Ma, this is my Liz," he said, in a drawl Liz had never heard him use before.

"Hi, Mrs. Talbott. I'm so happy to finally meet you."

The woman stared at Liz's multicolored mini dress with obvious distaste. "No need for that, child, just call me Miz. T., like all the folks here abouts." Seemingly oblivious to Liz's arms raised for an embrace, the woman leaned forward to give her a perfunctory kiss on the cheek.

13

Okay, Liz thought, as the woman steered Dwayne towards the house, chatting about how she'd squeezed all the lemons to make the cold lemonade waiting for them. *So that's the way it's going to be... I guess I can handle it.*

But Dwayne turned back and took Liz's hand. "C'mon out of the heat. Let's get you something to drink." He was extra solicitous, obviously trying to amend for his mother's lack of attention to her.

Once inside, Liz stared at the contrast. "This is lovely, Miz. T.," she said, surprised at the fastidious, Early Americana décor.

Mrs. Talbott's grey bun bobbed as she shook her head, obviously flattered. "Why thank you! This is *my* domain–the outside is Wilfred's. As you seen, he don't do a good job." She turned to her son with a singsong voice, "Dwayney, maybe you can be a good boy and help fix up the porch, at least, so's a body can enjoy being outdoors a bit when it cools down."

"Sure thing, Ma. I'll surprise Pa when he gets home. Meanwhile, let's get Liz set up in my old room."

Liz agreed. "I'd love to stretch out now. Maybe unpack later."

Alone in their room, she gave Dwayne a quizzical look. "I've never seen you like this. What's with the Ma and Pa Kettle stuff? You've never referred to them that way."

"Hon, they expect it from me – it's how I was brung up." He grabbed her and they kissed but were interrupted by his mother knocking on the frame of the open door.

"Better close your door for those shenanigans," she said without smiling. "Look here. I thought you'd like the drink I promised." She put down the tray and left.

Dwayne rolled his eyes. "She's very square. Sorry. Rest now. I'll see you later."

Hours later, when Liz walked down the hallway toward the kitchen, she couldn't help but overhear the woman's irritating voice say, "Oh, I put him to work outside, doing stuff his lazy pa don't do no more. Well, his wife... Who does she think she is, looking down her nose at us plain folk? Dwayne told me she

14

came from a ritzy family and I don't like her uppity-high-society ways." Pause. "No, not anything she said, just how she looks, dressing up like a baby-doll, putting on airs, turning my fine boy's head. Betcha she got pregnant on purpose to snare him in." Pause. "Well, I gotta go. I need to fix a fancy dinner for the princess."

Liz heard a guffaw, then the sound of a telephone being replaced. She scurried back to her room, closed the door, and threw herself down on the bed, rocking back and forth while holding her belly. Hot tears dribbled down as she punched the pillow. *What a witch! I can't believe Dwayne came from such common stock. How dare she talk about me, criticizing me to strangers, when she doesn't even know me; hasn't given me a chance. I'll never forgive her!*

Just then, Dwayne opened the door. "Hi, sleepyhead. Feel better? Your face is flushed, like you've been crying." He sat down on the bed. "Are you all right?"

She sat up as he wiped her cheeks and then flipped her long hair like a puppy coming out of the water. "Of course. I guess I'm too tired and didn't sleep enough. I didn't even know I was crying. How late is it? My watch is in my bag."

He hugged her. "Thought you'd like to come out and visit with us while we finish cooking dinner. Dad will be home to meet you any minute. I'm going to take a quick shower. I really need it."

When he left the room, Liz stood up and almost ripped the dress as she quickly took it off, then had second thoughts. Should she wear it to spite his mother? No. She remembered the ancient expression, 'You can't win for losing.' That woman was not going to ruin her marriage. She quickly decided to change, taking a pair of jeans and a shirt from one of the bags. After all, she thought, she should try to make a better impression on his dad because she could use an ally.

Wrapped in a towel, Dwayne returned and rummaged through his bag for fresh clothes. He seemed preoccupied and nervous.

Liz pulled out a shirt for him. "I'll take care of unpacking all this after dinner, but I'm exhausted, so you'll need to help, too, Dwayney."

"Now cut that out! I've always hated it when she called me that, but she's bound to say whatever suits her."

"Oh, yes, I definitely got that impression."

As Liz entered the kitchen, her face drawn like a mask to hide her feelings, she asked if she could help. In response, Mrs. Talbott pointed to the last cabinet on the left. "You can't wear such a wrinkled shirt to my table. The iron's in there."

Without a word, Liz took the iron to her room. She ironed her husband's shirt too, for good measure. When she returned wearing the freshly pressed blouse, she again offered to set the table.

"That's not necessary, Elizabeth, I've got everything in hand, and you seem plum worn out. Besides, it's more trouble to tell you where everything is. You'll just watch and learn."

Liz had never seen anyone set the table by simply putting a glass Mason jar containing silverware in the center of it. The dishes were left on the counter, but glasses of water, a bread basket and condiments were all carefully placed on the red and white checked tablecloth. Matching napkins were rolled in pewter napkin rings, each with its own pattern.

"Mind the design on your ring," Mrs. Talbott said, "we try to use them cloths more'n once."

A few minutes later, hearty shouts resounded near the porch, as Dwayne and his father hugged each other. The men talked for a minute. When they entered the kitchen, Wilfred nodded to his wife. "Veronica, smells good here." Then, with a broad smile, he enveloped Liz in his arms.

Liz felt he held on a little too long.

"You're a pretty scrawny thing, even with the belly, ain't ya?" he held her at arm's length, his eyes remaining on her chest.

Liz felt uncomfortable, but she kept looking right at him.

He winked. "But a mighty appealing one, at that."

So that's where Dwayne got his personality, she thought. Although, this man may need watching. Yet, maybe there's hope for a different atmosphere from that woman with him around. She seems to have perked up since they walked in. Either that, or it's all for Dwayne.

Mrs. Talbott brought in several beautiful roses which she artfully arranged into an attractive centerpiece. "Roses grow tolerably well in this climate," she said modestly when Liz complimented her. "I've got me a good scrap of a garden behind this ole house. You probably didn't notice it."

"I'd never have guessed they'd thrive in this dry heat," Liz said. "I'm amazed. Will you show me your garden after dinner?"

That brought a slight smile from the woman's plain face. She didn't wear any makeup and probably never did, Liz thought. I'll bet she'd never let me suggest anything like that, either.

Dinner was served on dainty porcelain dishes brought over from England by Mrs. Talbott's family, Liz was told. She thought they were a stark contrast to the hefty, simply dressed woman. The stew was tasty, filled with plentiful amounts of beef, generously spiced with home-grown herbs, served with vegetables freshly harvested from the garden. Seconds were offered, but Dwayne rubbed his belly, announcing that he was saving room for his dessert. His mother beamed with happiness over their comments about the dinner.

During the meal, Dwayne's parents kept referring to each other as Ma and Pa, never again calling each other by their given names. To Liz, the entire scene was reminiscent of Norman Rockwell's portraits of American farmers. All that was missing was the pitchfork that symbolically had already hit her. Liz couldn't have felt more out of place than if she were transported back in time to an earlier century. She wondered how she was going to cope with all this on a permanent basis and almost cried with pity for herself and her unborn child. If only Miz. T. could demonstrate some interest in her, some compassion, but it wasn't going to be forthcoming, so she knew she'd better adjust to the situation.

After dinner and a tour of the garden, they all sat on the cleanly swept, orderly porch. Dwayne had washed the furniture, but his parents hadn't said anything about it. Liz was surprised

Wilfred hadn't thanked his son for cleaning the area, repairing a broken rocker and hanging the gutters.

The evening desert breeze and cooler temperatures were a relief from the pressing heat of the day. Unhindered by clouds, the full moon illuminated the porch and lit profiles of the few trees and many species of cacti in the distance. Some of them had large buds, promising colorful flowers. A citronella candle flickered as tiny creatures fluttered and buzzed from a safe distance. The entire place was transformed as if by a paintbrush.

Dwayne's parents insisted on hearing all about Dwayne's former job and asked him about his future prospects. It was obvious to Liz they weren't interested in asking her about herself but she grudgingly acknowledged they hadn't seen their son in several years.

"Maybe you'll come down to the store and help me out a bit while you're here, son," Wilfred suggested, puffing on his corncob pipe, inhaling the smoke, coughing and spitting on the ground.

Liz looked at Dwayne, expecting him to suggest that he had planned to remain but he simply said, "Don't mind if I do keep you company, Pa."

Liz gulped and turned away so the others wouldn't see her tears. She thought. What's going to happen here? I can't believe him! He's not the guy I married, and here we are, out in the middle of the desert... Her heart felt heavy, like a building imploding.

Chapter 3

"No! Not there! Didn't I tell you that this morning?" The harsh voice was all too familiar, evoking painful memories. "Put the damn shirts on the next shelf. College sure didn't make you a better listener."

His face turning crimson, Dwayne looked away, inhaled deeply, and walked to the bathroom in the rear of the store. He resisted the impulse to slam the door shut. His mind raced back to his unhappy childhood, then as quickly as in a spinning top, flashed to his teenage years. It had always been that way. Soft-spoken with his customers – a little edgy yet carefully controlled with his wife – his father was always curt and didactic with him. Didactic? No, not just with a teaching or preaching voice, but impatient, bordering on angry. Dwayne had never understood the smoldering, underlying tension existing between them; keeping them at arms' length. The attention and bear hug he'd gotten from him yesterday was a freak occurrence; against his father's nature.

Years of therapy had helped ease the pain in Dwayne's heart. It led him to believe it wasn't his fault – he finally admitted the problem lay with his father – not with him. With all the trauma that had recently occurred in his own life, he'd tried to wipe out the past difficulties and had dreamed of a new mature relationship. His father had actually embraced him last night, hadn't he? After all, his parents were excited about becoming grandparents for the first time. They'd been disappointed when he and Liz had gotten married in a quiet civil ceremony in New York without inviting them but were thrilled when he notified them months ago that Liz was pregnant. They made him promise he and Liz would drive out West to visit at the first opportunity. Opportunity was not the proper word. The occasion was thrust upon them. Downsizing became more than that; their companies went out of business. Months of job hunting produced no results, only a few minor possibilities which quickly disappeared like the smoke from his father's corn cob pipe. Liz agreed to travel now before the baby was due. They certainly couldn't take time off right after they found jobs, could they?

With a jerk, he was roused from his reverie. "What the hell are you doing anyway?" he heard through the door. "Did you fall in?"

Nothing's changed, he thought, so why did he ever think he'd want to walk back into this?

When the two men went off to work in the morning, Liz kept biting her inner cheek to keep from arguing with her mother-in-law.

After breakfast, Mrs. Talbott suggested that Liz finish her unpacking and iron all Dwayne's shirts so he didn't have to think about his clothes. After lunch and a nap, Liz had asked if she could do anything to help prepare dinner, and the woman finally agreed. Several times, she criticized how Liz had prepared the vegetables, how she set the table, how she'd almost ruined the cake. How could she concentrate on following the new recipe using different utensils when the woman didn't stop yammering at her?

"How'd you get a job at the bank if you can't follow directions?"

Liz was too shocked to respond to the cutting remark. She knew she'd wake up in the middle of the night, thinking about a perfect reply. In the late afternoon, when there didn't seem to be any reason to try to have any normal conversation with the controlling woman, Liz mentioned she was going to take some time to write.

"Write? A letter to family back home?"

"No, I've been anxious to begin my new novel. I've got my laptop with me and I want to get started while the idea is so ..."

"You don't say. You write books? I didn't know you did that."

"I did some part-time editing and freelance work which didn't pay enough, so I worked at the bank. I have a great idea for my first ..."

"Well, that's nice, Elizabeth. I wish you good luck."

Yeah, I'll bet. Liz walked to her room. She lovingly stroked her laptop before booting it up, excited about beginning the new novel. It was easy to write the introduction; her thoughts flipped as effortlessly as pages blown by the wind but then she was stumped. She stared at the blank page on the computer. Should she outline several chapters, or dive into the book, and see where it took her? In the past, she'd been surprised at how the characters and plots seemed to write themselves.

Sitting up in bed, unable to focus her thoughts to the task on hand, she wondered how she'd be able to cope with her crotchety mother-in-law. Ordinarily, she wasn't argumentative, but now she berated herself for her silence. She was unsure of which tact to take. If she answered back to Miz. T., showing she wasn't going to take any shit from her, she was pretty sure she might lose, because the woman was obviously accustomed to having the last word. On the other hand, if she didn't respond in kind, the bitch would take advantage of her good-nature. She thought perhaps she'd talk with Dwayne about how to handle the situation, but she was unsure. What if he might react by defending his mother, not side with her? It was a conundrum.

She decided to wait to see what developed. What am I doing in this horrible place, she asked herself. No wonder I can't focus. I need the stimulation of intellectuals; I need the museums; the library; the theatres. I feel like a dead weight here. She shuddered. How could she use that term when she was carrying her dear baby?

More than a month later, they were still living with his parents. It was unbearable for Liz, confined out in the countryside with Dwayne's mother all day. Liz grimaced when the woman kept criticizing her without bothering to turn around to face her, as if she didn't understand. She couldn't get into town for an afternoon since the house lay more than three miles beyond the bus route and the dirt road seemed to have pockmarks larger than a whale's mouth. Their car had developed engine trouble and lay in the shop, waiting for parts. Liz never forgot the expression on Dwayne's face when the greasy-faced mechanic with a colorful spikey Mohawk hairdo had asked, "What's a Volvo?"

Occasionally, when different neighbors stopped by for a visit, Mrs. Talbott was an entirely different person, acting the fine hostess, showing off her son's pretty pregnant wife, even bragging that Liz was writing a book. In the evenings when the men returned, Veronica nodded to her husband with a slight smile, but gushed over Dwayne.

In the privacy of their room, Liz finally had to give vent to her emotions. Dwayne patiently heard Liz's complaints as she attempted to keep her voice down. Luckily, his parents' room was not next to theirs. "I've been trying to find some time to write, but she keeps interrupting me and doesn't let me breathe. I've held back as long as I could, but recently I've found it intolerable spending so many days with that cross, demanding woman. You've absolutely no idea of how differently she behaves when you're around. She's a female version of Jekyll and Hyde."

He listened without interrupting her; his usual lop-sided smile failing to dissuade her burst of indignation. He took her hand. "Believe me, I never figured she'd be so ornery with you. Dad and I have sorta-kinda worked things out, ever since I told him we were thinking of settling here, but I've had this odd feeling like I'm sleepwalking when we're together. For months, Dad seemed to encourage me to return and join him in the business. That's why we're here. Yet now he's ornery, acting like I'm in his way. I keep looking for some kind of reassurance that he loves me, even though he's never been able to demonstrate that. I've often wondered if he'd ever had a relationship with his own father but he never wants to speak about his childhood. Maybe he never witnessed the example of how a father should interact. I don't know how to deal with that."

"Well, doesn't he see what your mother does to make up for his lack of attention to you?"

"Obviously not."

It took Dwayne a long time to come up with a reasonable solution; something Liz would be able to accept. Something he'd be able to live with, too. "I haven't mentioned this to you before; Pa – OOPS! Have to return to our groove – SORRY! Dad hasn't been giving me much of a salary, calling me his intern, but I've been squirreling it away. I've also been looking into buying a small place for us in town, so can you please bear with my mother for just a little while longer?"

Liz squealed with delight. "Our own house in town sounds great, but where would we get the money for the down payment and the closing costs? Maybe we should rent something first?"

"I'll ask Dad to co-sign the mortgage. He's well-known here and has been dealing with the bank before I was born. Maybe I can talk him into taking me on as a partner. I'd pay him back a little at a time with my end-of-the-year bonus. And of course, when I prove myself, my salary will go up."

She hugged him tightly. "Do you really mean it? The sooner we move out, the happier I'll be. The best thing is I'll be closer to the doctor and the hospital."

"Yep, especially in your final months. I'm sorry I wasn't aware of how miserable my mother made your life. I'm sure she'd have been satisfied if I'd come alone; then she wouldn't have to share me with you."

That night, after telling Liz that he'd been looking for a home in town, Dwayne tossed and turned, unable to sleep. He kept thinking about what he hadn't mentioned to Liz. He hadn't really been happy spending all day with his father, who never seemed satisfied with whatever he tried to do. The store looked far better now that he'd organized the stock and kept the place much cleaner. The customers, who had immediately welcomed him back, noticed some of the changes he'd made, commenting on that. But his father vied for his regular customers' attention, almost unwilling to let him get into personal conversations with former friends and neighbors. It seemed like he'd become jealous of his son's popularity. The older man stubbornly refused to adopt some of his son's suggestions for modernizing, inflexibly keeping everything status quo. Their only one-time physical greeting when he'd arrived, and the recent early camaraderie seemed to dissipate more every day.

He recalled an incident that occurred a couple of days ago. "Hey!" his father replied when he'd tried to talk about upgrading the business, "This place did mighty well before, good enough to help send you East to college. It's stood the test of time and I damn well like it the way it is."

Wondering if he'd made the right decision to remain, giving up his independence and architectural career, isolating Liz in a small provincial community, gave him nightmares when he finally dozed off.

Chapter 4

In the morning, his eyes blurry from lack of a good night's sleep, Dwayne faced reality. He couldn't wait until Liz woke up so he purposely shook the bed as he turned a couple of times.

"I love you," he said, caressing her shoulder when she turned to face him. "I've been thinking a lot about our moving here, and now I realize it was just a pipe dream that we'd have a fairy-tale life with my folks. It's been horrible for both of us. I'm sorry I've been so selfish, and I think…"

She put her finger over his lips. He got the message and let her speak. "I was praying you'd come to that decision, but last night you seemed so positive about remaining here, I didn't want to burst your bubble. You can't give up your career for this small-town security. We'll have to get back to New York to find new jobs. We'll manage, somehow. I wish I could approach someone in my family but you know that's impossible. Maybe your dad will float us a loan. Let's tell them this morning!"

At breakfast, Dwayne carefully omitted the personal causes for their decision. "So, I've realized I just wasn't cut out to be in your business, Pa. I studied so hard to get my degree and I miss being an architect, so I've just got to keep looking for a job in my field. I'm sorry to disappoint you but we'll stay in close touch, and we'll flood you with baby pictures, Ma. Sometime soon, you both might want to get on a plane and visit us in the Big Apple, to see your grandchild."

His parents didn't put up the fuss that he'd expected. His father nodded in agreement. "We've known right from the get-go that you weren't going to be happy living here, so we made up our minds to let you figure it out. Stubborn as you've always been, you'd have fought with us if we said you were making a mistake, or you might have thought we didn't want you in our lives. You'd think we didn't have your best interests at heart. There's no future for you here. I didn't want to tell you I have to vacate my store within a few months. Only found out about it after you'd made your plans to come see us. That's why I didn't want any of your suggestions, good as they were. I'm so surprised nobody blabbed to you that the building's being torn down for a development – they're taking over the entire block and ripping it down like we're just a few old barns and outhouses – just for a stupid mall. Even though I thought maybe we'd open a new store there, I 'm plum worn out to do anything elsewhere, to start all over again. Time I retire and do some things around this here place, now you shamed me good." His eyes twinkled, "Valerie here's been right proud of the things you started, and I'm bound to keep her smiling by finishing them all. I'm even thinking of hiring some young fellas into helping paint our house It's beginning to look like a deserted mine shack."

Dwayne's jaw dropped open. "I'm flabbergasted," he said, looking at his parents in complete disbelief. "I don't know what …"

His mother interrupted, "Maybe we didn't go about it in the right way but I seen how you'd changed; you're not the young un what left for college. And when I spotted this dainty girl here, I knew, no matter what, you'd be miserable here. But it was good to have you here a spell, son." She wiped a tear, then turned to Liz, "I even got used to you, Elizabeth. I was hoping to help raise my grandkid, but it's not to be. I'd like to visit you in your own home, some day. That is, if you'll have me, after what I did to you here, to make you want to git out."

Liz hugged her. "You did a great job of making me feel so uncomfortable here – you might want to go on the stage or into the movies – you're a shoe-in to get the academy award for best character."

They all laughed a little too hard; it was best to end on such a high note, as far as Liz was concerned.

Dwayne and Liz were packed and ready to leave within a short time, hoping to get a head start before the intense heat of the day. Their car had finally been repaired and they were happy to begin the long trip with it in top shape. When his parents hugged them goodbye, his father gave him a large sum of money, saying, "Here, son, you earned this here 'seed money' and more. Hell, we can't spend what I've stashed away for when I retire. If you need more, let me know. After all, you'll get our money when we're both gone, so we'd like to see you spend some of it now. We know you really need it, with the baby coming, and all."

His mother handed Dwayne a large package. "This here is my travelin' goodie bag to tide you over a spell. And Elizabeth, no, Liz, you have to call me Veronica from now on, unless one day, you might want to call me Ma, and I'd be right honored by that, but I've got to earn it."

They hugged again. Everyone tried to hide the tears in their eyes – each person had a different reason.

As Dwayne drove away, he and Liz were enveloped in their own confused thoughts which whirled over their heads like balloons banging into each other. There was no need to talk.

In a pensive mood, Liz experienced tons of relief that she'd be back in their apartment in New York close to her obstetrician, writing her new novel as she tried to get freelancing jobs. She was scared about their future as parents. Her thoughts bounced like kittens playing and cuffing each other: she worried about Dwayne finding work; worried about how poor their finances were, despite his father's gift; and how they'd pay the hospital when she gave birth. They didn't have any health insurance. Maybe she should see a midwife and deliver at home. She felt strongly that the money Dwayne's father had given them should be set aside as their nest-egg. But she decided not to share these negative thoughts with Dwayne. He'd become so excited because of the drastic changes in his parents' attitudes, and with the money they'd given him to help them through this economic crisis – she wouldn't want to tarnish his positive attitude.

Ambivalent thoughts raced through Dwayne's head. Would he really be able to find a job? The recession hadn't altered since they'd left the city. How long would his father's money last? Did he have the temperament to be a good daddy? He'd certainly not be like his father. For sure. And he knew he'd better put on an upbeat face for Liz. She needed that more than anything – she was such a trouper.

Hours later, they found a rest stop on the highway with picnic tables in the shade. It was good to stretch their legs and eat the lunch his mother had prepared for them. She'd loaded them up with bags of fruit and vegetables. Whatever was perishable had been stored in their cooler.

Dwayne enthusiastically talked with his mouth full of his favorite chicken salad. "I can't get over this. I can't stop thinking about the abrupt change in my parents; how they worked it out to force me to make my own decision about our future. I've never known them to be so magnanimous. Must be because I'm settled down with a wife," he blew her a kiss, "an adorable one, and we're going to have a baby. They're tickled they'll be grandparents. And my Pa, sorry, Dad said we should choose the baby crib and chest of drawers and send him the bill. Can you believe that? And, I can't believe my Mom wants to knit for the baby and she insisted she's sending you a layette, whatever that is?"

Liz didn't feel like talking. She didn't want to remind him how mean his mother had been. No matter what the woman said today, her behavior had been totally uncalled for; truly unacceptable. Actually, Liz thought the woman suffered from distemper. Better not to burst his bubble; he'd faced enough. Well, maybe most of Miz. T's terrible behavior was play-acting to make them both so uncomfortable they'd decide that a move there was a bad choice. Whatever. Liz was grateful to be leaving.

Once again on the road, Dwayne focused on driving, and Liz fell asleep, listening to the soft sounds of country music. Hours later, as they approached an intersection, the glaring lights of an oncoming truck blinded Dwayne's eyes.

Liz shrieked, "Watch out!"

He blinked, jammed his foot on the brake, trying to maneuver the car as it careened across the road. But it was too late. They missed the truck which came hurdling toward them, but their car collided against the billboard.

Chapter 6

Dwayne jerked into consciousness when he heard his door being forced open. "Liz! Is she okay?" he screamed. "Help her!"

A handful of people gathered around, as two medics placed Liz onto a gurney and into the ambulance. Dazed, he felt someone strap him into a seat near her. Overwhelmed with fear, Dwayne watched as two strangers deftly moved the stethoscope across her chest and took her vital signs.

In the hospital, an older man and nurses took over. They carefully examined her for broken bones.

Satisfied, the man turned to Dwayne. "I'm Doctor Matthews. Your wife's just knocked out. She probably doesn't have a concussion but she won't like the big bump on her head. As far as I can determine, she hasn't broken anything. Her arms show that she deflected the airbag from her belly. Unless I have to, I'll try not to expose her to needless radiation from x-rays. I'd say she's about in the end of her sixth month, or just into her seventh, right? The baby seems fine, for now, but we'll keep her here in the hospital overnight."

Dwayne's knees began to buckle as he took a deep breath, relieved to hear the good news. Dr. Mathews steadied him. "We'll watch her awhile, but in the meantime, lemme look at you. Gotta be sure you're okay."

After his examination, Dwayne accepted a bag of ice for his aching head and sank back in the bed. The doctor had patients waiting in his office a few houses down the street, but he'd assured Dwayne he'd return within minutes when notified Liz had regained consciousness. Finally left alone, Dwayne breathed deeply and prayed his wife and baby would be all right. His mind wandered back to the first time they'd been here in this very town, just a short time ago, or did it really feel like eons had past?

Later, as he slowly opened his eyes, the bright lights made him blink. He realized these weren't the same lights he'd just experienced. There were more of them; they made his head hurt. The ceiling was moving like the lapping waves of an ocean.

Someone was squeezing his arm. "Why, hello. I'm glad to see you awake. I'm just inserting this I.V. Hold still now."

Dazed, he looked around. The bothersome lights were in a ceiling fixture. He shaded his eyes with his other hand. "What happened? Where am I?"

"You're in the emergency room," the pleasant, skinny-looking nurse said, putting a fresh cold compress on his head. "You're fine, though. I'm Agnes and I'll be taking care of you. If those ceiling lights are bothering you, I'll turn them out and we'll use the one over your bed."

"Tell me what happened. I can't remember…"

"You were in an accident. A truck lost its brakes and almost plowed into you. Your x-rays just show a slight concussion. I'll bet you'll be sore in a lot of places tomorrow."

Just then, Dr. Matthews entered the room. He checked Dwayne's chart. "You're a lucky guy. The airbag saved you from broken bones. You'll be able to function better as soon as the medication kicks in."

Jolted back to reality, Dwayne panicked. "My wife – is Liz all right? Where is she?"

Dr. Matthews put his hand on his shoulder. "She's got good genes, I'd guess. Just got shaken up a bit, but she and the baby are fine; resting on the other side of this curtain. We gave her a sedative to help her rest. She was mighty worried about you and I couldn't calm her down. Just let me check your eyes. Now follow my finger. Good."

He finished examining Dwayne and was pleased with his reactions. "Here, I'll draw the curtain open, so you can see her, but you'd better rest too."

Dwayne woke with a start. He looked around, finally remembering what had happened. He gazed at Liz's bed. She was sleeping on her back which made her snore daintily. That was reassuring. The bandage around her head and the neck brace worried him. She looked fragile like a child and seemed as vulnerable.

Agnes came in. "Did you sleep well?"

After he proved that he could drink on his own, she removed the I.V. "Let's get you out of bed."

While sitting up and looking at Liz across the room, Dwayne thought about how much he loved her and how his life had changed since they were together. An aide came by with fresh water for him, and he asked her for a sheet of paper and a pen. Within moments, he began composing a love letter to her, his way of engaging his emotions – something he'd done even as a lonely young boy yearning to define himself – but never sharing that inner part of him with anyone. It was his secret.

To my Liz
Where did she come from
this love of mine?
Did she float down from the sky
like a falling star
or – from a rainbow's end?
Did she come from the mossy side of a tree
in a quiet forest glen?
Did she appear when the pollen
from the wings of a buzzing bee
drifted through the soft summer air
to form this gentle being?
Was she found sparkling like a precious
jewel in the ever-changing sand
or on the tip of a lily pad
in a placid garden pond?
The angels must have touched her
and sent her down to me.
Wherever she came from
this love of mine
she is here,
Here with me.

Scribbling and erasing several times, editing and rereading, trying to capture the perfect mood, satisfied with his final results, he folded it and placed it in the nightstand drawer, praying that Liz would read it very soon.

When Dr. Matthews returned a short while later, Dwayne said, "I'm really concerned. She hasn't moved since I woke up, Doctor. I wanted to keep checking on her, but I'm afraid I dozed."

Dr. Matthews re-examined Liz's life signs, careful he didn't wake her. He was methodical and took his time. Dwayne took the opportunity to observe the good-looking man, at least into his fifties. Casually dressed in a western style plaid shirt and Docker khaki slacks, his snakeskin boots peeked out from under the pants cuff. Typical.

"Dwayne, the sooner you walk around to regain your strength, the better off you'll be. You might want to head to our cafeteria as anyplace else. Your wife will be just fine for a few minutes while you stretch your legs and maybe eat something. Tell them I sent you. I know you missed the last meal they served and just crackers won't do. You look pale."

Dwayne didn't wait for help. He stood up on wobbly legs. The floor beneath him seemed to be moving – he felt as if he stood on the epicenter of an earthquake. Yep. He remembered that feeling having lived through them many times in his life.

Agnes rushed to help him gain his balance. "Are you okay? Here let me walk with you a spell – help get your land legs to feel grounded. We'll head out into the hallway if you feel steady enough."

The searing pain in her shoulder woke Liz. She tried to open her eyes, but there was something covering them. When she lifted her arm to touch her head, a sharp pain jabbed her shoulder, forcing her to yelp. She sounded like a puppy. "What's happening to me? Dwayne! Dwayne!" She tried to call out, but it sounded like a whisper. "Where am I?" She felt a stiff collar encircling her neck. Clearing her throat, she strained her vocal cords enough to call, "HELP! Somebody help me."

Dwayne came rushing into the room. "Oh, you're awake! Thank God! I just this minute stepped out of the room." He embraced her and gently rocked her in his arms.

"Why can't I see anything? I can hardly hear you, Dwayne? What's going on? Where am I?"

"Shh, Liz, baby, You've got to rest. I'll get the doctor now. He was waiting 'til you came around. Lie still. We'll be back in a flash."

"No, don't leave me like this! Where am I?"

"Honey, listen, don't exert yourself. We were in an accident – you've been unconscious for several hours, but now you're fine. We're in a hospital and you're getting good care." He kissed her cheek. "Please don't move while I get the nurse. She just left."

"No, give me a minute to absorb all this. Are you all right?"

He laughed. "That's just like you. Sure, I'm great. I'm covered with black and blue marks and I've got a beaut of a shiner. Wait for me. I'll be right back."

Liz drew her hands down her body and gently caressed her belly. "I've got to know–is our baby O.K.?"

But there was no answer. Dwayne had already rushed out.

Liz tried to be brave and have positive thoughts. She whispered, "Thank you God, for helping us survive; please, please, dear God up in heaven, stay with me awhile and promise me that my baby's going to be strong and healthy. I'm going to be the best mother, the best wife, the best…"

Within minutes, when the doctor and Dwayne returned, they found her asleep again.

"That's what she needs, I guess." Dr. Matthews gently raised her head and removed the thin layer of gauze. "The cut near her eye isn't bleeding anymore." He felt her stomach and used the stethoscope, smiling at what he observed. He opened her lids and was satisfied that her eyes focused well. "As I told you, my concern was she might lose her baby. So, she was lucid when she talked? Yes?"

Liz's eyes fluttered open again, wide and colorless, as if reflecting the headlights of a car about to collide with her. She strained to blink several times and focus. "Who are you?"

"Howdy, Miz. Liz. I'm Dr. Matthews. Dwayne's right here with us. Here, let me take off that neck collar. You'll be more comfortable without it and you don't need it at all. We were just trying to be extra careful. You're a lucky lady the accident happened here, near my office. You've just got a superficial cut above your eye which wouldn't stop bleeding for a while, but it's good now. You have a minor bruise on your shoulder, and that'll heal real fast. The best news is you're able to hold your baby safely for now, but complete rest for several weeks will be the deciding factor whether or not you'll abort."

"Abort?" Liz fought to control herself. Dwayne sat down on the narrow bed next to her and took her hand.

Her face had turned white as she repeated, "Abort? What can we do to prevent that? I'm in my seventh month. I want my baby to grow full term."

"My dear, I'm doing the best I can. I've had lots of experience with all kinds of pregnancies and all sorts of problems and we've always worked them out. I suggest you stay right here in this area with complete bed rest and I'll monitor you every day. I'll be as close as the phone. Joan, whom I know you met, has offered to have you recuperate at her place. She's as good as any professional nurse."

Liz gently turned her head to view the room. "Is she here? Joan? Joan, from the restaurant?"

"You've got it! Accident happened right on her corner and she's planning to have you stay with her. She wants to be your first-hand nurse and has offered Dwayne a job to help her with the diner as best he can with her supervision."

As if on cue, Joan knocked on the open door to ask if she could enter. She embraced Liz, holding her for a long time. "When we met last month, I wished you were my daughter – it was as if we'd always known each other. Fate has been good to spare you and has brought you back to me. You'll stay as long as you need to, and I'll be your private go-fer."

"I felt the same way about you, Joan, but still…"

"No buts from either one 'a you. Besides, I can use the company and the help."

"Yeah, but where will we sleep and …"

"No problem. I've got a large guest bedroom and bath, so you'll both have privacy. I live in good quarters right behind the restaurant. If you feel all right, Dwayne, I'd be obliged if you can help me run my place and I'll do the best I can to help you watch out for Liz, here."

Liz shook her head. "I'm fine and don't need any coddling. If I'm ordered to lie still, I'll damned well be still, if that's what I have to do to keep my baby." She began to cry.

Dwayne had been quietly listening to the plans being made for both of them by perfect strangers. Overwhelmed, tears rolled down his cheeks. "This is more than I could ever have hoped for. How will we be able to thank you for all you're doing for us?"

"Hey, listen here. You're going to work your ass off. You're going to earn every penny. I'll even throw in free food. How's about that? Things here had been boring before you came that last time, but since then, the new highway's opened and I've had more customers than I can handle. So, Liz, you just rest and get well, and I'll take advantage of having Dwayne here, to help me out."

Alone at last, Dwayne presented Liz with his poem.

Chapter 7

When the alarm clock buzzer woke Joan, she lay in bed, luxuriating in the few minutes remaining before she began her busy day. Life had been so empty since her husband died several years ago. She never thought about remarrying, but that was just as well; there were no eligible men in their small town. Her sons had moved East and were busy with their families and business ventures. They seldom visited. Just recently, when the new highway had opened, business really picked up, so she didn't have time to feel lonely except during the long evenings. Having Liz and Dwayne in her home gave her an enormous lift. Now she had special reasons for getting up early to prepare everything before the breakfast customers arrived. She took a few moments to meditate – an old habit – it helped get her fueled for the long day. She had a few friends, but they had families and she was on the fringe of their busy schedules, hanging around like a loose thread, ready and willing to be woven into their lives. Which they often did. It wasn't enough.

She and Dwayne became a good team the first morning, and the regular customers seemed to like him. Everyone had heard of the accident and some enjoyed teasing him about his black eye. But Dwayne went right along with the joking; even seemed to enjoy the repartee. He checked on Liz and reported to Joan that she'd devoured her large breakfast and was feeling perky.

The morning went by quickly, and this was the first time Joan and Dwayne had the time to sit down to enjoy a cup of coffee before preparing for the busier lunch rush.

"Hey, Dwayne, are you feeling okay? Maybe this is too much for you, just outa the hospital."

He smiled to hide how tired he really felt, but this meant too much and he wasn't going to give in to the tiredness seeping into his legs. "Are you kidding? Do I look all in?"

"Yeah, a little. You're good. Betcha you've done this waitering before."

"You're right. I did all kinds of odd jobs while I attended Pratt Institute in New York. I had an internship with a large architectural firm after graduating from college, but you know what that means, 'nada salary,' so I had to work nights to pay the rent."

"How'd you happen to get interested in architecture – a country boy?"

"Blame it on my Lincoln Logs and Legos," he said, laughing. He paused. "Seems like a long time since I've found something to laugh about. My life turned upside down when I met Liz – I knew right away that I loved her – we were really happy. When I finally began to make a decent salary, I proposed to her. Then, soon after we were married, the economy went into a tailspin and I got laid off. You know, last in, first out. Bad josh was Liz had an agent, had just started writing articles for a magazine, and then lost her job at the same time. She worked at a bank for a while until she got the exit cue too. We've gone through our small stash..." He welled up and couldn't continue.

Joan put her hand on his. "Things are gonna be just hunky-dory. Not only with Liz and the baby, but I know our country's going to turn around, now we've got us a brand-new president. You'll be back designing office buildings and making a big name for yourself. I feel it in my bones."

Embarrassed because he'd gotten emotional, Dwayne cleared his throat. "I sure hope so! I'd like to think I'll be designing office buildings near the 9/11 site – give a boost to the neighborhood again. My idol was Frank Lloyd Wright, and before I met Liz, I spent a summer at his home and school, Talieson, in Arizona. I thought I'd died and gone to architectural and designer's heaven there. He wanted to complete the package by designing everything inside—furniture, fabrics, drapes, dishes, silverware, the works. I was lucky to be in California to see a retrospective of his great achievements in the large governmental center he designed outside of San Francisco. Even toured his famous house built over a waterfall, aptly named Fallingwater, in Pennsylvania. I followed his buildings all over the country. Almost didn't go back to New York."

"But then, you wouldn't have met Liz. Why don't you go keep her company while it's quiet here? I've gotta get things going in the kitchen, to be prepared for the next…"

"Thanks, Joan. Good idea."

He found Liz propped up in bed, reading one of Joan's books. "Hey! You look so much better today, Liz. Your color is back, and I'm happy you've gotten dressed."

"I plan to do that every day, then I won't feel like a sickie." She pointed to the bookcases. "Joan's built a lovely library here. I'm impressed with all the different genres. I guess she's had a lot of time on her hands. She told me this small town doesn't have a library, so she orders used novels on the internet, then exchanges them with her friends – even keeps records of who's got what, like a librarian."

Dwayne sat down on the edge of the bed and slipped off his shoes. "Yep, Joan's that way with her book-keeping records, too. I admire her independence and how hard she works."

"Looks like you're working hard, too. I'm sorry we're stuck here because---"

"Because I'm a damn jackass. Everything that's happened on this stupid trip is my fault."

"O.K., now – we'll have none of that. Promise? We're going to stay put until Dr. Matthews says I'm able to travel, and until then, we'll just do what we have to do. I don't want to preach, but we should both use this time to take stock of what we're going to do in the future and do some serious job hunting."

He sighed. "You're right. I'll have to find some time to use the laptop each day. I'll change my statement to – I should be looking for work and you should be writing your new novel. Isn't that what you mean?"

"Don't tell me what I mean, mister," she said with a teasing, light-hearted voice that wasn't very convincing. "I can do more than that. Maybe I can get a part time job editing while I'm writing my great American novel. I have some experience and good references." She patted the bed, encouraging him to lie down, and gave him a big wet kiss.

He smiled. "Not now, hon, I'm too tired." He ducked just in time to miss her playful slap but was able to grab her hand in midair. Laughing, they fell into each other's arms, kissing and undressing each other.

"We haven't made love in a while," Liz said, nibbling on his ear, "but don't you dare think this will make up for it."

His wide grin told her all she wanted to know. They had always enjoyed their love-making, but with their fear she might lose the baby, they were very careful. Afterwards, legs entangled, holding hands, they lay naked.

Just then, the smoke alarm went off in the kitchen, triggering the other alarms in the house to also go off. It was deafening.

Dwayne's eyes bulged as he jumped out of bed and pulled on his pants.

"Get dressed! And get outside!" he roared as he ran bare footed and without a shirt, through the apartment into the kitchen. He found Joan waving two towels under the smoke alarm, trying to disperse the smoke in order to disengage the alarm. The telephone rang. She was coughing and could hardly speak, so she pointed to the telephone and signaled Dwayne to answer the call from the volunteer fire station. He saw she'd already put a cover on the flame in the frying pan, smothering the fire, but the smoke had triggered the fire detector.

"It's O.K.," he yelled. "You don't have to respond. The fire's out! We just have to clear the place." He opened the doors to the restaurant to get a cross draft, and grabbing another towel, helped to clear some of the remaining smoke.

Still gasping for breath, Joan leaned against the counter. "I hate this sensitive alarm," she said. "It happens far too often. If you weren't here, I'd a stepped on a chair and ripped the cover off the damned thing."

She accepted the glass of water from him, then realized Dwayne was almost undressed. She winked at him. "I'm sorry if I ruined something…"

He laughed as he shook his head. "I guess we're getting to know each other faster than we thought."

"Go back to your wife and grab a nap, if you can. It'll be busy because there's a Little League game tonight."

He hesitated. "Sure you're able to handle all the preparation? I could get dressed and come right back."

"No way! I'm used to this and you're not. Get outta here."

Chapter 8

It was a busy night. Dwayne enjoyed seeing those young families with the energetic boys calling across the tables, discussing some of the notable plays, bragging about their game; the losing team consoling each other with promises to do better next time. Even the parents kidded each other. It made him think about the baby Liz was carrying, and he hoped again he'd have a son someday, but fervently prayed this baby would be strong and healthy, no matter what sex it was. As Liz had stated, young girls were into all the sports nowadays, and he promised himself to take an active role in his child's activities.

Hours later, after they cleaned the dining room and kitchen, Dwayne and Joan brought dishes of ice-cream into the bedroom to keep Liz company.

"Thanks for the delicious dinner, Joan. And the ice-cream. You're going to make me so heavy I'll be wobbling around with a cane."

"Not so. The dinner was healthy and full of protein. Unlike Julia Child and all her real butter recipes, I try to watch cholesterol. This ice-cream is low fat, so don't worry."

"Thanks for everything you're doing for us. You're an angel. Are you very tired, Joan?" Liz asked, her voice betraying how hopeful she was to get started with her new novel. "Do you feel like telling me one of the stories you've heard about the shoe tree?"

Joan laughed. She handed Liz her notebook and pen from the dresser. "If I'd a known you'd be asking me so soon, I'd of taken notes." When she saw that Liz looked disappointed, she said, "I'm allowed to tease, ain't I? Believe me, I remember all them tales because I loved them. So now just settle in and listen."

"All set," Liz said, delighted that she was finally getting some stories, even though they weren't first hand. "I'm not going to interrupt you so you can stay on track. Shoot!"

"Well, let's see which one I want to start with." Joan paused for only a moment. "There's this little ole lady who came in alone, quite a while ago, when the highway was just a dirt road. Her hair was kind of silvery, but I remember it might have looked that way because maybe she had a blue rinse. You know, women had blue rinses years ago, not so much now. Anyways, she was real skinny, wearing baggy, well-worn blue jeans. I took her for eighty, she looked so spry, but as we talked a little when the place emptied out after lunch, she admitted she was ninety-two. Imagine! Drove all the way out here from Chicago, pulling the kind of trailer which pops up into something like a tent. Seems like her and her late husband, twelve years younger, used to drive out here to the West to see a lot of the national parks and hike all around these parts."

When Joan stopped to take a drink of water, Liz gave Dwayne a knowing look which said they had to be patient.

"You know, those trailers are good because it's high off the ground, and you needn't worry about snakes and scorpions getting into your sleeping bag. Oh, I skipped a very important part. When she came in, she had a shopping bag – she put on the chair across from her–and asked me to set a place there, too. I figured someone was meeting her, so I obliged. No one came. The windup was, afterwards when we were alone, she told me it contained an urn with her husband's ashes."

"Really?" Dwayne said. "She carried it into the restaurant?"

Joan nodded. "Sure thing. Said she hated to eat alone. She was taking his ashes to scatter in the hills as she retraced their travels. He'd probably end up in the park in San Louis Obispo in California where they spent a lot of time a few summers ago. They loved watching the sea lions in that national park. Did you know that most bodies weigh six pounds of ashes? I think she even talked to him like he was really there the whole time – lots of people was busy gabbing – no one paid attention to her talking softly to herself."

"That's gross, eating with his ashes there!" Liz shuddered. "No wonder you remember her."

"Well, let me tell you what she told me. She was pretty lonely and needed to get some things off her chest. She said I was the onliest one she could tell this to. What the hell, I had the time and was feeling all alone in this world. I know I shouldn't talk this way, but many times when my friends and customers had gone for the night, I felt like I needed a soul mate. Anyways, it felt good to sit after serving all the meals. She told me her man had come down with Alzheimer's disease and was really losing it fast, so they had to stop traveling. He started wearing an ole pair of heavy hiking boots around the house and she was sick of seeing him wear those smelly things. One day, while she was cleaning up the place, she threw them out in the trash. Danged if he didn't realize what she'd done and got those grimy ole boots back. He said they were his good luck hikers and he was sure he'd get better and they'd go out to travel again. She threw them out another time when he was napping, but he didn't say anything about missing them, so she thought he forgot all about them. Here it was, a few years later, and he died. After a long time of readjusting to her life without him, she felt this was the right time to travel again. She said she was making this a journey to discover what she needed to do for herself. As she drove on the highway near here with his ashes, she had a flat tire. Poor thing waited 'til some good soul came by to help her change the tire, and when they opened the trunk to take out the spare, instead of the tire, there were his boots."

Liz's eyes widened in surprise. "What a smart old codger he was. I'm sure the woman realized…"

"Yep! I wish you coulda heard her describing her love for her husband. He must have had his good moments, found his boots missing, got them back from the trash and hid them well. So, she couldn't travel without a spare tire but she had a lot of moxie. She took a ride with the man who stopped to help her, came to this gas station here, accrosst the way, where she bought a new spare and had the flat fixed. That man was real good, helping her so much, driving her back to put on that tire. She said he wouldn't take a cent for his kindness. She talked about how she played tennis until last year. Imagine that. She had this great attitude about life and I remember what she said about her being an optimist; because she bought new tennis sneakers when she turned 89. Anyways, she'd gotten her car moving again, was driving down the road, and she saw the shoe tree, and--"

Liz clapped her hands in delight. "Oh, please let me finish this! She threw her husband's hiking boots up there. It had to be an emotional release, to finally let go of that physical part of him."

"Yessiree! That's what she did just before she got here to tell me her story. Funny thing is, I told her my own tale – I was in high school and I found my ma's saddle shoes from the year one in the attic. You know what they were – white shoes with brown leather where you laced them. Tough to polish the white without hitting the brown part. So, I started to wear them every day. My friends were so jealous. I plumb wore them out and every time my ma threw them away, I resurrected them until the leather sides were soft and laces wouldn't hold."

"Are you kidding me? This really happened?" Dwayne shook his head.

"Scout's honor. Ma got such a kick out of my doing that."

"Well, weren't you the lucky one. Thanks, Joan, you've given me another great story for my book, but it's not enough to fill a short chapter, so I'll just have to improvise and write the rest from my imagination. I'll give that couple lots of kids and lots of tribulations and---"

"Hey!" Dwayne said, "Show, don't tell."

"It's past my bedtime, guys, so I'll see you in the morning." Joan reached over to hug Liz and gave Dwayne a thumb up. "I can't tell you what a big help you are. And Liz, he's a born salesman – he even pushes deserts more'n I do. I'll have to bake more."

He wasn't going to let her leave without enveloping her in a bear hug. "Good-night, Joan. I'm enjoying it more than you know."

Totally exhausted from a full day of standing on her feet, working harder than usual, and suddenly seized with muscular cramps in her legs, Joan fell on her way to her room. In excruciating pain, she cried for help.

Chapter 9

Dwayne was almost in the shower when Liz heard Joan scream. She jumped out of bed, and holding her belly, rushed out into the hallway. In tremendous pain, Joan attempted to stand, but her right leg buckled under, and she fell again.

"Stay there, don't move!" Liz ordered as she ran to get Dwayne, who was toweling his body dry. He pulled on his pants and carried Joan to her bed as Liz called Dr. Matthews. The doctor arrived within a few minutes.

"We'll have to get you x-rayed," he said, after examining her. She winced in pain when he touched her ankle. "It may be broken, or it could be a bad strain; sometimes they're worse than a break. You shouldn't be working so hard, Joan. You're like the skier who insists on taking one last run and gets hurt in a nasty fall. I've been watching you and warning you about overworking these past couple of months."

Despite her pain, Joan smirked. "It's nice you didn't say I told you so, Doc. Please don't make me go to the hospital – some ice and two aspirins should do the trick tonight, O.K.?"

"No! Not O.K. If it's broken, I may need to reset your ankle. I'm on my way to the hospital now, so I'll meet you and Dwayne there. All right with you, Dwayne?" When Dwayne nodded, the Doctor's attention then shifted to Liz. "What do you think you're doing, young lady? Get back to bed. Pronto!"

"Yes, sir! I'm going." She blew a kiss to Joan. "Good luck."

It seemed forever for their return, but just as Liz began to doze again, she heard Dwayne and Joan arrive. Despite the doctor's orders, Liz walked to Joan's room as Dwayne wheeled her in and gently transferred her to her bed.

"Whew! This bed sure feels delicious." She lifted her leg to allow Liz to place a pillow under it. "Don't you love my walking cast? Bright purple is my favorite color. It's removable. I can take it off to shower." When she got comfortably settled, she became serious. "Good thing you two were here when I fell. Thanks! I owe you."

"You owe us?" Dwayne gave her an incredulous look. "Listen here, I heard Doc Matthews say you've got to stay off that foot to let it heal, so you better behave. I'll set my alarm clock for an early start, so don't you worry about business because I already know the morning routine."

"Are you sure you can handle everything alone?" Joan sounded uneasy.

"Give it up," he cautioned as he walked out of the room. He turned back. "You're absolutely not coming into the restaurant or kitchen, even in your wheel chair. If I have any questions, I'll be here in a flash. Better yet, keep your cell phone near you, and I can just double check things with you."

The next morning, Dwayne waited for a break in serving customers to bring the women their breakfasts. He found Joan with Liz, sitting in the lounge chair with her leg elevated. As he approached, he heard them talking. They spoke as if they'd been lifelong friends.

"Hey, ladies, I hope you like my omelets. My own concoction of Portobello mushrooms, fresh red pepper, onions and shredded cheddar cheese. Oh, yes, I even put in some eggs."

The look on Joan's face gave him the answer. "I can't remember when someone cooked for me. You're too good. I may have to take you in as a partner." She giggled, "But I'll be the senior one, in more ways than one, right?" She sipped her coffee. "I guess you'll find me here most of the time. It's better for me to be sitting here in this recliner, and anyways, Liz is lying down. I know she's going to pump me for more ubiquitous stories."

Liz smiled. She loved how Joan used new words she'd picked up while reading, sometimes using them inappropriately.

48

It was endearing – Liz hoped she could capture her capricious character and make it endure in her novel. "You better believe it, Babe."

The bell above the restaurant door jangled.

"That's my cue," Dwayne rushed back into the dining room.

When they'd finished eating everything on their plates, Liz looked at Joan, her eyes pleading.

"Yes, of course, I know what you're going to ask, so give me a moment to think…"

But Liz didn't have to wait at all.

"Oh, yes, this one is something I won't forget. At least a month ago, a woman, no more'n fifty-five, good looking, trim, nicely dressed, comes in just after my last luncheon customer left. I was really tired, ready to call it a day but just couldn't send her away. So, after I served her, I sat down at a table nearby to read the morning paper. You know how it is, sometimes it's the first chance I have to catch my breath and relax, every day. I always have the newspaper in plain sight and let everyone read it. Well, you should see the mess I get, when I can finally look at it myself. Some folks finish the jigsaw puzzles, the Jumble, Sudoku, even rip out ads or coupons."

Joan looked at Liz's blank expression. She sat holding a pen and pad but had jotted down the few notes when Joan described the woman. Joan chuckled, and said, "Yep, my pa always said I could talk flies off an elephant. I promise not to sidetrack but, you know it ain't easy to control my thoughts, to keep them in check. All right, as I was reading, I hear her scold herself – she's saying something like, 'Lies, lies! I've lied all my life and I'm sick of trying to keep most of it straight.' I didn't say nothing to her– just pretended I wasn't privy to her conversation with herself. I was just trying to concentrate on my newspaper. Then she's crying and that got my attention. I saw tears making those little dark eye-makeup-streaks down her cheeks. She looked so miserable I just had to go over to give her a napkin to wipe her face before she spotted her expensive looking shirt. She pointed to a seat at her table and I felt sorry for her, so I joined her. You know me, I don't charge nothing for listening. The lady took a deep breath and using a tiny voice which made me move closer, she said, 'My life is one big lie.' So, what was I supposed to say? I just sat there, like a bug on a dog. After a while, she said, 'I've never gone to confession or to a psychiatrist, but I've got to unburden myself to someone or I'm likely to burst. I'm just a stranger but if you can give me a little of your time, can I tell you something with a promise you'll never use my name when you repeat this to anyone? I could go to jail if you don't keep your word.'

"When I said I wouldn't think to get her in trouble, she gave out a loud whoosh of breath and then she began her story. I can still remember just about every word she said, just like it was yesterday. She spoke in a soft voice telling me she was a widow; had been for a few years. Her husband was a good man, and she loved him too much to see him suffer. He'd had a couple of heart attacks and was almost a cripple. He was always in pain and was addicted to pills. He got so fat, he couldn't walk anymore after his heart surgery. Needed to start using a cane, then a walker, and finally, a wheelchair. She swore he was eating himself to death, to ease the pain. She talked about the time she was walking back to their table in a restaurant – he liked to leave the wheelchair on the side once in a while and he was sitting on a regular chair – she saw only one third of him was on the chair, with just as much of him hanging out on each side. Said it was disgusting. Their children teased him when he was growing so big, saying he'd need Omar the Tentmaker to make his clothes. But no one could convince him to stop gaining weight, not even his doctor."

"This sounds like he was making a death wish by overeating and taxing his heart."

Joan stopped to sip her coffee. "I don't know if I should go on. Maybe it ain't right, to repeat this, 'cause I did give her my word... Do you promise to change it all around; you know, doctor it up so it can't be her true story?"

"Of course. I'll only take the general idea with every tale. Chances are slim that any of these people you tell me about would ever read my novel, if it ever gets published, because I promise to write my book just using the ideas and completely embellishing them so no one would ever get into trouble."

Joan nodded. "When this woman began talking, she really unwound, pouring out the story like a waterfall, almost as if she was afraid she'd never get it all out. She said, 'He begged me to help him die when it got real bad, and Hospice was coming to our house, giving him the medication which made him sleep almost around the clock. I helped him, God save our souls, and I've never let on, never told anyone, but it's eating me up alive. The doctor never questioned his death, knowing it was imminent in a matter of weeks, said his heart gave out. So, I lied to the world, again.'"

"Oh, my goodness, she was talking about euthanasia," said Liz. "She helped her husband die. She's lucky she's not in jail."

"I agree, but she didn't blink an eye. She was as cool as the proverbial cucumber." She smiled. "Great word, ain't it? Proverbial, not cucumber, that is. Read it in my latest book. Looked it up in the dictionary. Anyways, she skipped right past it like it was nothing and went on to tell me she'd spent her life lying about everything, big or unimportant. For years, she'd been lying to cover up things when her daughters were growing up, because her husband was just too strict – had a double standard. As a kid, he'd been wild and knew what guys wanted to get away with; so he made their daughters keep a strict curfew; and they couldn't date boys who weren't following their religion. She felt she had to do the right thing by the kids because they were ready to rebel and she hadn't been able to change their daddy's stubborn mind. She didn't want to lose them and loved her husband and didn't want to keep fighting with him, so she covered for them to let them have some freedom. Now it's years later, and she's on her way to her daughter's home up north of here. She brought her own wedding dress – all preserved in an airtight box, looking like the day she bought it – for her granddaughter's wedding next month. They're about the same size. Her daughter couldn't wear it because she'd eloped. Did it because her father didn't want her to marry that boyfriend. She cried then, said her daughter broke her heart when she was so impetuous. Yep, I store some of them words and it's fun to use them with you. My friends would laugh at me. Oops! I'm sorry; I did it again; I just wander off. So, this lady never got the chance to plan a big wedding like all her friends and relatives did. Back to that story. She was driving down our new highway and she saw the tree with all those shoes and boots on it. She stopped to stretch her weary legs and got a closer look at the danged thing. Said she never saw anything like it in her life."

Joan stopped to drink her coffee. "Anyways, I told the woman I'd been there and seen it. It looked positively wonderful to me. I felt it was probably the onliest one in the world. Then she tells me that she's not just a liar, but also a thief: always had been since she was a little kid when she stole little toys from stores; from her playmates; took change from her Mother's bag; even grew up and stole her girlfriend's boyfriend. Mind you, said she didn't love him; just wanted the challenge. I'm sitting and listening and nodding, afraid to say the wrong thing, afraid that maybe she's warning me she's going to hold me up, take everything from my cash register. She sure coulda fooled me – didn't look the type, refined and all, but who's to know?"

"It would never have occurred to me either," Liz said, scribbling to get it all down, "Maybe I should get a tape recorder; I don't want to miss anything."

Joan dismissed the suggestion with a wave of her hand. "The windup was she'd even practically stolen the ankle-strap shoes to match her wedding dress, which, by the way, she'd marked both things way down when the saleswoman wasn't looking. Carried a red pencil just in case. Well, she told me that after she got married, her husband turned out to be a penny-pincher and he watched every dollar she spent. But she had a big pocketbook with two zippers on the ends, so when she went into a department store, she'd stuff clothes like a nightgown or a shirt in the zipper panels in her bag, without a telling bulge. She even wore two bras home one day. No one was the wiser. This happened before the stores got smart and put those plastic gizmos on every item. She bought some things she knew her husband would criticize, claiming they were too expensive, so she scrounged money from the food bills, to pay part of the items in cash, and only charged what she felt he'd approve of. Then she told me she actually encouraged her little kids to walk out of the supermarket with things like books, telling them to wait outside. Sometimes, she'd change the prices on things, if she was able to take a sticky tag from a cheaper one."

"I'm surprised her husband didn't notice she had so many extra things," Liz said. "I guess some men don't notice. You know, don't you, you're acting like a priest during confession, or like a psychiatrist when you listen to all these people pour their hearts out?"

"Yep, or even a counselor, but I often feel I'm happy to be a sounding board for people who need to talk things out. I never knew I was such a good listener or that I could remember long conversations so much."

"Good for you! And I'm benefitting from all of this. I'm thrilled." She blew Joan a kiss. "And wasn't this woman enterprising? Not that she's a major criminal, but I've often thought that if crooks put their mind to something positive instead of all the devious stuff, they'd go farther."

Joan nodded. "Now, the day she came here, when she saw all the shoes on the tree, she realized she didn't want to pass many of her sins onto her granddaughter; she didn't want the young girl to begin marriage with a lie; didn't want her walking in her footsteps, stepping on her soul, if you get the two meanings." Joan laughed, pleased with herself. She shifted, shook her shoulders, then wincing with pain, lifted the leg with the cast, to stretch her thigh. She looked in need of more medication.

When Joan stopped to take a pill, Liz was able to add, "Yes! I guessed she'd do it! She buckled the straps together to throw the shoes up on the tree. I'll bet she'll take her granddaughter shopping for her own wedding shoes. There's a term for people who steal when they can afford to buy something and have the money right there with them. Kleptomaniac. She needs a psychiatrist—"

Liz stopped talking when she saw Joan leaning forward to scratch her toes sticking out of the cast. Before Liz could warn her that she looked precarious, Joan and the recliner tumbled over.

Joan couldn't stop laughing. She was all tangled up in the recliner, with her cast sticking straight up in the air. Liz was frightened, thinking Joan had hurt something, but when she realized Joan wasn't screaming in pain, she laughed at the sight, too. Dwayne had heard the crash and came running into the room. Laughing with them, he helped extricate Joan, sat her on the edge of the bed, and pulled the heavy chair upright.

"Hey! You guys scared me! I didn't know what to expect from the loud bang. It sounded like a chest of drawers had fallen…"

"Oh, mercy sakes!" Joan fought to catch her breath. "Couldn't you tell from our hysterical laughter that I was all right?"

Chapter 10

During the dinner hour, Dwayne was so busy, he didn't have time to bring the women their food, but they'd had a late snack and weren't hungry. When he had a few minutes, he sent a cheerful young man into the bedroom with their meals. Stu had offered to help Dwayne when he saw how harried he was. He said he'd done some odd jobs for Joan before going off to college and knew the layout of the back rooms.

"Hey, Joan, when I came into the restaurant for dinner, I heard about your accident. Are you O.K.?"

"Sure thing, Stu. Thanks for bringing this to us. Is Dwayne keeping up with the customers? He won't let me anywhere near the place."

"Yep, almost. But I chipped in and helped him some." The tall, willowy redhead smiled broadly, making it seem as if his freckles grew. "Cleared the tables and brought the food out. Dwayne's really working hard."

Joan's face flushed as she perked up. "Wow! You're the answer! You're on vacation now, right? Do you want to earn some money? Come work here! It'll be great for all of us. And you can eat all you want. Well, there is a limit, or I'll lose all my profit."

"How about that?" Stu beamed. "Fantastic! I'm only here for a couple of weeks before I go back for summer school. I can sure use the money and it'll be better than working for my Pa. I'll start right now." He ran off to tell Dwayne.

Obviously enjoying their roast chicken, the women concentrated on their food. Joan was thrilled with the seasoning. "Dwayne should have been a chef. The chicken isn't dry and the vegetables are crisp. It took me a while before I could tell what he added to enhance the flavor of the mashed sweet potatoes.

I'm sure it was grated fresh ginger. I'm so impressed with him! We're going to fly now that I've discovered his talents. So, are you in the mood for another story? I'm really excited about our new project."

"You read my mind! I've been trying to invent my own stories while waiting to hear your first-hand accounts. I remember reading a great quote by Ray Bradbury who claimed that his stories ran up and bit him in his leg and he reacted by writing down everything that went on during the bite."

"I like that. I've read some of his novels; great plots that really move and keep you wanting to read the next chapter. Now I'll have to put my head together to help you."

"After all, we're sort of stuck with each other, and I'm enjoying spending this time with you."

"Oh, sure!" Joan shook her head several times, resembling a bobblehead doll. "Spending time with me to pick my brain when I'm helpless and can't ambulate. I know when I'm being used." She ducked when Liz balled up her paper napkin and threw it at her.

Liz turned serious. "Joan, you're always talking about others and their stories, but I'd love to know all about you. Tell me about yourself."

"Me? Nothing much to tell. I'm here, running a busy place in a hick town, and that's who I am."

"No, there's more to you than that. You're special, so don't dodge the subject."

After what seemed like an extremely long minute, Joan settled in and admitted, "I was lonely a lot as a kid. My older sister, only eighteen months older'n me, we were close as twins, died of walking pneumonia when we were only eight, and my ma couldn't bear the pain of losing her child, and died right that same week. The doctor told us she died of a broken heart, and I believe that, to this very day. My pa was so busy working and was so miserable about how he lost his family, he couldn't even look at me and didn't pay me much attention, or know I was there, and I was alone, without my ma and my best friend, had no one to talk to, so I learned early on to just mind my own business and not count on anyone." She gulped hard.

Liz didn't know what to say. She waited while Joan collected herself. "Oh, I'm so sorry, Joan, that I forced you to discuss this. I shouldn't have."

"Hey! Maybe it's good to get some of this off my chest. I've always put up a good front; I heard it said that a smile begats another one, but now that I've opened up, I want to tell you about the most embarrassing thing that ever happened to me, which made me wake up and realize I had to take better care of myself. One night, this neighbor asked me if I'd like to stay for supper with her family. I'd been there, playing with her brood and it began to pour, so she called my pa and said I could stay over and sleep with her daughter. When it was time for bed, I put on a pair of her jammies; then took off my holey shoes and I was wearing filthy socks with big holes in them, and we had to go into the kitchen to say good night, so I took off my socks, and my damned feet were black, caked thick with dirt. I couldn't remember when I'd taken a bath and Daddy never checked up on me or tried to teach me anything. I felt so bad, I ran into the bathroom to wash my stinking feet, but their lily-white towels woulda gotten so ruined, that I just put my holey socks back on and marched into the kitchen, like a ragamuffin. What I shoulda done, was to put my shoes back on, but what was I to know? The looks on everyone's faces still bother me today and I feel myself blush even now. My face turned red and that heat went right down to my dirty toes. I knew they didn't want me to get under the covers with their sweet daughter. They thought I had cooties. I was worse off than that boy supposedly raised in the jungle by a chimp – at least, animals know how to clean themselves. I wasn't mad at my pa anymore – he just couldn't do for me – he wallowed in his own misery. So, I promised myself that from then on, I'd be as clean as a whistle; my body and my clothes; and I'm still compulsive. I have always showered every day, so I now I cover my stupid broken foot with a garbage bag when I take a bath. P.S. I never got the nerve to go into their house again, and of course, their charming flower-scented daughter never played with me again, much less than enter my house."

Liz couldn't find the words to assuage Joan's unfathomable suffering. She didn't want to say the wrong thing. They remained silent for a few minutes. Liz's mind went into overdrive: these strangers who told their stories were ordinary people living ordinary lives – they were not scientists who discovered something to add to mankind's future – they were not politicians monitoring world-changing events. They usually described mundane incidents which impacted their psyche and that sometimes gave them peace of mind; a sort of solace or mode of satisfaction, enabling them to deal with their memories. Who was she to judge?

Shrugging her shoulders as if throwing off the heavy weight, Joan broke the silence, obviously working hard to change their mood, talking quickly. "I was thinking about the middle-aged man who came in just before you arrived. There was an unusual look about him, like he wanted to talk to someone. He was a right nice-looking fella; tall, with a little pot belly. But, hell, I've noticed most men in their late fifties seem to be fighting that battle, like we women are fighting our growing muffin waists. Sexy beard, well-trimmed and all that, not like the I didn't feel like shaving today grubby look. He was very talkative, entertaining people at a table near him with some funny jokes. He had a sharp wit and a great sense of humor. I remember one funny short one – you'll love it. Did you hear the one about a guy who'd been sick and finally went to his doctor for a check-up? After many tests were analyzed, the doctor told him he had Canary-eye-tis and it was very serious. When he asked what the disease was, the doc repeated, 'Canary-eye-tis. It's not good.' The man said he never heard of Canary-eye-tis and asked what he could take to cure it. The doctor said, 'I'm afraid that nothing will help.' Joan had to laugh as she told the punch line. 'It's un-tweet-able.'"

The two women cracked up. Liz hadn't laughed that hard at a joke in a long time; she had tears rolling down her cheeks. The joke wasn't that funny to warrant her strong reaction – it served as a sense of relief from all the tension she'd been building up since the beginning of this trip, so long ago, it seemed – plus hearing Joan's outrageously intimate history.

When Liz finally stopped laughing, she said, "No wonder you remember that one. I'll have to tell it to Dwayne. Have you mentioned it to Dr. Matthews? He'll love it. Go on, what's that man's story about the shoe tree?"

"Hey, be patient with me and let me enjoy this."

"Patient, you say? Well, let me tell you about patience. I once read an article written by a psychiatrist who talked about delayed gratification –"

"See? There you go again – using them big words. I only barely graduated from high school, with low grades in grammar, so tell me what that means."

Liz looked forlorn. "I really am sorry. But give me a chance to explain the term. He took ten kindergarten children and placed a large bowl of cookies on the table before them, explaining that they could have a cookie right away, but if they could wait two minutes, they could take two cookies. He followed that experiment up twenty-five years later, interviewed the same people and reported that the few children who waited to get two cookies, ended up with more college degrees and made more money than those who satisfied their urge to eat one right away."

"So that's what it means, holding off."

"Absolutely! So, I was excited about that experiment because as a child, my parents would give me a penny to buy a fistful of candy at the tiny grocery store on the corner, and believe it or not, I'd wait until I had two cents so I could buy one piece of fudge."

"Yep, you're a winner. I'll remember – delayed gratification – wait for the better payoff. So, back to that man in my place. It's kinda sad, how he hung around, kept sipping his coffee until all the other customers had left. When he waved to me, I figured he was really looking to bend my ear, so I had nothing pressing to do except clean up, because for some reason, I hadn't seen Mary Poppins in this place yet, so things would be there when I was ready to tackle the mess. I sat down with him. He didn't stop talking. Said his wife had had a lot of mental problems yet wouldn't get some help, felt she could handle things on her own. Their kids had been out of the house for years, and she moped around a lot, not satisfied with anything or anyone. She'd been depressed off and on for months, had even threatened to kill herself. Since she wouldn't go to a therapist, he offered to take her on a trip across the country to visit some of the national parks and she perked up. He suggested that they take their golf clubs with them and play at some courses along the way. They watched golf together and always wanted to visit some of the places they'd seen on TV. So, he was making plans to get someone to cover him at work. The only time she didn't take pills is when she played golf a couple-a-times a week, otherwise she was onto many drugs, the new term is opioids. Filled prescriptions from different doctors at various drugstores. She and her three friends ate a leisurely lunch after the first nine holes before returning to the next hole. They always looked forward to spending those fun days together; gossiping, telling jokes, even shopping afterwards. One day when she'd been behaving badly at breakfast, he told her he was absolutely going to throw away her pills. He swore he was going to call their G.P. and tell him not to renew the prescriptions because they were making her worse. She left the house to meet the ladies for a round of golf. Afterwards, her friends said she wasn't so bad during the morning, not complaining as much as she usually did, sounding like a crotchety old spinster, and she wasn't grumbling about her partner."

Liz had been scribbling fast notes and hadn't even thought about interrupting Joan while she was zipping along, hardly stopping to catch her breath. "Well, it sounds as if she had a good time with the women and relaxed more."

"Not that day. He cried then, kept wiping his nose and could hardly talk. Said she'd gone to the golf course in her friend's car. After the ninth hole, they stopped for their usual lunch. She asked her friend for the car keys, saying she'd forgotten something. Next thing they knew, they all heard a loud noise, like a car backfiring."

"Oh, no!" Liz was too far away to lean over to take Joan's hand when she burst into tears. "That's outrageous."

"It's too terrible! The man said that his wife's girlfriend was a social worker for the state. She traveled around a lot to some pretty rough neighborhoods and felt she needed some protection. All her buddies knew she had a permit to carry a gun in the glove compartment."

"I can't believe this!" moaned Liz. "His wife shot herself in her friend's car?"

Joan dropped her head. "I'll never forget how he looked. He broke down again, poor soul. When he controlled himself to finish telling me the horrible story, he said he'd taken her clubs and golf shoes with him to tour the country, as they'd planned, and played golf, using her clubs in several different states. Of course, when he saw the shoe tree the day he stopped here, he'd tossed her golf shoes up there. He loved how they swayed back and forth awhile, as if she was telling him it was okay. Even left her golf clubs leaning against the tree for anyone who wanted them." Joan sagged as she wiped a tear.

Liz took a deep breath. "How awful. For the girlfriend who had the gun in the car, and particularly for the husband. Sometimes there's nothing you can do to prevent a tragedy. If not with the gun, his wife probably would have found another way to kill herself; maybe OD'ing on her opioids. Hey, Joan, I've noticed that some of these stories take a lot out of you. Maybe we don't have to continue. Unless this serves as a catharsis."

"It does. It's good for me to get some of these tales off my mind." She gave Liz's hand a squeeze when she left the bedroom. "Reconnecting with you has made my day. No. It's been the highlight of my life. Besides, you're cheaper than a shrink."

Chapter 11

Unable to sleep, afraid of disturbing Dwayne, Liz left the bed to work on her laptop in Joan's living room. She hadn't noticed the furnishings there since their arrival, when she'd been rushed directly into the bedroom. She'd anticipated a traditional mid-western room filled with artifacts, maybe a stuffed trophy head and a shotgun mounted above a fireplace. Not at all. It was delightful. Decorated in a colorful eclectic motif, it was cozy and comfortable. The window curtains were drawn to let in the daylight during the day, and the walls were covered with muted patterned wallpaper which contrasted with several whimsical paintings, done in primary colors of Western motifs. She admired the various collections of paper weights and antique silver napkin rings on antique tables. Small unusual frames filled with family pictures were casually placed around the room.

How lovely, and typical of Joan, she thought. She's such a warm giving person. I'm so grateful my baby's okay and she's taken us in, like lost puppies blown in from a sandstorm.

Stretching, she settled into the soft down-filled couch which seemed to envelope her like lying in a cloud, making her feel small and secure. Conflicting thoughts of how to begin her novel ricocheted in her head like captured fireflies in a glass jar. This was the first time in months she'd been so turned on by any writing project and she decided the best way to begin would be to start typing. She couldn't remember who said, 'I am not a writer unless I write.' How true. Having already written the intro weeks ago, she felt ready. She transcribed her almost illegible scribbled notes into three chapters, words flowing more rapidly than she'd ever experienced as she tuned into her best writing. Excited, she cut loose like Jack Nicholson's wish list in the movie, writing with a broad grin pasted on her face.

When finally, utterly exhausted, she closed her eyes, she felt warm and as safe as she did when she was a child covering her head with a blanket.

The next morning, after Joan had settled into her comfortable recliner in Liz's room, Stu brought in their breakfasts. He vibrated with energy and displayed a childishly teasing attitude. "Want to know what Dwayne's up to this morning?"

Joan gave him a know-it-all look. "Now what are you getting at, young man? Out with it!"

"O.K. I can't fool around with you, so I won't dawdle. Dwayne's been talking everyone into special French toast made with granola and all kinds of nuts. It's easier than filling all kinds of different orders, and more profitable. Wait 'til you taste these." As he uncovered a dish, his eyes shone brightly, his smile again seemed to make his freckles grow darker on the spot.

"Well," Liz rolled her eyes, "he did taste these once at John G's when we vacationed in Florida, but I never…"

They gobbled the first pieces. Joan looked as if she wanted to steal some of Liz's last piece, but Liz threatened her with her fork and stuck her tongue out.

"Dwayne's like a kid in Willie Wonka's candy factory," said Joan, "concocting new menus like Julia Childs. Did I tell you that I once met her at a fundraiser in New York? I'm sure you saw that recent movie about her with Meryl Streep, one of my favorite---"

"Ciao, my ladies. I'd like to discuss it with you, but I'd better get back to help in the kitchen," Stu said, backing out of the room with a flourish, as if he were leaving royalty.

After they'd finished their breakfasts, Joan gave Liz a knowing look. "Hey, girl, I'm ready with today's chapter, if you want, but…"

Liz plumped up her pillows. "Absolutely. You read my mind, but hey, I don't want to push you."

"Well, listen, I poured out my innermost secrets about my life to you, and now I've gotta ask you to share some of your life

63

and your thoughts with me. It's only fair." She snickered, "Besides, I took you and Dwayne in without any references and you might be serial killers, for all I know."

They giggled like teenagers. "Yep, that's what we do while you're snoring your head off. Have you noticed that there's a smaller population here?" When Joan finally stopped chuckling, Liz turned serious and said, "Nothing special in my childhood – my family life was ordinary and I grew up knowing I'd go to state college. I kept taking courses with the spare money I earned while working in nothing-special jobs; had a few affairs; but I was lucky to have a few good friends. I don't want to sweat the details, but my life became wonderful when I met Dwayne. Let's see, I used to be fastidious with my housework but now I consider myself neat. I don't sweat the small stuff and my hang-up is that when I wash my hands, I sing happy birthday to me like Larry David did in a Woody Allen movie."

Joan winked at Liz, "I'd say that's quite revealing."

"I'm really not interesting, not like some of the people we've been discussing. At my lowest ebb, I tormented myself that I'd like to shed my life like a snake leaves behind his former shell, but now I'm living vicariously through other people's lives and I feel damn lucky." On the verge of tears, she struggled to control herself by sighing deeply.

Joan waited. When Liz didn't continue, she finally said., "Okay, thanks for nada info, almost boring." She chuckled. Once again, they enjoyed spontaneous laughter. Joan nodded, "My cue. Last night, when I couldn't sleep – I'm not used to this damned inactivity – I thought about so many of the stories about the shoe tree all those new people told me. One woman, about your age, Liz – no, more like mine – had an unusual story. I really liked her and encouraged her to stay awhile after her lunch. She told me that while she was in college, she spent a year studying in France, where one of her new friends taught her how to flirt."

"Really? Like taking a course called Flirting 101? I thought it was inborn; it's part of a person's nature, or not."

"Hey! Not necessarily. Let me describe how I remember her. This woman, big-boned and strikingly attractive, wore a beautiful modern haircut, carefully applied make-up ..."

Interrupting Joan, Liz said, "This doesn't sound like you. I'm struggling to keep up with you already, and you're not even into the story. How do you remember so many details?"

Joan pretended to be hurt, couldn't do it, and gave up. "Are you accusing me of making up details like a literary professional? That's for you to do. So anyway, she, I think Ginny was her name, but you'll rename her anyways, Ginny had a great time in Paris, winning the bets she made with her friends by flirting successfully with someone every day. She said she never made love to the guys, just fooled around to get attention and have some fun. When she returned home, she decided that she'd try her sex appeal on young men here. She didn't get to first base for a while, but one day, while shopping, she went into a restaurant for a quick lunch. The guy behind the counter was cute, so she sat there near him, instead of sitting at a table. She described him to me as if he was sitting there in front of us. He had a dark complexion, with gorgeous dark wavy hair, and spoke with an accent. Emile told Ginny he was from the Baltic region, I think Serbia, and had been living here only a short time with his parents, who spoke very little English. He'd learned to speak English by watching TV. When it got too busy for their banter, he and Ginny exchanged telephone numbers and they dated awhile before he moved in with her. He told his parents he was going to share an apartment with a roommate. They never questioned him further. Of course, after a while, she became pregnant, but he still hadn't told his family about her. Unfortunately, when she was only into her first trimester, she had a miscarriage, and she was so upset, she went into a deep funk." Joan paused, realizing that she shouldn't have mentioned this last fact to Liz, but Liz was busy taking notes and didn't seem to notice.

"Now, during these many months their son wasn't living with them, the guy's parents assumed that he was living with another male from work. One night, when he had dinner with them, his parents informed him it was about time he got married to the girl back home who had waited to meet him all these years. They'd arranged a marriage with a young girl from 'the old country' when he was still a child. The two sets of parents were good friends before she was even born, and they pledged they'd cement their friendship by marrying their kids to each other."

"Wow!" Liz interrupted. "What a tough situation. I wouldn't want to be in Ginny's shoes. How did she take this news?"

Joan shook her index finger at Liz, as if talking with an impatient child. "Don't get ahead of me. Emile hadn't ever disobeyed his folks – they still had the old-fashioned European mentality – he never thought of refusing their marriage arrangement – and still didn't tell them about Ginny. When Emile told Ginny about his impending marriage with a woman who would arrive in a few months, she was distraught. She still mourned the loss of her baby. He remained in their apartment, hoping to somehow get out of his problem. During many months of delays in getting the prospective bride into this country, Ginny made up her mind; she wanted to become pregnant again, despite the fact they had no future together. The thought had entered her head like a screaming rocket, she said. I remembered that, word for word. She promised Emile he wouldn't have to feel any obligation to support her or the baby. Of course, I'm using her words the way I remember them."

Liz hardly noticed the fruit she cut into tiny pieces. "Yes, I noticed that. Well, she sounds like she knew what she wanted. It's not easy to be a single mother. How was she going to handle the finances?"

"Ginny told me her grandmother had died and left her a good amount of money. She was estranged, the lady's exact words, from her mother, her father had died, and her older sister lived in Canada, so she was independent. Right after she gave birth to Judith, Emile moved out and he and his parents went to Europe to bring back his bride."

"This is such a soap opera, Joan. I have to give her credit because I wouldn't have the guts to raise a kid completely on my own. Did Emile see his daughter at all?"

"Only when the baby was born. Ginny moved to Texas and raised Judith there. She never married but dated a bit. Emile had three sons, and yet had deep feelings for Ginny. He'd call occasionally and sent birthday and holiday gifts to her and his daughter. Ginny took her daughter to visit her father once she was old enough to handle the unusual situation but he still didn't mention any of this to his wife, or his parents."

Liz looked up. She smiled. "I have a feeling you didn't mention that Ginny's daughter was here with her. Right?"

"Yep! I was saving that. What a lovely young woman she was, with her mother's looks and Emile's dark complexion."

"How old was she? Was she sitting there all the time her mother was telling you all this?"

"I'd say about fifteen. Judith had heard her mother repeat this story before and she wanted to explain to me how she reacted to all this. She told me she felt shy the first time she met her father. Didn't get emotional. More like curious. She didn't object to meeting with him again the next summer. She said she'd only seen her dad for a few days each year and he was nice, but they hadn't really bonded. She'd talk to him about school, her interest in sports, and friends. That was all of their conversation. He only showed her pictures of her half-brothers when she asked about them. So now comes the fascinating part of the story. This last visit was the eye-opener for all of them. Emile finally told his mother about Ginny and Judith after his father died this past year. Seems as if his mother never did like the European wife, and when she heard about Emile's other life, insisted she meet his American family when they traveled East again."

Glowing with pleasure, Liz clapped her hands; a childish habit she'd never outgrown. "This is fascinating! Please don't leave out any details!"

"I won't, because I was really getting emotional, picturing the grandmother meeting her teenage granddaughter for the first time. By the way, the two of them sat here a long time telling me everything. The meeting had just happened a few days before I met them. They were touring this part of the country before going back to Texas and I was the first one to share their story."

"So that's how this all came about. Go on, I can't wait to hear the rest."

"Here's the best part. Emile's mother accepted Judith as a granddaughter, and immediately took a liking to Ginny. She was upset with Emile for not telling her years ago that he was living with a woman whom he loved. But she also knew her husband would not have wanted to renege on the wedding arrangement he'd made when Emile was young. Family pride and tradition, you know. All their lives could have been different if Emile had only demanded that his father let him choose his own wife."

Shaking her head, Liz said, "Quite a conundrum. If he'd only had guts, and loved Ginny enough, he'd have faced his father and told him the truth and insisted on marrying his lover. Then they'd have had a beautiful life together. It could have been a wonderful romantic story, but what does it have to do with the shoe tree?"

"Aha! I'm coming to it. Emile's mother met Ginny and Judith a second time. She called them her family. She brought them many gifts, including her own gold bracelet for Ginny and an heirloom locket she wouldn't give to Emile's wife because they never had a close relationship. Instead, the woman wanted to give it to her granddaughter, Judith. She gave them handmade shawls and fancy crocheted slippers, then made them promise to visit her each year when they came to see Emile. The two of them had tears in their eyes when they told me the slippers were too small, so when they drove here---"

"I know how this story ends. They tied them together and threw them up on our shoe tree." Liz sighed. "I'm not sure I like this story. It's bittersweet. What a different story this would have been if Emile had been man enough to stand up for his love."

Chapter 12

Joan was finally able to hobble around in a temporary cast and crutches. Recuperating well, in a complete turnaround, having undergone physical therapy twice a week, she'd spent a few hours each day assisting Dwayne while sitting at a counter. Now that her strength had returned, the therapist finally felt she was ready to handle the kitchen.

When their routine returned, Dwayne sat down to talk with her. "I'm happy you're all right now, Joan, and Stu is top-notch, so it's a good time for me to fly to New York to try to get a job. If it's okay with you, Doc Matthews says Liz needs to stay awhile but I can't wait any longer. I've got to provide for us when the baby comes."

"Hey! Don't you dare think twice about her! I love her like she's my daughter, and I know you need to go get yourself set with a proper income to prepare for them. I know Liz wants to go with you, but if Doc feels she needs just a little more time here, just to be sure the baby is safe, I want her to stay as long as she needs to."

"I'll pay whatever you feel is right…"

"Are you kidding? You worked so hard while I was laid up, and your salary wasn't enough to keep a family going. No ways are you giving me money to feed her for a while. You'll need your money while your job hunting, Now git! Make your plans and I'll have someone drive you to the airport. I'll need Stu to help me, and there's lots of folks here owe me a favor It's about time I collected some of those."

It had been an exhausting day for Joan, who had single-handedly cooked and served both breakfast and lunch. She thought how much she missed Dwayne. *He'd taken over so much of my responsibility. He spoiled me rotten. We didn't tell him that Stu would be leaving for school within a week of Dwayne's leaving. He probably would've stayed. Now Stu's left for summer school. Somehow, I've gotten through the day, but by the skin of my teeth. My mouth almost hurts me from forcin' a smile to hide how much I ached.*

A young man had been watching as she worked at a feverish pace, yet she'd managed to keep up a cheerful patter with all the customers, many of whom he seemed to know. He waited until the last customer left.

"Hey, Joan," he said boldly. "It's obvious you need some help. I'd be obliged if you'd hire me as your waiter and all-round assistant. I'm a hard worker and I can learn fast."

Her heart told her to grab the opportunity. She looked him over. Squat and muscular, Greg had a pleasant enough look about him. She'd seen him around for a while but had never gotten involved in a conversation with him before.

"Is that a fact? Tell me about yourself."

When he explained who his parents were, and that he'd just returned home from college for the summer, she eagerly hired him, figuring a smart boy like him would quickly learn the ropes.

The next morning, they worked together very well. Greg anticipated her needs and offered to do extra things, like loading the dishwasher and slicing or chopping vegetables; which took some of the burden off her. She noticed that he had a great rapport with the customers, who joked around with him and took his suggestions for ordering more things, like soup or dessert.

When the final group left, it was mid-afternoon.

"Hey, kiddo," she said when he'd cleared the last table, "you have a sharp wit and sense of humor and better yet, you know what to do without my saying anything. You've got to stay here forever. Forget college and marry me! I need you!"

His laughter sounded like a pig snorting as they both howled at her preposterous proposal. Tired, they spontaneously sat down near the kitchen. Joan offered him a beer, winking as she muttered something about the sheriff being away. It was easy talking and gossiping about the local folks and the out-of-towners who'd dropped by demanding quick service, but then stayed on for a longer time to sit and talk with Joan and each other when it quieted down.

"Funny thing about having outsiders come in," Joan told Greg as they unwound. "Some of them can't wait to talk to me about being there at the shoe tree. They've told me some pretty personal stuff that you'd hear about on Dr. Phil's TV program. I never knew people would unburden their hearts to strangers like that."

"That tree sure is an uncommon sight. Have you gone over to see it lately?"

"Nope! Can't say that I've had the time in a dog's age. Haven't you noticed how busy I've been here?"

He grabbed his snack with one hand and took her arm, getting her out of her seat before she realized what had happened. "You're in for a surprise! I stopped there yesterday, on my way to my grandma's. Grab your hat. You need a break."

"I can't!" Joan protested. "What if someone comes by for an early dinner?"

Instead of responding, Greg wrote a large sign stating they'd be open at six o'clock, placed it in the window, and guided her to the door. She ran back to tell Liz where she was going. As he drove them in his open, dusty twelve-year-old dented jeep, he kept a running dialogue about how he and his friends used to stop there at the unusual tree to drink and carouse for hours, making up stories about the reasons people had for throwing their things up there. Sometimes, the kids would steal a note which was attached, or exchange their sneakers or boots for better ones, but they never felt guilty. It was all part of the game.

When the shoe tree was in sight, she gasped. "My word, there's twice the stuff there since I saw it!"

"Isn't it great?" he chuckled in a proprietary way as they got out of the jeep and circled the tree.

They sat down and leaned back against the large trunk.

He smiled as he pointed to a branch high up in the tree. "I've thrown my own worn out boots there, still stinking of cow dung. No way will I return here to be a cowhand for my ol' man. I'm going to be a vet and practice in town. No farming for me."

Joan took a few moments to think of the proper advice to give him. "Well, since you've passed it by me, I reckon I'm going to have a say-so. Have you squared your plans away with your pa? I know your whole family well. Seems to me, as his only son—"

"Didn't you hear me, woman?" He drew a deep breath. "I don't mean no disrespect, but I've got to live my own life. I've chosen my path. It's a narrow one, and I wish it was as wide as the Yellow Brick Road, my favorite movie. That's why I'm saving to be on my own someday. I've worked hard to get my scholarships and not feel beholden to anyone. I want to get hooked up with some pretty young gal and live in an apartment in the center of town, with all the new appliances and modern contraptions."

His decision resonated in her heart. She'd raised herself and had encouraged her own kids to have his same dreams of independence. *Yep. He's serious about it and he's sure to do it all. I do feel sorry for his family. For sure they've wanted to pass the farm to him, but maybe his younger sisters will marry and live on their homestead; raise their kids there. I hope so.*

There was nothing further she could add.

Neither of them spoke for a while. It was quiet and peaceful there. A good place to sort their dreams. The desert wind came up now and again, rustling the leaves and moving some of the smaller items on the thinner branches. Joan felt a sense of calmness oozing from the rhythm of the objects in motion. It seemed like an aura surrounded the entire tree. With a perfunctory wave, she murmured, "Things and people ain't always what they seem. I've learned that the hard way."

He straightened his shoulders. "Waddaya mean?"

"If all these things here could talk, they might tell you about some of the times they've run into, different than what their owners may have told me. There's always another side to a story. Or things that might have happened in the past, that weren't mentioned by some folks in telling their stories, not necessarily lies, but stuff that was bound to be forgotten. I mean, the WHOLE story."

Lost in thought, he didn't respond. *Wow! This is a whole other side of Joan that I've never known. Was she actually philosophizing? Is that the right word?*

In the distance, they heard a motor and saw the dust swirls from an approaching car. Within minutes, the speeding red convertible pulled up near them. A stunning woman, dressed in expensive-looking designer jeans and sweater quickly joined them. Her short white hair was beautifully styled, serving as a halo to her well-lined face, but her taut figure was that of a more youthful person. She exuded boundless energy.

"Well now, this is the famous tree I've heard about. I've come miles out of my way to look at it. It is something, isn't it?" Her well-modulated voice didn't have any semblance of a local accent.

"We're about to leave in a few minutes," Joan said, "but you're welcome to sit with us. This here's Greg, and I'm Joan."

Disregarding the sandy ground near the base of the tree, the elderly limber woman sat down facing them. Her wide-set eyes shone. "Thanks. My name's Frannie. I'm happy to find someone here, to share this moment with me. I'm celebrating my eightieth birthday with my family in Reno, and I wanted to enjoy driving alone through this great country."

Joan gave her a long approving look. "Aren't you wonderful to drive all around alone? I've never had the chance to do that, and I guess I never will."

"I've been on the road for five days since I left Texas, and I've loved every minute of it. I'm a real tourist, stopping in interesting towns, even ghost towns, and National Parks."

"I'm curious, Frannie," Joan said. "What did you do in your younger days, that makes you look so great?"

"I'm proud to say that I taught school for about thirty-five years, during good times and bad, but I always felt I did something worthwhile. If I touched even two children every year and gave them the incentive to accomplish what they dreamed of doing, then I'm pretty proud that I've had a purposeful life. I raised three kids who all went on to become professionals, and I always worked hard balancing my family life and taking courses for advanced degrees while working full time. Hey! We didn't have computers like the kids today, who look everything up on their smart phones." She laughed. "Siri, the iPhone voice who gives them the answers, is one of their best friends."

Greg nodded. "You're inspiring me. I count on Siri, too. I have all kinds of plans to continue my education."

"Do you want to hear my pet peeve?" Frannie didn't wait for an answer. "When I meet pampered women who never worked a lick all their lives and they tell me that they're entitled to their easy life because, and I quote, 'I paid my dues, raising my family.' I could just puke. I didn't ever do any of my necessary household or school work until after the kids fell asleep. I felt they needed my attention, so I often wound up with five to six hours of shut-eye."

"How'ja hear about this tree?" Greg asked. "If you don't mind my asking."

"I think someone down in Las Vegas mentioned it to me. I have a real purpose in coming here." She strode to her car at a brisk pace and took a pair of small well-worn shoes out of the trunk. "These were my Buster Browns. I wore them to death when I was seven years old."

The laces were barely long enough to go through the last holes. They were knotted half-way up the five rows, the ends of the knots all frizzed. Frannie turned them over, to show that the soles had immense holes in them. Parts of the soles hung where the stitching had worn apart.

"I was a Depression child, and when these shoes got so holey that I swore I was almost walking barefoot, my folks put cardboard in them. My socks hurt because they were darned so much. Even fine snow as soft as flour that spouted from a sifter would penetrate. People don't know about sifters any more, I guess. Especially you, Greg. My feet were always cold and I had a perpetual runny nose. Even when I outgrew them, Mom saved them. Somehow those sad brogues never got tossed out no matter how often we moved." She sighed. "I have to admit the truth that we sneaked out in the middle of the night from a lot of places because we couldn't pay the rent. Years later, our fortunes turned and we were really in the money, but my mom told me she kept my shoes as a reminder of the hard times, to keep us humble. She was right – these torn things inspired me to succeed in life and to never worry about taking care of myself or my family. When Mom passed, I kept these shoes like she did, to always keep me grounded, you might say." She smiled, pleased with her metaphor and quickly continued, "I almost thought about having them bronzed like people do for their baby's first shoes, to use as bookends, but that would have spruced them up and spoiled the tattered look."

Frannie didn't look as if she wanted any response. She seemed to be content with an audience for her thoughts and Joan and Greg were wise enough to sense that and didn't say anything.

"One thing I always remember about Mom was how devout she was about praying at the oddest times, when she'd orally thank God for the ability to think, and question. She'd say, 'Thanks, my dear God, for giving me my life, thanks for giving me my health, and thank you for giving me my family.'" Frannie hugged herself and almost whispered, "I've outlived most of my siblings, my wonderful husband, and some of my friends. I miss them. My kids have their own lives, and sometimes I feel that it's a lonely life now."

Reaching into her alligator boots, Frannie pulled out a bright red ribbon to tie the worn shoes together. With a great show of dexterity, she threw the shoes as high as she could. They caught on a branch midway, swaying back and forth for several minutes, looking just as if a hypnotist was waving them in front of his subject to cast a spell.

Joan broke the mood as she stood up, dusting her pants, ready to get back to the restaurant to prepare the dinner menu. "I'm glad we were here to share this with you. It's a fitting place for them." She looked up at the tree and waved her arm about the lower branches. "You know, I think I recognize some of these things from the tales people have told me when they've stopped by my place after they were here. If you don't mind, I'll repeat this story to my friend who's writing a book about all this. I wish this tree could talk. Better still, I wish I had the time and smarts to write the stories I've heard. Some of them, like yours, were really interesting and uplifting." She shook her head. "But, some were down-right heartbreaking."

Chapter 13

Joan noticed that Greg's presence attracted more young people for late dinners. Some of his friends even stopped by just for a drink and dessert. She wasn't sure she liked having to work later, but she certainly liked the increase in her business since he'd started working for her. Greg was a blessing. He'd made her life much easier – she wasn't as exhausted as she had been, now that she didn't have to drag around her cast. He suggested they write up menus which he printed on his computer and designed a jazzy logo; it added class to the diner. All in all, she was grateful to have him around, and gave him an increase in salary after one week.

A few days later, during a slow afternoon, a middle-aged man came in alone, read a book while eating, and dawdled over the last of his lunch. He was thin, almost gaunt, with sparse hair combed over his bald spot. He had a strong, masculine-looking face but the dichotomy was that his face was pale, with a shiny, almost-like-plaster coating. He was wearing well-worn jeans with a button-down white dress shirt, not the usual combination in this county.

The restaurant was quiet after the few remaining customers left. When Greg offered to refill his cup, the man said, "This is my first stop after spending the morning at that weird shoe tree. I've never seen anything like it in my damn life. Do you know anything about it?"

"Do I? That's my favorite place hereabouts. It's not so long ago, a year or so or more, since a guy tossed the first pair of shoes up there, but it sure has become famous. Joan, my boss can give you the particulars but she told me it all started when a couple who stopped there to stretch their legs had a terrific row.

Joan's the right one to give you the particulars. They made up in this restaurant."

The man smiled. "That's a pretty romantic way for a legend to begin. I'd like to write a column about it to submit to my newspaper back East. It sounds like a great human-interest story."

Coming in from the kitchen, Joan overheard the end of the conversation. "For sure. My friend's a writer, and she's just begun a book about some of the stories floating around here. You might want to interview her; give her a leg up on getting it published."

"Sounds good to me. My name's Jonathon Vance." He gave her his card. "As you can see, I'm a reporter. Out of New York. Does she live around here?"

"As a matter of fact, she's staying right here in my home for a while. I'll check to see if she'd like to meet you."

Joan took a long look at him before leaving the restaurant. She was pretty good about sizing up people. When she gave Liz the newspaper reporter's card, Liz insisted that she go out to meet him.

"No way, girl. The Doc said you're to have complete bed rest and I promised Dwayne before he left--"

"Hey, Joan, I know I was told to stay in bed, but it won't hurt if I sit out there for just a little while. I'd feel funny having a total stranger come into my bedroom to interview me. Even if you're here to chaperone. This is my chance for some great publicity and I can sure use that wind-fall."

Without waiting for Joan's approval, Liz slowly walked into the restaurant and approached the stranger. "Hi, Jonathon. I'm Liz Talbott. I hear you're interested in the shoe tree. Funny, I've just started writing--"

Jonathon stood, shook her hand and helped her get seated. "I think you've got a hot topic here, and I don't want to usurp your idea; just want to write a feature article about the unusual tree and its background. I'll plug your book as a human-interest story and give you some advance publicity. It's a win-win situation."

Liz glowed. "I'd love that, but you must know most of the stories are being retold to me by Joan, who seems to be the sounding board for the people who stop by here after their visit to the tree. When I can, I'm going to sit out here to interview some of these people myself."

Jonathon nodded to Joan, "Can you join us?"

"I was planning on it." She sat down. "Greg's left, and I don't serve dinner for several hours." As she launched into details about the people who'd come to tell her about their personal stories after driving away from the tree, Jonathon scribbled notes. He never interrupted her.

When Joan signaled that she'd nearly exhausted her information, he turned to Liz. 'Your turn, Liz. How about your story? What's your background?"

Reluctantly, she summarized some facts. She added, "I'm a writer, but I don't want to write about myself. I'm paying my good luck forward and giving you the chance to editorialize."

He put his pen away. "When I was sitting under the tree, I felt some pretty strange sensations. The stuff there wasn't unusual in any way, but I'm sure, neither were most people who left their things. The tree is strong and healthy, growing right in the middle of a highway in a desert, reminding me of the dust bowl in Steinbeck's book, *The Grapes of Wrath*. I saw some of the most dilapidated shoes and boots I've ever seen, yet, there were many hardly worn items, which must speak in a different voice." He looked at Liz. "You know what they say, about the past being a prologue." His face was open, as if he were calibrating her response.

Liz smiled. "I know what you mean. I was struck by the entire scene, too. So, where do we begin? I must say from what I've already heard, these people are ordinary folks who've either lived through some simple life-changing experiences or some extra-ordinary ones. I care about them and want to develop them into real characters in my novel. I'm hoping each of these stories will hook my readers and they'll become incredibly involved and anxious to read the next chapter to meet new people with their different reasons for adding to the mysteries of the shoe tree. I'm sure everyone will love this as much as Joan and I do."

"Your enthusiasm is compelling. I can't wait to read all the stories. My paper has a wide circulation. It just might bring you lots of attention. Now give me an idea of your background so I can maybe make you famous, like Joyce Carol Oates."

Liz beamed. "Don't I wish. When I get this published, I'll send you an autographed copy."

As the interview came to a close, Joan asked, "By the way, how did you hear about this? What really brought you into this area, so far away from the regular tourist destinations? Sounds like you're not being totally honest."

"Well, that's pretty much to the point, isn't it?" Jonathon took a long drink of water. "You'd make a good journalist, Joan. So here it is — one of the guys at the paper had stopped here recently and gave me a heads-up. I didn't expect to ever see it, much less write about my experience there."

Joan gave Liz a nudge with her good foot and rolled her eyes.

He sensed their reaction. "To be honest, I just came through a horrible glitch in my marriage. There we were, living in a beautiful house, our responsibilities to our kids over with, celebrating our thirtieth wedding anniversary. I'm really a contented guy, a dependable homebody. So, one Saturday, I gave my loving wife a nice bracelet, took her to a high-end restaurant, and I thought we were lovey-dovey. I came home from work the next Monday, and there was my wife, sitting in the living room with several suitcases. She told me that she was leaving me. The woman never acted like she was unhappy or needed more excitement in her life. Nothing. Do you know what she told my attorney? She said she was sitting there in our home with me, night after night, watching TV, and she felt lonely. Walked out on me just like that."

When he stopped talking for a moment, to control his emotions, Liz patted his hand. "Sorry. I promise you I won't write a chapter about this."

Joan shook her head and gave him a strange look. "C'mon, we're talking personal stuff here, so I have to ask you – you must have had some idea that she was unhappy."

"Believe me, I've gone over it many times. We didn't argue over anything – not the kids, not money."

Liz looked doubtful. "It's better to feel your emotions than to bury them. You must have been in denial about something missing in your marriage."

"I'll bet anything she was fooling around behind your back," Joan said with a knowing look. "At our age, a woman doesn't usually strike out on her own. She left you for another guy, right?"

He nodded. "You've heard the expression; the spouse is the last to know. In hindsight I realized she'd been fooling around with one of her guys at work for over four years. They must have had torrid lunch hours. I knew the man! We even socialized. She used to invite him and his wife over, or we'd go out together. Some of our friends later told me they suspected something, but I never had any idea of what was going on. The four of us took vacations a couple of times, for Christ's sake. He and his wife split, too, and now they're living together. My wife and him, I mean. We sold the house, got divorced, no big contest, and I was at loose ends, in a new place. So, I needed to get away and decided to take some vacation time to put my head together. I drove out here, not even thinking of this as a destination. Then I thought, what the hell, I'll check out the crazy shoe tree my buddy told me about."

"Did you leave something there?" asked Liz, "You know, to add to the mystery?"

"Nope, did the opposite. It took me awhile, but I climbed up and took a pair of disgusting lady's shoes to remind me not to get involved with anyone again. I'm going to hang them in my bedroom, facing my bed. I've been cuckolded for the one and only time."

"Have you gone for help?" Joan had absorbed this from listening to Liz when she analyzed people's motivations.

"What kind of help?"

"To talk with a psychiatrist," clarified Liz.

Jonathon stood up for a moment, stretched out his lanky body, then sat down again. "No, I probably should."

Liz waved her hand, "Well, we've sorta been behaving like counselors for you here, and maybe you'll follow up and get a real professional point of view."

He shook his head. "You've no idea what talking with you has done for me. I've never exposed myself like this to anyone, not ever. That tree must open a lot of hearts for strangers to come here afterwards and talk so freely about personal, painful things they've experienced. After reading so many self-help books about putting my life in order, I'm really okay. After all, if she and I had an affair years ago, while she was married, wasn't it foreshadowed that she'd end up doing that to me? Know what? I've figured I stole her away from her husband when I met her, and now, it's like divine retribution. I'd never felt guilty about destroying her marriage. So, now I'm getting my payback. That's why I don't need help. I'm really doing well. And at least she isn't claiming alimony. Our kids understand that we, my former wife and I, will still be friends and won't embarrass anyone when we're attending family functions. And I'm a happy-go-lucky guy without any restrictions."

Joan gave him a playful jab in the arm with her fist. She grinned. "I'll bet you sing a different tune when you begin seeing another woman within the year. Funny how the heart heals itself. There's lots of great women out there who'd love your company and would like to share your contented home-loving life."

Chapter 14

After Jonathon Vance left, Liz was totally keyed up and refused to go back to bed.

Joan was adamant, "Now see here, my sweet pregnant one, I'm giving you just two seconds to get out of here. You know what Doc said."

"I know exactly what Doc said, but what if I just put my legs up on a chair and you could bring out the vegetables and stuff you want to peel for the soup, then we can keep each other company?" Her face turned pink from the rapid way she blurted out this question.

Joan relented. She moved over an armchair to make Liz more comfortable with her legs supported. "All right, but only for a little while. I guess it's the same as if you were sitting up in bed. After all, it's not like you're going out jogging."

Liz laughed. "Hardly. As a matter of fact, bring a lot of stuff out here for the salads, whatever so I can help you instead of sitting here like a phlegmatic---"

"Whoa! Now that's a new one on me, kiddo. What's phlegmatic mean?"

"Oh, sorry. That word was ubiquitous when I went to college – one of the guys did absolutely nothing to help plan anything for our group, or even add to our conversations, so we called him 'Phleggie,' short for phlegmatic. It meant, he was like a bump on a log; passive and a follower. But that's how he liked it, and we really liked him, so it was a perfect deal, and more intimate than his ordinary name."

Joan grinned as she nodded. "I like that. My new word for today; phlegmatic," she repeated while slowly pronouncing the first syllable. "Sorry to say, there's some folks hereabouts who suit the word right fine." She walked into the kitchen and returned with a tray of vegetables.

"Be right back with the chopping boards and some knives," she murmured to herself, shaking her head in disbelief. "I thought I was the boss here."

In a short time, all the preliminary work for the dinner menu was completed. Joan brought out a glass of milk and a small piece of her homemade Toll House cookie pie. "Time for an afternoon snack. Can't let this last bit of pie go to waste, now, can we?"

Just then, a woman entered the restaurant. She noticed the place was not occupied by other customers. "Sorry," she said. "I thought you were open. Just wanted an early dinner before I complete my trip up to Reno."

"Yes, we're open," Joan said with a broad grin. "Just wasn't expecting anyone here so early."

"Well, in that case…" the woman began to back out the door.

"No! Hold it. We're very flexible around here. I'm sure I can rustle up something to tide you over. I just can't offer you soup yet. Let me clear this out of here so's I'll be back to tell you what's on the menu tonight."

"Great! Thanks. I'll just freshen up. Take your time."

Liz took advantage of the fact that Joan had forgotten she shouldn't be there, resolving to remain as long as she could. When the woman returned from the ladies' room, Liz noticed her beautiful posture and the refined way she handled herself. She passed by Liz's table. Their eyes met for a brief moment.

What a homely woman, Liz thought, but her eyes are so remarkable; they draw your attention to them.

Liz nodded to the woman and she responded with a wide smile as she sat down at a nearby table and waved, "Hi, I'm Rhea. I was thrilled to find this place open." She noticed Liz's legs propped up on a chair. "You look comfortable. When are you due?"

Liz stroked her belly. "In two months, I hope. I'm supposed to be lying down all the time but I escaped from the bedroom for a little while. I need to see and speak with people."

"Funny–I came here for a different purpose–I'm so tired of feeling stressed with deadlines… and I'm tired of being with a roomful of people." She stopped. "I'm sorry. Give me an audience and I'm carried away." She laughed. She was enchanting.

Liz's first impression had been so wrong. The woman wasn't homely; she was animated and interesting and her startling blue eyes took your attention away from her plain features. She might even be called cute.

"I'm Liz. Your name is interesting. I've never met a Rhea."

"Most people say that. My mother always loved Greek mythology. Rhea was Cronus the Titan's wife. Actually, they were brother and sister. She gave birth to the Gods Zeus and Poseidon among others. The unusual name sort of suits my career. I run a dancing school." Her voice dropped an octave as she emoted, "Woe unto those who don't toe the mark! I spit thunder from Olympus."

When Joan came in from the kitchen she had to smile at the two women who were laughing at some joke. "I've missed something here. I'm jealous."

"It does feel good to just let go," Rhea said, accepting the glass of water. "Takes fewer muscles to smile than frown. So, what's for dinner? I'm famished."

"You're in luck. I've got some dill chicken salad, there's spinach and mushroom quiche, the usual house salad, and there's always a hamburger."

"Sold! I'll take the quiche and salad." She turned to Liz. "Won't you both join me? I'd love your company, and I'd like to tell you about the strangest tree."

Joan guffawed. "I knew it! You've just come from the shoe tree, haven't you?"

Rhea looked perplexed. "Yes. How did you know?"

"Wait!" Joan held up her hand. "Liz, we're having an early dinner, and don't say one more word about the tree until I bring it all out."

"She means it, but we can talk about other things, like where do you teach?"

Rhea shook her head. "Nope, she'll want to hear all that. So, Liz, tell me about you. You don't have the local accent."

"You're right." Liz talked about her life as an editor and writer in New York, how she and Dwayne happened to be here, and now she was writing a book about the shoe tree. As she brought Rhea up to date, Joan appeared with their dinners.

During the meal, Rhea talked about her ballet school in Greenwich, Connecticut. "Obviously," she laughed at herself, "I always loved to dance, especially ballet. I was heartbroken when my instructor told me I was too tall, and I knew I didn't have the beautiful face to become a professional ballerina, but I had the talent. I loved dancing more than anything, so I was willing to help others by teaching. I've experienced doubt and despair in my lifetime but it has been replaced by the joy of living and knowing that I have a purposeful life. Greenwich is close to New York. I'm called there frequently as a consultant for a new play. They choose me first because they don't have to pay a full-time choreographer. I'm small potatoes, but I've really enjoyed working on Broadway."

Liz said, "I notice you're not wearing a wedding band. Do you have family back there?"

"Until recently. My husband left me a few years ago for a bimbo in the chorus line. Ours was not a strong marriage; we had so little in common. I thought that it was good to have opposite points of view, but I was wrong. It's hard to imagine that when I met her, we'd been introduced by some friends, she said I was the most intelligent woman she'd ever met. I guess he found her the more interesting one. But he and I did have some good times before she came into the picture. We did things as a family; travelling together; stuff like that. I had a daughter..." She choked up and put her head down on the table.

Liz reached over and patted Rhea's head. "Hey, we don't have to know any more than this. It's okay if you want to skip the subject. Let's talk about the shoe tree."

It took a few moments for Rhea to control herself. She wiped her eyes with the napkin. "No, it'll be better if I talk about it. I'm grateful that you're letting me share this with you." She hesitated, "My daughter, Audrey, was petite and gorgeous. She walked like a ballerina from her first steps and always danced around the house. Energetic and vivacious, she commanded attention, entering a room with an attitude of 'Ta-da, I'm here.' When she was four, she was very sick with fevers and swollen glands. The doctor diagnosed her with rheumatic fever and kept her in bed for months. It was a particularly rough time for me, because my older sister had died of a heart attack at thirty-three and I was scared for my daughter. I closed my studio to spend time with her, to make sure she'd be totally inactive. We played school and she learned quickly. I taught her how to sew and knit. While she was bedridden, all she asked for was a ballerina doll – my mother bought that for her. We read as many books as I could find about dancers and bought her the movie *The Red Shoes*."

"I remember that classic – Moira Shearer was gorgeous and talented – right?" asked Liz.

"Exactly. Well, luckily, Audrey completely survived the illness. When she was strong enough, she joined my classes and became the star of every recital I gave. I tried not to push her and it wasn't that she was my favorite, mind you, she had to work harder to prove herself and she earned it. What a natural, gifted dancer, the best I ever had. I finally sent her to New York to study with the New York City Ballet. Meantime, she'd become close to her father, who came through when she needed him and their relationship worked. When he was killed in Iraq, she felt compelled to join the service. I didn't want her to go to war. She said it wasn't in retribution for his death; she felt she needed to finish the job he started. She was only there five months," tears streaked down her face as she spoke in a whisper, "when she was killed by a sniper."

Both Liz and Joan stood next to Rhea and stroked her shoulders. They couldn't help but cry along with her.

"Such a waste. What can I say?" Joan asked.

"I'm so sorry," Liz added.

"I know. It's been a horrible nightmare. I still can't accept her death. I closed the studio and have been wandering around out here, stopping off to see family and friends across the country. My cousin lives in Reno…" She broke down again.

"You don't have to continue, Rhea," said Liz, "but I'd like to hear your reaction to the shoe tree."

"Of course. I've treasured the last pair of ballet slippers Audrey wore, and had them in the car, to keep me company as I traveled. When I saw the unusual tree today, it seemed a perfect monument, keeping company with other emotional or painful stories. I knew then why I was fated to drive this highway. I sat there for a long time, talking to her, and then I hung her ballet slippers on a low branch. It may sound insane to you, but a strange wind seemed to make them do a pirouette. I felt the very best place for her favorite shoes was to hang them there, for however long they'll last, or if some young girl wants to take them to fulfill her own dream."

Chapter 15

Early the next day, Dr. Matthews stopped by to check up on Liz.

"I'm glad you're here, Doctor, because I had planned to call you. I've been in bed just as you ordered. I feel great."

"Good. Keep it up."

"Well, why can't I sit up for a couple of hours to have my breakfast, lunch and dinner in the restaurant? Dwayne's in New York and I'm going stir crazy lying here alone all day. Please say it's okay."

The doctor examined her. "The baby sounds good to me. I'm sure it's because you did stay put." He shook his head. "And if I say no, you're not going to listen, anyway, so just don't overdo it. You can sit up for your meals and don't do any lifting, and definitely don't plan to help Joan. She's fine without your physical input. Promise?"

"Oh, of course! Pinkie swear." She raised her right pinkie and kissed it. "Thank you. It means a lot to me."

"I wish I still had Joan's wheel chair, but it's been long gone. You know what? I've got an old wheel chair which was donated to my office, in hopes that someone could use it someday. I'll bring it over when I stop by later. You're welcome to use it and I'll feel better that you're not walking around too much."

"That's terrific! When I wake up each morning, I feel so exhilarated, thinking, will I hear another story today? What an experience it's going to be, sharing someone's life. I won't overdo anything, I promise. I'll be able to look at people, maybe judge their personalities and while talking with them, find out why they come here to the shoe tree, and what they leave there. Hopefully, I'll be able to listen to some conversations about someone's experiences instead of getting the new stories second-hand from Joan."

"So that's what it's all about. Heck, my daughter's staying with me while her divorce comes through, and she's got a story to tell. I'm sure she'd like to share that with you. She drove over here just yesterday. I'll ask her to stop by."

"I'd love to meet her. And thanks, Doc, for taking care of us." She patted her belly.

"Don't mention it. You give me something to do when things are slow and;" he winked as he touched his protruding waistline, "it's a good excuse to come by and get some of Joan's famous pies."

Liz laughed. "Come by any time and it'll be my treat!"

Just as Dr. Matthews was leaving, Greg knocked on the open door. "Hope I'm not interrupting but I thought this was important. There's a letter here from a certain Mr. Somebody from New York." He crossed the room within a heartbeat and the two men left Liz tearing open her envelope.

Reading her husband's poem made her spirits rise, yet she cried, hugging the paper to her breast, rereading it several times to memorize every word.

Dearest Liz,
You are so much a part of me
And I am a part of you —
Our daily lives are so intertwined
that when we are apart
there is something missing —
The presence, the touch, the loving,
the gazing into each other's eyes.
And when you return
the parts are back
where they belong and
We are
Whole
Again.
I love you.

With her tears still damp on her face, she decided to call him right away and not wait until that evening. He surprised her when he answered the phone and they became emotional together. After their exchanges of love, he went into detail about some of his promising interviews. She sounded so grateful that he had a positive attitude and mentioned that Dr. Matthews was going to allow her to use a wheelchair to spend a little time in the restaurant, meeting some people herself, instead of learning their stories through Joan. She added, "I'm really nothing but a sounding board, absorbing other people's words; after all, who am I, to sound judgmental. Sometimes, if it's warranted, I hope to offer any suggestions to them, but I'm afraid that most times they don't want anyone's opinion; they simply want to be heard. In my wildest dreams I couldn't make up some of these plots. I'm actually using these incidents to help me be more creative, weaving in my interpretations."

"Sounds good to me. With all your free time alone, what have you been reading?"

"I'm reading John Updike's *Bech* and I'm amazed by his vocabulary and intellectual references. His tongue-in-cheek style is positively mind-boggling – every sentence is an anomaly of Thesaurus metaphors. He's sensual and eloquent with full page paragraphs ending in a glib poke in the ribs. He must have had a good time throwing in those subtle slings. He makes me want to interpret the characters with a deeper vision, getting into the essence of their personalities."

"Well, that's terrific, hearing you expound about Updike and learning from him. Many people can't get into his style. I'm happy that Joan had that book. I've gotta go, now, Hon. I'm sending you tons of hugs until I can deliver them myself."

Later, when Liz wheeled into the restaurant for lunch, there were several people already seated. A few waved to her and mentioned they'd heard all about her and hoped she was feeling well. Liz felt overwhelmed with this outpouring from well-wishers who all promised to buy her book. She laughed when a woman suggested that after her book was published, she should come back for an official book signing. One of the steady customers brought Liz a dainty hand-embroidered handkerchief. She had just gotten settled when a perky thirty-something woman walked into the diner. Many customers greeted her warmly; she hugged and chatted with them before spotting Liz, who recognized her immediately. She had her father's unmistakable handsome features.

"Hi! You must be Liz. I'm Jaimie Matthews. Dad said you might be interested in talking with me. Mind if I join you for lunch?"

Liz beamed. "Do I mind? I'm delighted. Oh, here's Joan. I haven't given her my order yet. Hey, Joan, look who's here."

Joan enveloped Jaimie and held her for several moments. It was obvious that they had a special emotional relationship. The three women talked for a minute before Joan suggested that they order her fresh vegetable soup and left them to get acquainted. Liz felt she had to put Jaimie at ease by explaining that she was writing a novel about the various objects thrown onto the shoe tree and that she hoped she was correctly portraying the personalities of the people who were involved. She planned to fictionalize the stories after basing them on the actual events and promised not to use names or exploit the people she'd met.

Jaimie brushed all that away with her hand. "Suits me fine, although it would serve him right, the bastard, if I smeared his name. Here's our story. Jim was older'n me. We were married ten years last spring and until just a short while ago, I thought we were still lovey-dovey and I was happy, even though we didn't have kids. He was a widower, had two sons, but they were grown and gone. I got along with them okay whenever they came by. We lived in Utah. Did everything together; you know, skiing, hiking, walking, skating. He liked his beer and his good times. It showed on his belly. Let's see, you'll want to know what he looked like … Pretty decent when we first met, but now, he's … Here, I'll show you a recent picture on my cell phone."

Liz studied the face. He had several flaccid chins and sparse grey hair, altogether not a pleasant looking man. She silently handed the phone back to Jaimie, who continued. "I always loved family. Only thing was he wasn't close to his older sister, Marie, who didn't even come to our wedding. It took quite a lot of my talking with him over a long time before he admitted how his sister was mean and made trouble for them. He was an adult, the father of grown children when she told him he was a bastard, not the swearing term, but that he was born without a father's name listed on the birth certificate. In those days, that was really taboo and people didn't talk about it." She laughed. "Hell, today, nobody cares who the father is; sometimes even the mother doesn't know."

Liz laughed with her, thinking that Jaimie was so down to earth, so wholesome, her father must be proud.

"So, that was a shock to Jim because he never even really looked at that paper, his birth certificate, that is. Never knew that the man he had lived with wasn't his real father; that his mother had lied to him all those years. Jim was real mad at her. He didn't understand why she was so spiteful, to hurt him, when they'd always had a good relationship. They had a terrible fight and never spoke again."

Liz nodded. "I'm so sorry to hear that they'd waste their years by not communicating. We all need as much love as we can get. Too bad. Okay, let's talk for a moment about Jim not having his father's name on the birth certificate; but you know what's been going on with all the professional sports players, famous actors, and celebrities having babies without getting married. There's no stigma attached in modern times. Sometimes the couple gets married years later. Or not."

"The 'not' was not in those days. From what I remember of what she told him, when Marie was real little, her parents were still living together, but weren't sleeping in the same room. Said her ma couldn't stand his snoring. Well, the short of it was, her ma had an affair; the guy disappeared, she had the baby boy, and their pa said he forgave his wife and he'd raise Jim as his own."

"That's commendable. When and why in heaven's name did his sister even tell him about this overwhelming secret after all those years and hurt him so much?"

"She did this only a few years ago, after their parents died. He got depressed over the news and I didn't blame him. It wasn't fair to tell him after all the time had gone by. What difference did it make? But Marie's meanness didn't cover the fact my husband was going off the deep end for the longest while before she even skewered him with the terrible facts. It was only in hindsight did I put it all together. Back when we first married, we were friendly with four sets of his cousins, visited them out of town, they'd come to us, we had good times with each of the couples, then poof, Jim cut them out, one by one. They'd each been nice to us, but he wouldn't give me any reasons, just said he didn't want to be with them again."

Liz held up her hand to interrupt Jaimie. "Since we've just met, and you're getting into pretty personal stuff, do you want me to express an opinion about what you're telling me, or do you want me to listen; be a sounding board? This discussion doesn't ever have to be repeated to anyone, especially Joan, who knows you so well. Scout's honor."

Jaimie cleared her throat. They'd been talking softly, so they wouldn't be overheard by other diners. "Hell, I'd be interested in your opinion, if you'd like to venture it. I took it for granted that you'd keep my story from Joan. This is a small town, and I'm glad you're not going to use my name in your book. My Dad would never forgive me; you better believe that. It's my business, after all."

"As I promised, I never planned to use actual names in my novel. In fact, when someone tells me their personal thoughts or discusses anything with me, it's understood that that person is giving me permission to use the story but not identify them. All right then, you must understand that I'm listening to you as a new friend, and I care. I'm not a psychiatrist, but I'd like to ask questions, if I may. It's up to you. When Jim began to pull away from everyone in his family, shouldn't that have given you a clue he was changing and had a personal problem?"

"Nope. Call me stupid, I didn't even think about it. He'd been sorta depressed from time to time and he began having headaches, but no, the man wouldn't think about seeing a doctor.

It had nothing to do with throwing away money to get help – just male menopause, I thought. Then he starts up with, I didn't iron his shirts right, didn't cook like his ma, just kept picking on me."

"What was your reaction? How many years were you married when that started?"

"Oh, it only started about last year or so. I was in love with the guy and tried to make our marriage work, you know, so I tried to let some of his crap go by. After a while, when I talked back, I told him I wasn't gonna take any more of his guff and we stopped talking for days on end. Have you ever lived with someone who wouldn't even look at you for days? Funny thing is, I wasn't feeling so hot myself. I began to get these dizzy spells–"

Liz interrupted, "Like vertigo?"

"Yeah, that's it. I thought that maybe I'd see an eye doctor, because I still wasn't wearing glasses." She stopped talking when she saw Greg approaching. "Oh, here's our soup. Thanks, Greg. How'd ja do in school this year?"

The two women kibitzed with him a while, then ate some of their lunch.

"So, as I said, the eye doctor told me my eyes were fine, that I wasn't dizzy for that reason, and that I should go to an ear man; maybe I had an inner ear infection. First thing that new doc asked me was, did I have any stress in my life? I thought my job was good, and I was getting along with Jim for a while, so I said, 'I'm O.K.' He did all this testing, said the results were all negative, and the next step was that I should see a neurologist, have an MRI, or was it a CAT scan? I can't ever get them straight. Then I became scared – did he think I had a brain tumor? Jim wasn't takin' me to the doctors. He didn't believe in all that stuff. He complained I'm spending all this money for nothing."

"I hope you don't mind my saying this, but Jim doesn't sound very loving – and you were in denial if you said there wasn't any stress."

"For sure. It's just that when it's happening you just don't see it. We were still good in bed sometimes and going out together and seeing our friends. So, I went to this neurologist and he also asked me if I had any pressure in my life and I told him the only pressure was my worry about feeling dizzy once in a while; I even said part of it might be worrying about his fees. He laughed. I had the MRI or whatever it was, and that doctor told me there was absolutely nothing wrong with my brain, no growth or anything. So, I let everything go. Then as time went by, Jim got more ornery, just didn't talk to me, disappeared without a goodbye or a hello. You know, that idiot would get a phone call, and I'd tell the caller to wait while I got him, and damned if I couldn't find him in the house, the back yard, and when I looked in the garage, his car was gone. Do you realize how embarrassing it is to tell the guy that I didn't know my husband wasn't home? I finally told Jim we needed marriage counseling, but he'd have none of that, so right out, I said I wasn't happy living with him anymore and that I needed a divorce." Jaimie lowered her voice to a whisper, making Liz lean across the table. "You know what? Since I'm away from him, a free woman, I don't have dizzy spells. What does that tell you?"

"A lot! How long do you plan to stay here with your Dad? Does Jim know where you are?"

"I'm only here a few days. I didn't tell him or no one else I was coming here, but if he's a mind to, he could figure it out. I don't rightly care if he does show up. He's a mean SOB and I don't want no more part a him."

Liz was silent, absorbing what she'd heard. Then she leaned forward again. "Do you think he had another woman and was trying to get you so angry that you'd ask for the divorce?"

Jamie laughed so hard, she snorted, sounding like a dog barking. "Do I think? Sure thing. He'd been fooling around off and on for a while, and I figured it out. Did he think I was stupid? He had these nights out with the boys. He said he was bow-ling, whatever. I tried to make things work 'cause I still loved him or thought I did, and hoped I'd win him back. Took a while, then I smarted up. I didn't need him or his attitude. I found me a nice little apartment near work. I've got my girlfriends for company. Life's too good to just go around bawling and wasting it."

She stopped talking when Joan came over to offer some tea and desert, but they'd filled up with the hearty soup and delicious home-made bread. The customers had come and gone, but the two women had been so busy talking, they hadn't noticed.

After Joan went back into the kitchen, Jaimie continued, "I guess you see a lot of difference between me and my Dad, don't you? He was always upset with me because I didn't want to go to school and get a diploma. I dropped out of high school when I turned sixteen and he was really mad. But I always had a hard time with school and he loved me enough to respect my idea to just go to find a job. We love and understand each other, you know."

But having spent this time listening to Jaime and her western expressions, Liz already surmised that Dr. Matthews' daughter wasn't as refined as he, but Liz felt that this woman was a sweetheart, a sincere person, worthy of her father's attention and love. She liked Jaimie and felt determined to befriend her and try to help her in any way she could.

Jaime went on; "The shoe tree, that's why we're talking, isn't it? Well, it seemed to me, that he really wasn't with the guys all those nights, and when I packed up my things because I wanted my own place in my new life, I took those damned smelly bowling shoes outa his closet. I'd heard about the tree the last time I visited here, so guess where I was, yesterday? I'll lay odds that Jim won't even miss them, the liar." Jamie took Liz's hand and admitted that she'd never opened up her heart to a stranger before. "It's just not like me – I don't know what possessed me. You must think I'm foolish."

"No way! I guess you really needed someone to listen to you. You've had a lot to cope with lately. It isn't easy to face a traumatic marriage breakdown." Liz had concern written all over her face as she looked closely at Jaimie. "Are you still in love with the guy, despite all this?"

Jaimie shook her head several times to emphasize the point. "No siree. He wiped that love clear out. You know, someone once said to me that life is like an open book and we write the pages as we go. That's so on, don't you think?"

She didn't give Liz a chance to reply because her pretty face lit up when she quickly smiled. "You know, one of my friends was complaining that she was gonna shoot her husband because he was running around with a real young hippie, and I didn't have to think about it for a second when I told her, 'Don't do it – your kids would be orphans when you're sent to prison. Just wish him a slow, painful death.'" Again, she couldn't control herself – she laughed heartily. Liz spontaneously joined her.

Chapter 16

It was Presidents' Day weekend. The restaurant was constantly crowded with young people. As Liz and Joan chatted in her room one evening, Joan mentioned how much harder she was working. "Of course, they're mostly Greg's friends. This place has become a hangout for them in the evening, so I'm keeping later hours." She wearily propped her feet up on the recliner.

"Aren't you standing on your ankle too much? Are you in pain?"

"Not exactly in pain, but sure bordering close to it. The brace is wearing me down and forcing me to use other leg muscles. Greg's a terrific help, but I've been living on pills. I'm pooped."

Liz sat up straighter. "I've got it! Bring me some of the easy things to peel or dice to take the drudge work away from you. I can peel some stuff at a table in the diner, or the kitchen, sitting in my wheelchair. I can cut apples, potatoes..."

"Naw, that's too much for you. Doc wants you resting in bed. Besides, I've learned to sit at the counter to do a lot of that stuff." She chuckled, "I'll tell you one thing – Greg's friends are a hoot. Always joking around; a laugh a minute. Makes me feel young again."

Liz pouted. "I'm missing everything."

Joan laughed, "There's the perfect example of the old expression, 'You can't dance at two weddings with one rear-end.'"

That made Liz smile, "I'm getting large enough to do just that."

They both jerked when her cell phone rang. "Oh, it's Dwayne."

Joan signaled that she'd be back and left the room to give Liz some privacy.

"Hi, Honey. Did you get the job? Pause. Oh, that means that you'll have another interview soon." Pause. She repeated what he said, "Fifty-eight applicants; they called you back as one of ten, then they'll whittle it down to a final three. Of course, you'll make it." Pause. "So, what about my writing? Well, some of the stories seem awfully wild. There's no way I could have conjured up some of the things I've heard. Maybe they're not all true. Who thinks these kind of thoughts anyway? I'm not educated enough to analyze the meaning behind someone's words. Are they conjuring up these stories to hold my attention and maybe get some kind of notoriety when all they did was take an old pair of boots they kept in the trunk in case they needed them to walk through a big puddle or through unexpected snow? Who am I to judge truth from fiction?"

Liz shifted in bed, dropped the phone and scrambled to retrieve it from the sheets as she said aloud, "Hold on, I dropped… okay, now…" She listened to his pep talk about her exciting novel. They talked for a few more minutes about her condition and how much they loved and missed each other. She told him how deeply his poem affected her and recited it by heart. They kissed each other over the wires before she turned off her cell phone. "Damn it! I can't stay here any longer. I'm…"

When Joan returned a moment later, she found Liz crying. "Is Dwayne all right?"

Liz wiped her cheeks. "You've been terrific and I guess I have to stop feeling sorry –"

"Hey, kiddo! It's just for a short time, and you're entitled to miss him and want to be there, but just think about keeping your baby safe and anyways look at another part of all this; all the stories you've heard. You've got a great head start to your novel."

They hugged and said goodnight.

At lunch the next day, some the same kids returned. Liz got there in time to hear Joan lecturing them about their order of pies and soft drinks. "If you're short of cash, drop the soda and order a couple of sandwiches to share and I'll make sure you don't leave hungry."

She left to prepare their sandwiches. Greg brought out their tall glasses of water with lemon. Liz smiled as she watched them use packets of sugar to sweeten the drinks, which now became lemonade. No other customers came in, so the gang hung around and told Liz about some of their partying at the shoe tree and talked about the beat-up sports shoes they'd added. Some bragged about climbing the tree to get to higher branches to deposit their worn sneakers.

When they left, one of the boys hung back. His face was covered with generous freckles and his curly red hair flopped on his forehead. He turned to Liz. "Hi, I'm Pete. Have you been there lately? Did you see the fancy black patent-leather men's dress shoes on one of the lower branches?"

Liz asked him to join her at her table. "No, Pete, I didn't. Someone must have grabbed them Were they yours?"

"Forget that. I thought you'd like another bit about shoes that are left on the tree."

"You bet!"

"Well, my grandma lives in Florida, and my Mom sent me there for a week last summer to check up on her. It was the first time I flew, or swam in the ocean, and we had a blast, going places to see alligators and iguanas. Even went to Lion Safari and one got real close to the car."

"Oh, that sounds great. I've been to Florida, but I've never been to the Lion Safari."

"It's one of the only places you can touch a camel's face. They built a ramp you can walk up and you're eye-level with them. It's a feeding station. They eat out of your hand."

Liz laughed. "That's exciting!"

"You know, my grandma's got style; she's pretty, perky and very busy keeping in shape at the fitness center. I never saw so many old people as where she lives. Scary! And it's dangerous with all the old timers driving crazy and taking chances to beat the red light. On the road, I'd see a big caddie up ahead with what looked like no one at the wheel. She called them the 'No-heads.'"

"I'm sure they were all delighted to see a handsome young man. Your grandmother must have been thrilled to show you off."

"Oh, yeah, you can bet on that. So, one reason I went was to meet this guy she'd been seeing a lot. Every time she'd call us, she'd use this freaking high-pitched unnatural excited voice. Mom was worried that he might take advantage of her, and maybe move in with her. He was all she talked about for a few months. She said Ken was the best dancer, the most fun she'd ever had. He made her very happy and he said he loved her. Mom asked her if she had given him any money and Grandma swore she hadn't. Who knows? We were afraid that maybe he'd get around to ask her to give him money or let him borrow some; she doesn't have a bundle but she's comfortable. So, I flew over there, you know, and met him at a whopper of a lunch buffet, the first one I'd been to. In Florida, old folks eat out most of the time, especially cheaper early dinners called "Early-bird Meals." Mostly before 5:30 or 6. And everyone leaves with a doggie bag. Let me tell you, Ken was a very tanned handsome man. Younger by a long shot and dressed real fancy with those loud Hawaiian print shirts. He didn't sleep there while I was around, but I saw some of his clothes in the closet, and all his personal stuff, like his after-shave lotion. My Mom called him a 'gigolo' and was scared Grandma was being taken in. I was there as a spy." Pete smiled with a self-deprecating grin.

"You obviously didn't like him. Did he spend a lot of time with you?"

"Yeah, too much. He drove this big really old Caddie, and when we ate out or did anything, he let Grandma charge the bills, saying he'd give her the cash later – said she needed the mileage to fly out here to visit us sometime. Sure! I never saw that happen. Him paying her the money, that is. While I was there, they were invited to a fancy sixtieth anniversary bash, and he brought his own tuxedo over to get dressed—"

Liz held up her hand. "No! You stole his formal shoes and threw them up on the tree?"

She laughed so hard, that she hiccupped and Joan limped out with Greg to see what they were missing. They sat down for a few minutes while Pete filled them in.

"Jeez, what a pack of lies that guy told, and everyone around there would just eat them up, like they believed him. But they were too far-fetched. He was always talking, like he was the master of ceremonies or holding court."

"What'd he talk about? Did he tell jokes?" asked Greg. "I've never met a gigolo."

"Of course, he knew everything! Do you know what? My Mom asked a friend of hers, a retired P.I., to do some background work-up on him, and the man couldn't even find anything out. He said that we should warn Grandma that the guy was hiding something, or he'd have a valid Florida license and plates, but we decided she'd never listen and she'd only be mad at us for checking up on him."

Liz leaned forward, "No record of anything? Maybe he falsified his name. That's really strange. Did she ever see his place?"

"Yeah, she said it was small and had cheap furnishings that he said he bought and paid for the apartment for his mother, and when she died, he just moved in, temporarily. You wouldn't believe his stories! He said he retired at sixty, bought a fifty-foot sailboat and sailed around the world one and a half times in twelve years. Bragged that there were three young girls who were the crew. They walked around topless; just wanted to see the world; worked for the chance to travel and for food and a place to sleep. Then, get this! Ken swore to everyone that he was celibate – I liked that new word – 'cause if he slept with one, the others would get jealous. Grandma told me she knew he was telling tall tales – everybody else knew it too–but he was so entertaining, that people wanted to be around him. So did she."

"So, what made you take his shoes?" Joan asked. "Wouldn't he miss them?"

"Naw, he forgot them when he packed up his things just before I left. You won't believe what he said he was going to do – he was going to Costa Rica to help put together a deal. He was supposed to have spent time there when he was sailing, and some guy he'd met there called him about flying down and even sent him a ticket. I never saw it. He forgot his dancing shoes in the back of the closet, and I didn't want Grandma to find them."

"Sounds like you suspected that he was really pulling out." Joan stood up to clear the table.

"You know what? When I got back here, I'd call her every week to say hi, and she'd tell me he also called her often from Costa Rica and told her he loved her. After a few months, she let it slip and told him that she couldn't wait until he came back, said that she wanted him to move in to live with her."

Greg leaned forward to pick up some dishes. "How'd that go over?"

"You guessed it. She never heard from him again. She took it real hard. I suspected that he never did go away, just made all that up. I figured he needed someone with lots of money to support him, maybe buy him a nicer car. He must have found a new victim. Months later, when Grandma realized it was all over, she wrote him a letter, told him she never regretted the time they spent together, but she did regret that he wasn't man enough to tell her the truth; that he had to move on."

"Good for her," Greg said, shaking a fist. "She'll meet someone else."

"It's tough to get jilted," Joan stood up to hobble back to the kitchen. "Been there, done that."

"I feel sorry for your poor Grandma, Pete." Liz said. "No one deserves to be treated that way. But at least she did have a good time when they were together. My guess is that she's a survivor and will get past this experience. Did she ever admit to giving him money?"

"Guess we'll never know, 'cause she's too stubborn to admit it." Pete walked towards the door. "But anyway, he won't dance with anyone else with those shoes; I got my revenge."

Chapter 17

The following day, Greg came rushing into Liz's bedroom. "Hey, Liz, I knew you were planning to come out for lunch, but you've got a visitor now."

Fully dressed, Liz pretended to cover her body with part of the blanket. "Did you forget to knock, young man?"

He backed up. "Sorry, the door was open. An old lady named Meg asked for you." His face lit up when he realized she was teasing him.

Liz winked at him as she slowly got out of bed, fully dressed. "I'll be there in a second."

The petite woman with an alert expression and bright shiny eyes didn't fit Greg's description. She couldn't have been more than early-fifties, but Liz realized that to a young boy, anyone older than his mother was doddering on the brink of death. Liz held out her hand and was pleased to be looking into the bluest eyes she'd ever seen. They truly looked as bottomless as a clear Bahama ocean. If she were a painter, she'd begin to sketch that lovely face with the shy enigmatic smile. They exchanged greetings and Liz settled down at her favorite table as she asked Meg to join her.

Joan arrived with a tray of coffee and a breakfast menu. Without waiting for their invitation, she sat down. "Greg will be right out, ladies. I'll just sit a minute or two."

"Before you talk about your visit to the shoe tree, tell me something about yourself."

"I'm nothing special. I taught school for 35 years and always loved elementary grades. I always felt I was accomplishing something meaningful if I touched even one child's life every year."

"You must have many wonderful stories stored in your head."

"Absolutely, but most of them are ubiquitous and have already been written. Strangely enough, just yesterday, something triggered a funny memory. When I began to teach, we wrote a paragraph for each subject on the report cards but one year, the report card system was totally changed to using the alphabet: C was the standard for a second grader who was working at grade level; B was given to a student doing advanced work; A was the reward for a child who read at the next grade level. The average student earned a C for reading. The elderly teacher who taught next to me didn't like the new system and refused to adapt to it. After the first report card came out that year, I was outside on recess duty, when a girl who received only C's in my first grade the previous year, ran up to tell me she'd gotten an A in World Mystery. It took me a moment to realize that the mystery was that she'd been given an A for WORD MASTERY."

She grinned as they laughed.

"I'm curious, Meg," Liz said, "How did you know about my novel?"

"Oh, it was that newspaper article. I was planning to come out west for the winter, meet some old friends, and ski in some real powdery snow for a change. We get too much of icy man-made snow in New York State. Since I'd be driving through your area, I made this detour. I just came from your famous tree, after tossing my grandson's tennis shoes up there. Almost like new, they were. He hasn't played in years. They ended up in my trunk and I just never got rid of them. That tree sure is the most unusual thing I've ever seen, and I'm proud to add something useful that some kid might use, so I hung them from a lower branch. I even left a note inside." She sipped her coffee after adding cream.

Liz grinned, "I'm sure you hear this often, but you don't look old enough to have a grandson who was a tennis player."

Meg's bright eyes sparkled. "I don't mind telling you I'm sixty-nine. I became a grandmother at forty-six, but you should have seen me prancing around the hospital with a license plate tied around my neck that boasted, 'Grandmothers have Something Special.' Wore it for a week before I attached it to my car. He was gorgeous, my Paul. Looked just like Tom Sawyer or Huck Finn. No hair until he was two; it grew in almost white and so fine that everyone stroked his head. Always at the center of everyone's attention; he covered the room like a professional politician. We bought him a play gym for his second birthday, and that's when we began to call him 'Chicken Much.'"

"You mean 'Chicken Little,' don't you?" Joan stood up when a couple entered. "Excuse me, gotta get to work. Liz will bring me up to date later. But only if that's all right with you. After all, I'll probably read about it when the book gets published."

Meg nodded, then turned to Liz. "Chicken Much best describes what a scaredy-cat he was. He loved the swings and the glider but refused to go down the little slide. It took months before we talked him into it. I even held his hand to take him down the first time. He did fine alone after that. Then, I'm sure you remember the movie, 'The Wizard of Oz'?"

She stopped talking long enough to thank Greg for serving her food and took a bite of her toast. "This looks good, and I'm starving. Paul was about three when my husband and I took him to a revival of that wonderful movie. That night, my daughter had a tough time getting him to take a bath. He'd always loved them, but suddenly he became a monster, fighting and crying. Finally, maybe after a week, he was able to verbalize why he was so frightened. He said that in the movie, when Dorothy threw water at the Wicked Witch of the West, she screamed and melted down the drain."

"Wow!" Liz stopped eating. "What a sensitive child! He thought he was going to dissolve and disappear like the witch! I never suspected that kids wouldn't love that movie, with the adorable Munchkins and the flying monkeys."

"And there was the other thing that bothered him during the movie. He shrieked and went under his seat when the monkeys were harassing Dorothy and flying at her. I always thought that Grimm's *Fairy Tales* was too violent for young children. But those were only the beginning of many incidents. The kid was literally afraid of his own shadow, to be trite." She paused to take another few bites of food, and the two of them watched as more customers entered the restaurant.

Liz finished her lunch and accepted coffee from Greg, who was busy with the other customers but remained attentive to her needs. "I'm more than happy to pour more coffee for you, Liz, but shouldn't you switch to decaf, if you don't mind my suggestion?" She nodded.

"Now that's great. I think he has a crush on you, Liz," Meg said when he disappeared into the kitchen. "My, what a lovely young man. He's really working hard. So, back to Paul. When he was five, we took him to see the Ice Capades; sat in front row seats. Five minutes into the show, when Captain Hook came skating close to where we were seated, Paul gave out an ear-piercing screech and dove under his seat. Captain Hook actually lost his balance and fell down! We were mortified. How could we know that Paul had seen him in the movie on TV and was scared that the crocodile that followed Capt. Hook around would then come over to bite off his arm?"

Liz fought to control her laughter, thinking she'd be disturbing others, but only a few people near them noticed. Several of the regular guests just smiled her way, as she waved to say hello. She gave her attention back to Meg. "It's obvious that you're crazy about your grandson."

Meg beamed. "You're just starting your family now, and I know you'll adore your children, but someday you'll understand when I say that a grandmother has such a different love for her grandchildren. He's twenty-three now, and my heart still flutters when I think about him."

"Your Paul must have grown into—"

"Oh, I'm not getting into that just yet. Then there's the hysterical time that we were invited to see him playing soccer the Saturday before he entered kindergarten. Now, you must understand that my son-in-law, Mike, was the star soccer player in college. He played in the all-American Soccer Tournament, was voted MVP, and became a professional soccer player for years. He and my daughter skied, biked, jogged, played tennis, you name it, they were active in so many sports. Even had kiddie seats attached to the back of their bikes. Mike played soccer in the local thirty-something league, which is no small feat; it's so exhausting. So, he became the coach of the little tykes' soccer team, hoping to get Paul to get more physically involved. What a riot! We couldn't believe that when the teams were playing in the center of the field, there was Paul, running up close to the fence, away from all the action. No one was going to kick him or bump his precious body! Can you imagine how Mike felt?"

Liz's eyes grew large. "Hey! Imagine how little Paul felt. He obviously hated contact sports."

"Well, he found his own niche in tennis and golf and did well on the teams in college. He also became a fantastic dancer, having taken lessons in jazz, tap and ballet. Did I mention that he developed into a handsome six-footer?" Meg chuckled. "We grow them tall in our family! He always outgrew all his clothes and his shoes."

"That's why you had his tennis shoes. Thank goodness! I try to anticipate how a story ends and thought you were foreshadowing something else, quite…"

Meg's face betrayed her emotions. "I was! He joined the air force, was sent to Iraq…"

Catching her breath, Liz was afraid to verbalize what she was thinking.

When Meg realized what Liz might be imagining, she shook her head. "Oh, no! He's doing all right now. He's walking with a cane. Has gone into the advertising business. He hasn't any active interest in sports, just watches it on TV. A long time later when I found his tennis shoes in my old car, I planned to drop them off in a clothing bin, and never got around to it. I discovered your shoe tree. Maybe some lucky kid will come across them soon."

Chapter 18

That same evening, when most customers had left the restaurant, one person remained in her seat, staring at her coffee cup. Sitting in her wheelchair nearby, Liz had noticed that the small woman furtively glanced at her during dinner, but quickly looked away when their eyes met. Finally, with the pretext of moving to the counter to pour herself some water, Liz addressed the stranger, offering to top off her cup.

"Yes, thanks, I'd love a refill, but let me pour yours. I don't think the owner will mind. I'm Annabelle." There was an embarrassing moment of silence. "You must be the lady who's writing the book, right?"

When Liz introduced herself, Annabelle asked if she could join her. "I'm from a small town near Santa Fe that no one's ever heard of, filled with lots of nobodies. Heard about the shoe tree from a neighbor and decided to drive out here to see it myself."

Liz smiled. She liked this person with a benevolent demeanor. "That's a mighty long drive just to see a tree. By the way, there's a shoe tree in Albuquerque, New Mexico, much closer to you. When I researched shoe trees, I read that there are at least fifty of them in twenty states."

"No, I didn't know that. Thought this is the only one. Fifty? Yep, this one sure is far away, but I'm off for the summer, so I've got lots of time. I've always wanted to see Las Vegas. My husband and I just spent a couple of days there, now we plan to go to Colorado and see Utah on our way back, and visit Bryce, Zion, and the north rim of the Grand Canyon, which is supposed to be spectacular. There's so much to see in this glorious country. We've been trying to see most of the national parks. We even have a special little book to fill with stamps from the parks we get to. I just left him napping at the motel and came over to meet you. I think I have an interesting story for you."

The woman spoke quickly, almost breathlessly, and seemed to nod her head often to emphasize certain words. She had a shy smile; almost a mousey look. She looked as if she were wearing someone else's clothing, almost like she hadn't chosen the outfit which didn't seem to flatter her. Liz thought she was in her late fifties, because of the wrinkles around her eyes, and there were a few streaks of gray peeking through her dark wavy hair. Altogether, Liz sized her up as a sweet, sincere person.

"I'll bet you're an elementary school teacher?"

Annabelle's smile made her eyes crinkle into slits. "Yes, I teach elementary school, several different grades, sometimes a combination of two of them. Keeps me on my toes. How'd you know that?"

"You said you had time off this summer, and it was just a lucky guess. So, what's the scoop?"

"Well," Annabelle looked around to see if anyone had come in and was eavesdropping. "I've been afraid of reprisal and felt it was a good time to be scarce from our town for a while. First, I must give you some background. Do you remember reading about the fights during the Democratic Convention in Chicago in 1968? There were riots with hundreds of people outside the Convention Hall and there were reports about police brutality while handling the mobs to break them up?"

"I sure do," Liz said. "I've seen reruns when the stations talked about past political conventions." She waved to some customers who had just entered and asked how she was feeling. Joan and Greg came out to take their orders and set the table.

Annabelle waited for Liz's attention and kept her voice so low that Liz had to lean forward to hear her. "During that convention, when the chairman wouldn't let certain people speak if they weren't in agreement, one of the delegates ended up by banging on the podium, demanding the right to address the assembly."

"Yes, that was broadcast many times." Liz said, while nodding to Greg, who approached their table with a coffee pot.

Annabelle's coffee had gotten cold, and she was happy to accept a new mug. She thanked him. Greg attempted to hang back to overhear their conversation, until Liz surreptitiously gave him the high sign to leave. When he walked away, Annabelle continued, "Well, to get back to our own time frame, our school district was fighting for a raise in pay, among other demands, and a judge had ruled that there couldn't be a strike until the parties had gone through arbitration and mediation. It was in all the news broadcasts and in the newspapers. The Teachers Union, also called the Federation, held a city-wide meeting which every teacher was required to attend, member or not. I had dropped out of the Union many years ago, because I couldn't agree with their policy that I couldn't buy supplies from nonunion distributors. I really do believe in unions and they've done so much to help workers in industry and teachers to get a good pay scale and benefits and all that, but I was also idealistic and realized there was a point where I had to do the right thing, too. No one was going to tell me where I could shop. I always spent some of my own money for supplies in my classroom. So, I joined the local branch of the National Education Society. Now, back to that special required assembly with hundreds of teachers and administrators; almost everyone wanted to vote to strike. Mind you, I'm not into politics, but I was so furious, I got up to speak. You'll find this hard to believe, but the chairman wouldn't recognize me because he knew that I wasn't a Federation member. I don't know what possessed me, but I brazenly demanded that they turn on the microphone so that I could address the group. I didn't even know what I was going to say. I actually thumped the podium and yelled for everyone's attention."

Liz interrupted. "Our lives are all entangled in a metaphysical bond. I've just met you, but I absolutely would never have guessed that you'd do such a thing. I'm amazed that you'd–"

"Yes, I amazed myself! I had to shout over objections, but I was concise. I remember exactly what I said. I identified myself and told them where I taught. Then I said that I was ashamed that they weren't setting a good example for our students but instead were flaunting the law. I asked them to go through mediation and arbitration before striking, as the judge had ordered. A short time later, the group overwhelmingly voted to strike. So much for my input. After the meeting, while driving home across town, I heard my voice on the radio with my short speech played over and over again. It was on a local broadcasting station. Mine was the shortest speech of that afternoon and the only one who spoke out in opposition to the union's demands. It was scary, hearing myself over and over again. Our school was one of a few that remained open the next day, and when I drove into the parking lot, other teachers from striking schools were screaming 'Scab' at me. Someone pounded on my car. It was completely unnerving."

"Wow! You are one rare, brave woman! What happened then?"

"That day, a teacher who was new at our school, Jack was his name, told his class that they could do whatever they wanted to their classroom, and they trashed it. Later, our principal found out that Jack had been thrown out of his previous school for inciting poor behavior. He had him transferred. In the meantime, because of my speech and the fact that my school was open during the strike, I was considered a rabble-rouser. Again, you won't believe this, but a couple called to say that they wouldn't keep our plans to go out that Saturday because they were involved with the Federation and didn't want to be seen with me."

'Yes, I can see you were considered a traitor."

"You must think I'm crazy. In retrospect, I was. You probably don't believe me."

"I certainly do. I realize you're offering to tell me a secret that's close to your heart and I trust you."

Joan came out of the kitchen to check with the remaining customers about dessert and stopped by their table for a moment. Rubbing her belly, Liz passed on her suggestions. "Oh my, Joan, dinner was great and I couldn't think of dessert. I'm sorry you weren't able to hear Annabelle's powerful story, but I promise you'll be the first to read it."

When Joan walked away, Annabelle said, "Well, now I'm getting into the best part. That teacher, Jack the trouble maker, continued to defy authority in another school, was finally fired from our small school system, and was actually hired to teach in Santa Fe. Obviously, they didn't check on his past employment in my town; never vetted him. The next time I heard about him, there was an article in the paper stating that he had been arrested for brawling in a local tavern and resisting arrest. He was fined and given community service as a penalty. Some slap on the wrist, don't you think? I'll wager anything that he never complied with the sentence and no one ever checked to follow up."

Liz smiled as she shifted in her seat to get more comfortable. "My baby's anxious to come meet everyone, I suppose. So, that man, Jack, still kept his teaching job?"

"Oh, yes! Then a year goes by, and I read that he's running for the Board of Education in Santa Fe. I couldn't bear to think about what he'd propose."

"Really?" Liz squeaked. The last couple caught her attention by waving good-night but even though she waved back, she didn't get distracted from this conversation. "I can't imagine that someone didn't research his background before allowing him to run for such a crucial position."

"That's where I came into the picture. I spent a few sleepless nights trying to think of what I should do. I finally got up the nerve to call the newspaper that ran his ad and asked to speak to a reporter. I said I had an interesting story that might be newsworthy."

"No! You didn't!"

"I sure did! I was so angry that he'd be in a responsible role making important decisions for children's education. What kind of a job would he do? The receptionist at the newspaper said no one was available to speak with me, but someone would get back to me soon. In the meantime, I had very serious misgivings. Jack must have had a lot of political pull to be able to be considered, and to think of running for office in Santa Fe, where he lived. I had nightmares about being beaten up or my house set on fire, all sorts of retribution from that guy, who might even have owned a gun. I finally decided that whenever a reporter did contact me, I'd just say I changed my mind."

"You actually thought the reporter would tell anyone who his source was? There are laws about that. You were doing the right thing by exposing someone not fit to serve in office to the public."

"My imagination went wild, I admit, but I was afraid of my name leaking out. I was sorry I'd started anything. The long and the short of it is – don't laugh – no one ever contacted me from the newspaper, and I simply let it drop." She smiled without engaging her eyes.

Liz looked doubtful. After a moment she asked, "Well, if you never told anyone about Jack's background to try to prevent his election, why do you worry about retribution?"

"Yeah, you guessed it. When I was so worried about the whole situation, I did spill the whole thing to our custodian, Al, one time when he was cleaning my room. I had to talk to someone about the fact that that troublemaker Jack was running for…" Annabelle shook her head.

"Okay. Maybe Al has kept his word. You must have really trusted him. So, did Jack get elected?"

"Of course! He's now serving on the Board and I just hope the kids don't suffer."

"So, it's over. No newspaper expose, no repercussions. What does all this have to do with your stop at the shoe tree?"

Annabelle gave her a knowing smile. "I wasn't going to forget the epilogue. That's what brought us together, after all. One day, when our custodian Al read about Jack in the paper, winning the election and all, he brought the newspaper to my room after school. He gave me an earful about the horrible condition of the classroom when Jack left. He told me that when that guy was packing after being thrown out of our school, he filled several boxes with our equipment and supplies. That's akin to stealing. He actually had the nerve to ask Al to help him load the stuff into his car. Jack had never treated him with respect but always demanded lots of attention, he was that kind of guy, so to get even, our good-natured Al admitted that he sneaked one of the boxes and hid it in the storage room to force Jack into coming back to find it. But he never did. 'Funny thing,' Al said, 'I finally opened it and found a nice cashmere sweater, along with an expensive pair of hiking boots. Now I feel guilty about what I did. You might be driving near where he teaches. Suppose I give his stuff to you, and you drop it off. Okay?'"

Liz laughed. "Shame on you. I know what you did! You gave Jack's sweater to a place like Goodwill, and our wonderful shoe tree is now decorated with his fancy boots."

Chapter 19

The restaurant had been closed for the evening but the lights weren't out and the door hadn't been locked. Dr. Matthews stopped by and found Liz and Joan still sitting at one of the tables. He joined them and ordered coffee and a piece of his favorite pie from Greg, who had just begun to wipe down the tables to set up for the early breakfast crowd.

A few minutes later, Greg served the dessert to the doctor. "Please put that on my tab," Liz said, grabbing the check.

Dr. Matthews acknowledged the offer, but turning to Greg, put down his money. "Thanks, my boy. I'm happy that you're here to help Joan. I don't know how she'd manage without you." The good doctor shook a finger at Liz. "You can't buy me off, young lady. And how long have you been out of bed? I expected you to eat and chew the fat for a little bit. Aren't you overdoing it?"

As Liz began to speak, a woman opened the door, peeking in, checking to see if she could enter. Liz could hear her panting as if she'd been running. She was striking – wavy jet- black hair, pale complexion and the darkest eyes which commanded attention. Her tight-fitting spandex outfit showed off her svelte figure.

When Joan began to explain that the kitchen was closed, the woman drew a deep breath. When she spoke, her Southern drawl made it obvious that she wasn't a local woman. "Actually, I didn't come for dinner. I rushed over here because I understand that there's a woman here who's writing about the shoe tree, and I wanted to tell her about my experience. It might make a good chapter for her."

Liz identified herself while she shook hands, asking the newcomer to sit at a table across the room, to ensure some privacy. She turned to Dr. Matthews. "I promise that I'll be in bed for the rest of the evening. You can see I'm not running around, and I spent all afternoon resting in my room."

She didn't wait for his reply.

When Greg approached them, he told the woman that there was still some hot coffee if she wished, and plenty of dessert choices.

"Yes, I'm grateful, if it's not too much trouble. The man at the inn down the street raved about your pies. I'll have hot decaf coffee with milk, and I think I'll splurge with some apple pie a la mode." She laughed as she sat down. "I know, milk instead of cream and then I order ice-ream. I'm Wendy, originally from South Carolina, but recently from San Francisco. I know this is presumptuous of me to barge in like--"

"I'm delighted that you feel you can trust me. I'm always on the lookout for new material. That grouchy man over there, Doc, isn't my father, but he is my boss. I'm supposed to be on total bed rest, on his orders, but I'd love to hear your story."

Once again, Wendy drew a deep breath, and then proceeded to speak in her Southern patois. It was obvious that she was trying to talk quickly so she wouldn't keep Liz too long. "My husband got transferred out to California about six months ago. My last kid just entered college, so we were empty-nesters and didn't have to worry about taking our family away from their friends. Actually, our daughter Carol wanted to go to Berkeley, so moving out west worked out for her. I have a feeling that our son, who attends college in Philly, would want to transfer out here, too."

She thanked Greg, who served her with a flourish, sipped her coffee and continued. "I'll try to be brief. It's probably an old situation that you've heard before. Back home, my husband and I moved to another section of town because I found out that he'd had several affairs, mostly with our best friends and he was even shtupping our next-door neighbor. He just couldn't seem to keep his pants zipped. We went for guidance from our priest and followed that up with seeing a marriage counselor for months. Even though we were warned that Marriage Encounter is meant to help happily married couples renew their bonds, we took a chance and went to one of those weekends, sanctioned by the church. You've probably heard about it?"

When Liz shook her head, Wendy continued, "They confiscate your watches, there's no telephones or TV, they deprive you of sleep, give long lectures about loving relationships, and then ask you to write a letter to each other daily about your feelings. I could do that, but Justin couldn't express his emotions; he wanted to specifically write about incidents that were sort of argumentative, specifically bringing up old issues. So that approach didn't work, either."

Dr. Matthews had already left. After explaining that everything in the kitchen was shipshape, Greg said goodnight and left. Joan came by to say she was planning to stretch out her weary body and read in bed. She invited them to sit in the living room where they'd be more comfortable.

Sensing that Wendy had much more to say, Liz leaned forward. "I have lots of time, and if you want to, we could get out of this bright room into more comfortable furniture."

Wendy hopped up. "Terrific! I promise not to keep you up much longer, but I would like to finish my story."

Settling into the soft sofa, Liz felt grateful to be lying down.

Drawing a deep breath, Wendy didn't skip a beat. "This is almost like sitting in front of a psychologist, isn't it?" She laughed. "Except our positions should be reversed. It took a while for me to forgive him for having affairs with other women. I know all the trite expressions about the fact that if I don't forgive, I'll become burdened with a heavy heart, be depressed forever, and all that bunk. I had to work it out – I didn't know if I could honestly trust him again. He'd had several affairs and I was lucky that I hadn't gotten any horrible diseases. He'd betrayed my love with my best friend who betrayed our friendship. It's hard to believe, but at one point, she actually told me that she mentioned to her husband that if she died first, he should meet someone like me, in fact, she said, get me to marry him. Can you believe how uncomfortable I was with them after that. So, back to my philandering husband. He'd lied so many times about working late, about being sent out of town by the company, about losing money somewhere or other, to try to explain how his pocket money ran out; money he spent on trysts. Telling lies was too easy and smooth for him. They say an alcoholic will be one forever – I had to ask myself if he would chase a pretty face the rest of his life?"

Almost breathless, Wendy stopped to take a sip of her drink and smiled. "With Viagra so readily available, would he grow old and carry the pills in his wallet in hopes of an amorous score? But I loved him, and the kids were still young and they adored him. How could I destroy our family? So, we never let them know our problems and we made up for their sakes. We began to find new interests and that helped somewhat. You know, the family that bowls together, skis together, stays close together and all that shit. We went on vacations and had fun. It lasted for several years. So, recently, when he was offered a fabulous promotion if we relocated, I thought the move would renew the spark in our love, what with being together more, fixing up the place and all. So, now that we were settled out there in California, Justin comes up with a new wrinkle. A few months ago, when our kids were home from college for vacation, he suddenly decided to get into better shape by taking up jogging. Our son offered to run with him, but Justin claimed he had to go out much earlier than Rob would get up, so he'd be back in time to have breakfast with us. The kids kept saying that it was unusual for a man their father's age to be jogging for two hours every – what?"

Liz was giving her a funny look. "Weren't you getting suspicious?"

"No, I didn't think anything of it, because Justin was always a health nut. He liked to keep in shape at the fitness center, worked hard to get a deep tan like that movie star. You know the type. He even had hair plugs when his hair began thinning. He looked terrific. I had to work hard to keep myself toned up to match his image, but I wasn't going to have plastic surgery all over my face and body. So, a couple of months ago, when the kids left for college, he wined and dined me to celebrate our anniversary and then sat down in our living room and told me that he was leaving me. Some anniversary present, don't you think? He said he'd always had more women than he'd admitted to me previously in our former neighborhood; that he'd waited for several years until our kids were in college; and that now he planned to live with a younger woman who had two little babies. I couldn't believe that he'd already had an affair in our new town, when he'd always been home every evening, but he then admitted that he hadn't been jogging, he was with that bimbo each morning." Wendy choked up and turned her head.

Liz reached out to pat her hand. "I've heard stuff like this before, but it's always hurtful when you're the one involved."

Wendy's accent became more pronounced as she got more aggravated. "Did anyone ever mention to you that the woman's so-called devoted husband said he'd never loved her? How could he say that to me? He was always so –"

"No, but I'll bet that he said that to hurt you, so you'd hate him and not fight the divorce." Liz remembered that she had to be impassive and keep her opinions hidden.

"I just can't picture that vain, that selfish bastard, that narcissistic man getting involved with babies and diapers all over again. He wasn't that helpful when we were raising our family." Wendy began to cry more openly but became embarrassed and tried to control her emotions. "I've had many sessions with a psychiatrist, but I've told you more now than I did in half a dozen sessions with him. I can see why folks pour out their guts to you. You're a good listener. Now, one of the reasons we're going to have trouble legally settling things, is that we'd just put so much money into our new home. The landscaping alone was way over ten thousand dollars. And the housing market's so bad, how could we sell it at a decent price and not lose money? To make matters worse, the developer is still trying to sell the houses he's been building. Buyers would want to make their own selections, not take our choices, no matter how recently we moved in."

"I don't know – someone might be happy to move into a home that's already built, not having to make decisions about all the kitchen appliances, counters, cabinets, not having to start with grass seed."

Wendy smiled through her tears. "Now I know why you're the writer – you've got a good imagination. Well, I have to sell my home because I can't afford the mortgage, and besides, I'd be happier to be in a small place, closer to work."

"Sounds like you've worked it all out."

Wendy stood up. "You bet. So, you know the ending to my tale."

"I sure do. His unused jogging shoes are hanging just as high as you were able to throw them."

Chapter 20

From the moment she opened her eyes, Liz panicked. Disoriented, she clung to the mattress. Then the baby began kicking and she shuddered with relief that she was still pregnant; that she was safe in bed in Joan's home; that she hadn't fallen out of bed as she woke with the horrible dream with a sickening sensation of falling off a cliff. She'd had so many of those dreams when she was a child. This jolt was as frightening as it had been in those years, except this time her parents weren't around to hug and reassure her. Her mother, especially, would have negated the trauma and transformed it into a positive happening.

Mornings were always tough. She moaned when every muscle hurt as she attempted to rise. That audible sound brought Joan hobbling into the room without knocking on the door.

"Hey!" Joan stopped short when she saw Liz getting out of bed. "I was walking by. Was that a call for help? Everything all right?"

Liz's bright smile was the answer Joan needed. "Yessirree! All's right with the world. I'm sorry if I scared you. Just had a nightmare. Don't be so jumpy."

Joan nodded. "Guess I'm nervous as your time gets closer."

"I'm really indebted for all you're doing for me, Joan, but I wish the doctor would give me permission to fly to New York. I need Dwayne – I miss him terribly."

Joan sat down on the edge of the bed. "I know you do, Liz, but you can't take a chance on delivering the baby prematurely while traveling, and it's important that Dwayne finds a job. From what you've told me, you'll certainly need his income now."

"I don't mean to sound childish, and wish my life away, but I –"

"Of course! Listen, I'm ready to make the first pot of coffee and I'll bring some as soon as it's ready, so just stay put."

"I will, as soon as I shower and get dressed. It's important that I don't feel like an invalid. Besides, I promised Dwayne I'd get up and about every day. I can nap later, if I want."

Joan slowly walked into the kitchen. She hummed to the music on the radio as she ambled around on her brace, then said out loud, "Oh, I can't wait to be outta this monster boot. I feel as if my knee is acting up from the additional strain of that weight. I hope I don't get arthritis out of this deal."

Greg walked in just then. "Are you going to keep talking to yourself all day? You're getting mighty cantankerous lately."

"Hey, eavesdropper! Why so early?"

"I couldn't sleep, thinking about how you're so crippled…"

He ducked as she threw a towel at him. "Crippled? Crippled? I'm still …"

Greg caught the towel and flicked it at her arm as he teased, "Well, slower, maybe. Here, let me grill that bacon, so you can chop veggies sitting down. That's why–"

He stopped talking midsentence when they heard someone enter the restaurant.

"Wow, that's the first customer," Greg said as he walked out to greet the older man. "Morning, sir. Sit anywhere you wish. You'll have to wait 'til the coffee's brewed, but I can take your order."

The newcomer walked to the table next to the window. "Right here's fine with me, son." He looked at the handwritten menu on the chalkboard. "What's the omelet of the day?"

Greg was struck by the older man's posture and smooth gliding walk, like that of a professional dancer. He had chiseled Grecian features and a head full of thick wavy white hair that made Greg think of Apollo. The man smiled at Greg, waiting for his response.

"Oh, I'm sorry I was staring. You remind me of someone famous and aristocratic. The kitchen's loaded with many veggies, like broccoli, mushrooms, asparagus, all kinds of cheese–"

"Fine! I'd like a medley of all those vegetables and just a small amount of cheddar. I'm hungry, so add some bacon and multigrain toast, if you've got it."

Liz appeared in her wheelchair just then. She winked at Greg, looking like a child getting away with something, and he scowled in return, knowing she shouldn't be there until much later. "Hey, I couldn't wait for room service," she said cheerfully.

When she settled down at a table in the back of the diner, the man realized that she had entered from the rear and was not a customer. "Good morning," he said as he chivalrously lifted himself off the chair a few inches.

Liz nodded as she got comfortable.

In a deep baritone he said, "We're the only ones here, and I'm used to sharing breakfast with a partner, so I'd be honored if you'd join me. I'm Charles. You're safe with me. I'm certain that young man will chaperone us."

His demeanor transmitted calmness. "I'd love your company. I'm Liz. It might be easier if you come here, please. I still find it difficult to manipulate this. It's not powered. Yes, Greg will definitely watch over us." She smiled at the picture of the boy's reaction to her sitting with the stranger. Greg was so protective, yet he knew Liz was anxious to hear stories first hand. "You're a New Yorker, aren't you? I recognize just a hint of---"

"You're perceptive. I was, but when I relocated to California, I worked hard to get rid of that, and now, I'm retired. Just touring." He seemed to exude refined gracefulness.

"You're so energetic. I'd guess you were a dancer or an actor."

"Both. I'm unapologetic. Many years ago, in my past, eccentric life. Who'd want a crusty old guy like me around? You must be the famous author in residence here. You don't need an agent because the desk clerk at the inn raved about you and told me all about how people flock to this diner to talk with you. I was at the shoe tree yesterday. It was quite an experience sitting beneath it, contemplating the lives of all the people who left their possessions. And while I meditated, a wind came up. The tree seemed to come alive in sections. First, a small pair of ballet slippers performed, then tap dancing shoes clicked against each other, followed by a pair of lady's boots twisting, all following a silent tune as if they were in a dance recital. It was extraordinary. Some of everything imaginable is hanging there. Something must trigger all those people to leave their things, and then it's a sincere compliment to you that complete strangers want to unburden themselves to you and bear their souls."

"What a beautiful description! Oh, you can't believe how grateful I am for this experience. I've met some fantastic people who've shared their inner secrets. Thank you for this tremendous compliment. And now you're here for the same reason. Tell me, what did you leave?" She stopped talking when Greg came out with juice and coffee for Charles, and juice for her. She disregarded his stony look. "What's cooking now? Do I smell oatmeal? I'd love that, please. And add a dish of fruit with a dollop of yogurt, thanks. I hope that the coffee's decaf. I'm trying to cut back on my coffee consumption. Never had so much in my life."

"So now, instead of coffee – don't yell at me – I'll bring you some warm milk."

When they were alone again, Charles continued, "As a child, I knew I was different from other boys. At six, I was the only boy in a dancing school with a hundred girls. I was one of four children, yet I was often alone after school. I don't know where my family was, they just weren't anywhere around. Maybe that's why I crave company now. Yet, when I am alone at home, I'm fine, don't even turn on TV to keep me company. I've always loved music. It moves me."

"Are you a classical dancer?"

"Some of everything, mostly ballet. In high school, I didn't participate in contact sports but I loved golf, dance, chorus, and I was lucky enough to win all the leading roles in every play. Then I went to college. I met James and we immediately connected. He was a gifted violinist. He was my only partner. It took me awhile before I finally told my family, but they knew I was a one-man guy – no gay bar scenes for me. They didn't have to worry that I'd get AIDS."

"I'm going to be presumptuous, and if I'm stepping out of bounds, you can stop me. Do you mind if I ask you what their reaction was when you came out?"

He paused, lost in thought. Charles seemed to have turned inward., trying to read a blank page. He wondered why he was talking about his life, his love, his deep emotions, with this young woman who didn't know him, who couldn't understand his deep love for a man who was gone from his life, leaving him an empty husk? Could she possibly fathom his pain; the void in his very soul?

Liz waited for him. She actually shuddered. What should she say? What could she do?

She waited.

Charles shook his head. "No, not at all. My father took it hard, but he'd always sensed it. He reminded me that when the guys were wearing baggy pants, I wore tight jeans with my shirt tucked in. I was always with a gang of kids, boys and girls, but never dated anyone in particular. My mother didn't object when I confided in her; she just wanted to be sure I was happy. I was, for the first time in my life. I gave up worrying about those people who couldn't understand or approve. Hell, California voted for gay marriage, then rescinded the law, but hopefully that'll change. So, to get back to those early years, times were tough in New York; it wasn't easy finding jobs. I was busy going to auditions for one play or another, always living on the edge. Even tried to get into TV; had bit parts but never a big break-through. And even with his tremendous talent, James had trouble getting his violin concertos published and performed. We decided to pursue our careers in L.A. Those were good years for us both. He worked in studios, playing with different orchestras, and I had many minor parts, nothing like lead roles, but I was happy. Then I hurt my back during some strenuous dancing rehearsals. It was a real setback."

Liz thought she already knew what he'd left on the tree. It had to be his ballet or his tap-dancing shoes. "I'm sorry to hear that. You must have been devastated."

"It wasn't easy, being laid up for weeks, then undergoing bone fusions with the long recuperation and months of physical therapy. James and I became even closer. Seems as if he had a fractured childhood, too. We talked a lot, and celebrated every birthday and the anniversary of anything, just the triumph of life itself. I realized that I never remember anything special about anyone's birthday when I was growing up – no cards, no cake, no party. Never questioned why? James was the best caregiver, attending to all my needs and sacrificing an opportunity to tour with the L.A. Symphony. He absolutely wouldn't hear of leaving me. He did appear in many local venues. And a youth group agreed to perform one of his orchestral pieces. People began to call him Maestro. Believe me, it was great when a waiter or someone in a store would come up to him and acknowledge his performances. He was thrilled. You should have seen the expression on his face when a man in a drugstore told him that he and his wife attended his last performance and would he come out to the car to meet his wife. There wasn't an arrogant bone in his body."

A few customers straggled in and waved to Liz. She acknowledged their greetings.

As they talked while eating, Charles was gracious and attentive to her; she glowed with his interest. His voice was well modulated and it easy to listen to him. "The paltry parts the studio offered me weren't exciting, so I waited it out, but nothing promising came along. I realized I had to seek another outlet for my talent. You've heard, 'Them who can't, teach?' Well, that's what I did when I realized my dancing days were over. I eventually opened an acting studio and loved being with young people; learning from them, too."

Greg kept coming out of the kitchen, ostensibly to offer coffee, and to take orders and service the customers who arrived, but he also checked up on Liz. The diner became busy, and Joan appeared a few times. She gave Liz the high sign, motioning that she wanted Liz to go back to bed, but Liz couldn't wait to hear how Charles's story would fit in with the tree. He finished his meal and settled back to complete his narrative.

"We'd been living together all these years and were married several years ago, when it finally became legal. It's a good thing we did, because James came down with lung cancer last year. His family fought with us, but then when he insisted, they had to allow me to help him make the important decisions. His disease had metastasized. He was in hospice awhile, then decided to come home to be with me. Hospice was there round the clock and kept him comfortable. He was happier living in our home with our paintings, our memorabilia and our collections, away from the clinical atmosphere. It was horrible, watching him die, but he was brave and upbeat until the end."

Charles covered his handsome face with his napkin. Liz waited for him to compose himself. He looked up, apologized, and drank his coffee. "I loved James so much. He was such a beautiful man, and so talented. He should have lived years longer. I miss him. I still picture him, practicing for hours, sitting in his shorts, wearing his favorite tasseled, lined L.L. Bean slippers. I kept those slippers. I felt good wearing them, like he was still around. I packed them for this trip, to use in motels. When I drove by the tree, I had this gut-wrenching feeling that that's where they belonged."

Chapter 21

Dwayne picked up his cellphone to dial Liz, then realized that there was a three-hour time difference. *She'd kill me for waking her up at four in the morning.* He'd wanted to share a moment he'd had today while he was watching the construction of a skyscraper. He noticed a giant crane hovering over the skeleton frame of the building and he thought it resembled a praying mantis. Just such a simple simile, but he'd wanted to tell Liz. He felt empty, thinking he'd been living life as if sipping through a straw instead of gulping and drinking deeply. No, like sucking a long string of spaghetti as a child, getting sauce all over his face and usually his shirt. He now ordered ziti or cut strands of the pasta and enjoyed a mouthful of it instead, eating a full measure without incident, or accident. He smiled at the pictures he'd conjured. Why hadn't he applied that to gaining control of his future? That was the metaphor he was missing, mastering his problems with finesse. That's what he wanted in life and he'd be damned – he would nail that interview today!

When Dr. Matthews came by that morning to check Liz, he sounded optimistic. "I think you and your baby are just fine. You don't have to stay in bed so much anymore. Take some walks, get some exercise. It's good for both of you. Just don't get tired or overdue anything. Promise?"

Liz hugged him. "I will! I've hated being bed-ridden, even sitting in the wheelchair, and I was worried I'd gain some unnecessary weight with all this inactivity."

He smiled and shook his finger, "I know you've been sitting up in the restaurant more than I allowed, but---"

"C'mon, Dr. Matthews, I've heard really good stories for my book. I wake up in the morning anticipating who I'll be with today. It's so wonderful to meet these people instead of trying to picture then from Joan's perspective and memory. I didn't strain my body and I've sat with my legs up in the wheelchair. Don't you think I'd be careful not to take any chances with my baby?"

He laughed. "Just so's you know – you can't hood-wink a hood-winker. It's O.K. because you've used the wheelchair. I've known all about your extra forays into the diner, and I don't blame you. Being cooped up twenty-four hours isn't much fun. So, now I want you to go for short walks in between meals but make sure you rest, too. Let's get some lunch before all the tables are taken. Unless you want to sit alone, thinking I'm cramping your style."

She laughed. "What do you think?"

They were too late. Every table was occupied. A portly man stood up near the center of the room, signaling them to join him and a woman. Liz and the doctor made eye contact, and nodding, he steered her towards them.

"Hi! I'm Norm and this is my wife, Gladys," he said as he pulled out a chair to make room for Liz. "We were looking for you."

The doctor shook hands with them. "I'm Doc Matthews and this here's Liz, the famous author." He ducked a playful jab from her. "Be careful, there, lady. I bruise easily."

The host couple got acquainted by chatting about themselves and the merits of touring the country by car. They had a small notebook put out by The National Parks which listed each National Monument by state and flipping through, showed how many stamps there were on the pages of where they'd been. Gladys said, "Did you know that if you're over 60 years old and register with the government, you get a free pass to the national parks? Actually, each state gives free passes to seniors, too."

"We've just had coffee so far, haven't yet ordered lunch yet. What do you suggest, Liz?" asked Norm, pointing to the daily chalkboard menu. "You must eat---"

Liz sighed as she looked at her belly. "A lot! Everything's great and made to order. I love the freshly sliced turkey sandwich, and the sweet potato fries, but I've been eating more salads now. Either cold fish or chicken on it for protein."

Dr. Matthews laughed. "Don't say all that on my account. You know what's good for you."

Liz leaned forward and looked as if she were going to poke him. "Honest, I'm ..." She stopped talking when she realized it was all a joke. When Greg came to take everyone's order, she studied this new couple while they made their selections and liked what she saw. Interesting. She guessed they were in their late seventies. Their grey hair framed their tanned faces and they were dressed in sporty attire, but very tasteful, like Banana Republic casual.

"I'll bet you're from the southeast coast, aren't you?" Liz said after they all gave Greg their orders. "Your accents and suntan give you away."

"Yes-siree," Norm answered. "We're originally from New Jersey but retired to Florida. Nevada used to be the retirement capital, but we've taken over, I guess. Although real estate values have dropped these past two years, we're beginning to notice a slight turnaround."

"We had a chance to rent our place for a couple of months, which gives us the money to travel," added Gladys. "Thought we'd see our own country. Our dollar isn't worth much against the Euro and it's almost winter down in South America, so here we are. Our neighbor showed us that article in the newspaper about the shoe tree nearby, so we took along something to add to it. Thought you'd like to hear about it."

Liz beamed. "Would I ever! I'd give up lunch ..."

"Don't believe her!" Dr. Matthews warned as he winked. "The only way she'd give up a meal would be to upchuck it, in the kid's vernacular. Watch that she doesn't sneak your pickle."

"Oh, you!" Liz pretended to be hurt, but then quickly turned to Norm. "Please disregard the interloper and go on..."

"You may have heard stuff like this before," Norm said. "We live in a gated community, which is large in small-town gossip. It's a medium-priced over-fifty-five community. After tennis or golf, almost everyone goes to a shaded area where we can sit and get drinks and schmooze. There's this mousey-looking woman, let's call her Susan, can't even be sixty, whose husband travels on business, and then there's this good-looking fella, we'll name him Bob, who's retired with all the time in the world. His wife had been up north, taking care of sick elderly parents. Now, you understand, we knew most people at the club, also knew that Susan's husband traveled every week. In broad daylight, out in the open, we'd see Susan and Bob playing golf together, then sitting off to one side to have a cold drink, so when our group invited them to join us, they'd say that they were expecting another couple any second, but it didn't happen, so we got the gist of what was going on and left them alone."

He stopped talking when Greg brought their lunches. They all took a few minutes to taste everything.

"M-m-m, good choice," said Gladys. "Now, my turn. It didn't take long before this stupid couple began holding hands and mooning around obviously not caring that we could see their shenanigans. Mind you, we all knew them and their spouses, but they didn't seem to care. Oh! You've got to hear this! I didn't know it until I was told about this after their affair began, but Bob and his wife had divorced when their kids were grown and gone. Then after a few years apart, they began to see each other again, and reconciled. They moved into our block, right down the street, telling all the neighbors the divorce didn't take. They were living together again, but they never saw the need to remarry."

Liz ate slowly, listening very carefully, as always, wishing she could tape these interesting stories. She'd sensed that most people became intimidated when they heard they'd be talking into a machine. She vowed that she'd go right back to the room to jot down notes while the story was fresh.

"Didn't the spouses suspect anything?" Dr. Matthews asked. "That philandering couple would have to be serious actors when Susan's husband came home weekends. Also, didn't they think that their spouses could hear about their adultery?"

Gladys lifted her eyebrows. "Would you be the one to tell their mates that they were being cuckolded? I sure wasn't going to. You know that, centuries ago, the king would have the messenger killed if he didn't like what he heard?"

"Oh, yeah, I have." Liz nodded. "Today with all the guns around, there'd be lots of fireworks. Who would want someone's death on their hands? It's always been a philosophical question – would you tell your best friend that her husband was cheating on her? Is someone obliged to help her friend and let her know what's going on behind her back? I don't think even clergymen have an easy answer to that conundrum."

Intrigued, Dr. Matthews asked, "Did they all live in the same development or whatever you'd call that community?"

"Very close, a few blocks apart," Norm said, "but you know, the way they carried on right in public sure beat that TV soapbox, *Desperate Housewives*. Maybe even *Brothers and Sisters*. This couple didn't care who saw them eating lunch in the clubhouse, real cozy, sitting close to each other. You remember the adage, 'still waters run deep?'" He almost sneered, "Waters weren't too still with them. It's always the quiet ones who surprise you."

Gladys' face lit up. "I couldn't believe this, but when Susan's husband finally found out, he came over to my house to ask me what he should do. We hardly knew each other, but I guessed he needed someone to talk to. I just happened to be the first one that he bumped into that day, and he asked me if we could have a chat. Said he knew all about what was going on while he was away, that he didn't blame her for wanting company. He still loved Susan and was willing to forgive her shenanigans. Of course, I wouldn't give him any advice. I was just a listener. He seemed relieved to get that all off his chest." She took a sip of water.

Norm took over. To Liz, it was like sitting at a tennis match, watching the ball being hit from one court to the other. "But, Bob's current ex-wife came back and had no intention of putting up with their adultery. It was her house, her car, her money that supported their life-style. She even paid their club's dues. He was broke. One afternoon when I was driving home, I saw all Bob's clothes thrown all over the lawn, including all his toys—golf clubs, tennis racquets, all up for grabs. But of course, no one touched the stuff. I'll bet the neighbors kept an eye out to see his reaction when he saw that he was thrown out."

When Greg came by to talk about the dessert menu, Liz told him, "This story is sweeter than the best gooey concoction you have. I promise you can read my version of it tomorrow."

The kid grinned.

"No desert for us," the doctor said. "We're watching our waists."

"What waists?" asked Liz. "Speak for yourself. It's not that I don't want some rich chocolate concoction, but I'm actually full, and will pass."

The others did too. That settled, Norm said, "So, after Bob came home and found his stuff thrown out, he rang our doorbell to ask if we had any boxes or suitcases he could put his things into, and he's desperate, because his wife demanded the keys to the car. Gladys here, feels so sorry for him, tells him she's not taking sides, he can put his stuff in our guest room, even sleep over if he needs to, until he can straighten out his life."

Liz leaned forward, no mean feat, with her large belly. "You really got involved with these people? Took him into your home? You're something."

Gladys beamed. "Wait! This gets better. As we said, Bob's wife had all the money — an inheritance – Bob lost his shirt on bad investments after they were divorced. He'd sponged from a woman here and there, but I guess he was tired of his escapades. Sometimes he and his ex-wife had to see each other at their kid's affairs or what have you. They decided that they loved each other enough to give it a go. When they began living together, the house and the cars were in her name. He confided all this to us and complained he had *nada*. He slept at our home but he'd be out all day, looking for a job and a new place to live. His handsome face had 'jackass' written all over it. So, after a week, Bob took most of his stuff out of our place, got a room somewhere and bought a Tin Lizzy..."

Looking perplexed, Liz interrupted, "Tin Lizzy?"

"Sorry, you're too young for that term. It's an old clunker of a car, held together by mostly rust. Bob told us he'd found a job and would be back soon for the rest of his belongings."

Gladys paused to accept hot coffee from Greg. She took a moment, then continued, "Susan and her husband seemed okay, behaving themselves like they always did in public, but of course, they weren't talking to us because we helped Bob. I don't know what he would have done without our help. He really needed us and I had to—"

Norm guffawed. "My wife also takes in stray dogs and cats, you know." Gladys pretended to smack him, but he grabbed her hand and kissed it. Still smiling, he said, "So, the wind-up is, Bob's ex-wife was living it up at our country club, dissing Susan and Bob every chance she had to discredit them, and then she began to date the assistant tennis pro among others. In the meantime, because Bob was working and her husband travelled, Susan is left alone during the week again, and I don't have to tell you what she was up to. Her milquetoast of a husband eventually heard that she'd been sneaking around, meeting Bob in his new digs, even going to restaurants and movies where people saw them together. He finally had it, told Susan to leave, and of course, she ran to Bob."

Delighted, Liz clapped her hands. She pulled her head into her shoulders as if apologizing when she noticed people nearby looking at her. "Sorry! This is wonderful. It can't be a true story! So, let me figure this out. Susan, the plain Jane, leaves her lovely home and breadwinner husband, goes to live with gorgeous no-money-Bob in a room somewhere – Bob's former wife, his betrayed wife, is wining and dining, sleeping around, while Susan's husband, the jerk, is left alone in his castle."

Gladys patted Liz's shoulder. "You're a quick study. You've got it! Here's the finale – It's been more than a year, Bob still hasn't claimed his junk from our guest bedroom, and he finally told us to give it to any organization. We saved his ski boots to add to your famous shoe tree. Lord knows he can't ski in Florida!"

136

Chapter 22

After lunch, Liz rested and wrote notes to remind herself of the last wickedly funny story about the adulterous affairs of the two couples. She planned to embellish it, to make it even more enticing, something on the order of the New York Times bestseller, *Peyton Place,* which morphed into a popular sexy TV show. Then she took a twenty-minute nap, and woke up refreshed, raring to take on some exercise outdoors.

As Liz enjoyed her first outing, she stretched and warmed up by walking slowly, and when she felt comfortable, then advanced to a brisker pace. As she walked along, happily breathing in gulps of fresh air, she reminded herself that she should have taken her small notepad with her, so that she could jot down her latest thoughts about the last few stories she'd heard. It had happened so many times before – important plot changes or variations on someone's personality ran rampant through her mind when it was inconvenient for her to jot down these thoughts, but when she'd finally sit to pursue those new ideas, her page was blank or not as vibrant as her original ideas.

Of course, she had overdone it and walked too far. She was forced to sit on a stone wall to rest and was exhausted by the time she returned. Suddenly, it felt as if a hot wave washed over her, sapping her strength. Sharp pains stabbed her sides as she barely made it back to her bedroom.

Back in bed, breathing deeply and softly massaging her body, the painful jabs slowly subsided. *Wow, this has never happened to me before. I've been lying around so long, I've lost my rhythm. I know better than ---*

She fell asleep.

137

Hours later, when Joan came in to chat, she woke Liz. "Hey, I'm sorry," Joan said, backing out the door, "I didn't mean to wake you. I'll knock more softly next time."

Liz yawned and checked the clock. "Oh, I can't believe this! I really conked out. Please stay. We haven't spent much time together lately."

"Are you all right? You look pale to me. And you're still wearing your jacket."

"Yes, I'm fine now. Doc said I should get some exercise and you know me—"

"Yep! I sure do. You should tell me when you're going to go out for a walk. In fact, I insist upon it. He told me to keep an eye on you, and I haven't."

"Joan! Now cut that out. I'm not your personal responsibility, but I will promise to tell you when I'm leaving, okay? You're busy enough without taking me on, too! As a matter of fact, if your ankle were totally healed, I'd drag you out with me. You're the one who's looking peaked. We'll chat another time. Go take a nap before dinner."

Joan nodded. "I think I will. I'm bushed. Come early for dinner; it's a surprise."

When Liz entered the aroma-laden dining room, she noticed a young teen-aged boy waving to her. He had a ponytail and looked too pale for someone who lived in this area. His radiant smile seemed to reach to the back of his head. "Would you please join us? Joan told us you'd be interested in our story."

The other boy, olive skinned, stood to pull out a chair for her. He had a wisp of a shy smile. "I'm Jake. We'd be happy to eat dinner with you, if you'd like to?"

Liz grinned. "I'd be delighted. If Joan checked you out already, you must be all right. She's as sharp a judge of character as any detective I've ever read about."

The first boy leaned forward and shook her hand with a firm grip. "My name's Troy. We're from Detroit."

"You're a long way from home, guys. What brings you out here?"

"We're on vacation," Troy said, "thought we'd see the wild West. Maybe you're wondering how two hot-shots like us had the money to do this. Bet you thought we robbed a bank, huh? Well, we've borrowed a car, sleep in it at night, and we worked for a year to be able to do this after we graduated from high school. Sort of a present to our friendship."

"I'm proud of you, boys. You had a dream and worked to make it happen. Listen, we just met, but I'd like to help you, so eat hearty, your dinners are on me."

"No, thanks," Jake said, "we've been earning extra pocket money as we've traveled about. Maybe we can treat you."

Liz gave them a tough look. "No way, kids. I mean it. Just don't mess with a pregnant woman. We get downright nasty." She gave them a disarming smile. "So, tell me, isn't this country great?"

Troy's eyes grew larger. "It's been a fantastic wonder. We've taken some great pictures to show off when we get back home. But mostly we wound up here on our way back because we'd read about the shoe tree and the fact that you're writing a book about what people throw up there." He stopped and laughed at himself then stammered, "I sure didn't mean throw-up there, I meant leave there... Or ..."

Liz laughed as hard as the two boys.

Jake lost some of his reserve, "Yep, we heard about the book and wanted to meet you. You're famous, even before your book gets published, so we wanted our buddies to be a part of it."

"You've come to the right place. I'm becoming a regular story factory." She looked around. "Are your friends here?"

Jake looked uncomfortable, "Well, in a way, they are." He stopped talking when Joan stopped by to take their orders.

"I've got you covered," she said, winking at Liz. "My special tonight is something to die for. What'll you have, boys?"

"We'll both take today's special, and two cokes," Troy said. "The man down the street said you're the best restaurant here-a-bouts. Tell you the truth, with what we've been eating lately, this will be the most like home-cooking we'll have had by a long shot."

Joan seemed pleased. "Must have been Jim, the gas-station owner, right? He's a bachelor. Eats here regular. My best advertisement. You won't be disappointed."

After she walked away, Liz gave Jake a reassuring look. "So, spit it out! Where are your buddies?"

But with a sad face, Jake deferred to Troy, who shook his head, then let out a torrent of words as if he were being chased. "They're gone. Let me start from the beginning. A bunch of us grew up together in the same neighborhood. You know how it is… Jake and I stayed straight – if you knew our mamas, you'd know how hard they pushed us – and our two best friends moved on in a different direction. Early on. One of the guys, Darren, half-black, had trouble adjusting to either the Black or White communities. Jake, here, was different, you know, black, and his family fit in. He played a trumpet and boy, did he rock. But the kids bullied Darren, saying he was mixed-breed mulatto and he had a rough time growing up. He was sharp, with good ability but didn't want to use his brains. I'd talk to him about college and he'd go, 'Fat chance I'll be going to any school.' He joined a tough gang way back in junior high. They made him feel like he was a somebody, a somebody who belonged. They made him feel protected and wanted – so he told me. He'd been raised by several different foster-parents and tried hard to find his real mama. A couple a' years ago, when he was 14, he finally found out the truth. He'd traced her to a nearby city. When he called her, she refused to have anything to do with him, said she'd only drag him down, and she didn't have any kind of a life to offer him. When he tried to push her to give in, she told him she was a prostitute; admitted that he was an accident. She wouldn't even meet him, explaining that she didn't want the pain of sending him away again."

Liz shook her head. "Oh! That's heartbreaking. At least Darren had you two to lean on."

Watching as Greg took orders from new customers, Jake realized his mind had drifted, but he finally found his voice and continued with the story. "Naw, only for a little while. You see, in our city, in high school, we're all segregated. It's a fact of life. In the cafeteria, I sit with all the black guys who want to make something of ourselves; study, go to college. Then there's another black group; they dress like the guys in jail to show their solidarity, wearing loose pants, no belt, you know, showing their stupid underwear and half their bare butts. For a while, they didn't even wear laces in their sneakers, but that's not so popular any more. I always thought they looked like they was hobbling, like Frankenstein. The white crackers, like Troy, here, sit separate, so do the Hispanics, and the Asians. We're more comfortable with our own. It's that way wherever you go." His voice threaded off to almost a whisper as Greg brought out their dinners.

Liz had been holding back tears. As she listened, her mind went on a rampage, questioning the future, worrying about what her baby might be facing. Was it fair to bring up a child in New York where he would be in the same kind of social situation if he attended public school? Good preschools were so overcrowded that babies had to be registered at birth for some of the better ones. Could she afford private schools? Maybe she should home school her child? When Greg put her piping-hot dish of stew in front of her, she had to brush away these negative thoughts. She inhaled the delicious blend of spices and sauce. "Oh, does this look fantastic! This was Joan's surprise. Tell her I'm…"

Joan appeared with hot bread. She grinned. "Tell me yourself! Am I the greatest, or what?"

The two boys spoke simultaneously, "You are!"

The boys scarfed down the buttered rolls. They were quiet a for several minutes while they attacked their meals, then Troy put down his fork, took a long drink and continued, "Our other buddy, Ellsworth, was real white, almost looked like an albino, but he was lucky that he had Paul Newman's sky-blue eyes. He hated his name and got into fights all the time even when he was only five years old, hitting kids who called him Ellie. They kept tormenting him, telling him he had a girl's name. We liked his guts, called him Chuck, and helped him way back then, but

141

Darren defended him the most, all through the years. He loved Darren so much, that he tried to join his gang, but they turned him down. They called him a white pansy–told him they were never going to accept whities. When we talked about it, he would go, 'They're the losers.' He wanted to prove that we're all brothers, so he turned to another black group, and he was accepted because he really acted tough like he belonged all the way. Say, do you know what they call white guys who want to be part of the black community, dressing and talking like them?"

Liz was caught with a mouthful and just hunched her shoulders and lifted a hand as if to say, "I don't know."

Troy grimaced. "You won't like the word–he was a 'Wigga.' Get it?"

Liz groaned, "Yeah, I sure do. That's one word I haven't heard before. So, with all that going on at school, did you four boys get together these past couple of years?"

Troy pushed his empty plate toward Greg, who was quietly bussing the table as he attempted to catch parts of their conversation. "Chuck would sneak over to one of our houses late at night, 'cause his gang said he wasn't supposed to have anything to do with us," Jake said, his eyes welling up with hot tears, "but it wasn't smart. We were always scared we'd be found out. His gang would kick his butt. Darren always came, too. Then, last month, Chuck and Darren got caught up in a gang blowout and when a bullet hit Darren, Chuck dived to help him and got caught in the crossfire."

Liz yelled, "Oh, no!" before she could stop herself. She covered her mouth with both her hands as she sobbed.

The two boys didn't speak, thoughts whirling, fighting to control themselves. They had already cried many times.

They waited for Liz.

Greg had alerted Joan that there was a small problem, so she came out of the kitchen to sit down at the table, waiting to see if she could be of any help.

After several minutes, Jake had the strength to conclude the sad tale. "Troy and me took one favorite sneaker from each of Darren's and Chuck's families. When we got to the shoe tree, we tied them together, and I climbed that dam tree all the way up as far as it was safe. Now they're hanging out together again and maybe they'll be in your book so the world could meet them. No one would want two different sneakers anyways."

Chapter 23

The next day, the lunch crowd had thinned when a young girl entered the restaurant, asking for Liz. Greg was clearing empty tables but put down the tray as he looked her over. She was only a few years older than he but was not in good shape. He thought a good haircut would do wonders with her bland-looking hair, and some makeup might help to make her plain face more attractive. Her worn designer jeans and Ralph Lauren sweater smacked of big bucks. Her boots were polished, but looked well worn, so she wasn't pretending to be elegantly casual.

"Well," she said, flashing a broad grin, "have you finished judging me enough to answer my question?"

He burst out laughing. He liked her flippant remark. "I'm sorry. I didn't mean to do that. I'm almost dead because I just finished hustling for the past six hours. Sure, Liz is in her room, but I'd have to check to see if she's napping."

"Take your time. And may I please have a cup of coffee while I'm waiting?" She sat down and stretched out her legs while she arched her ample back.

"Hey, Joan," he whispered in the kitchen. "An interesting girl out there wants to talk to Liz. Do you want to see if she's up for it, or should I go ask her?"

"I'll see if she's asleep," Joan said, "Is that coffee for the customer? I'll take it out so I can check on that 'interesting girl' while I'm at it. It's funny how folks are coming out of the woodwork to pour their hearts out to Liz. I never thought so many people would opt to talk about their personal lives and bare their souls with a complete stranger, just because she's writing a book. I mean, she just brings that out, doesn't she?"

Just as Joan left the kitchen, Liz walked into the restaurant from the back rooms. The girl approached her. "Hi, you must be

144

the writer. I'm Janine. Do you have the time to talk with me? I've just come from the shoe tree."

Those were the magic words always made Liz perk up. "Oh! Sure. But I'm out of here. I was just going for a walk. Want to come along?"

The two women were silent while they stretched and set their pace, then Liz said, "You don't sound like a Westerner, even though you look like one. How can I help you?"

"Well, I don't exactly need help. Just need a good listener. I read about your upcoming new book…"

Liz laughed. "Someone must have posted billboards on the highway. Yes! I'm always on the lookout for a new chapter. Tell me about yourself."

"I'm from Philadelphia, where I grew up in a dysfunctional family. My home was oppressive, filled with conflict because everything revolved around my gorgeous twin sister. I've just tied one of my twin sister's damaged boots onto your famous tree." She took a deep breath then continued. "My sister Jackie possessed everything I've never had. Even as a preteen she had a beautiful, mature look like Elizabeth Taylor, with a gorgeous head of wavy hair; she's really smart; she's got a drop-dead figure, and--"

Liz stopped walking and looked into Janine's eyes. She recognized the ache within them. "You're painting a great picture of her, but you're sure belittling yourself. Talk to me. What's the angle?"

Janine's face contorted in pain. "Let's continue to walk, O.K.? I've lived a more insular life and have always faced rejection because of her. We're fraternal twins, and I've been aware that people have always compared us. When I was old enough to understand, I realized that she was the center of everyone's attention because she was so perky and petite." She held up her hand when she thought Liz would interrupt her. "I had an inferiority complex, some might call it a handicap. I've seen pictures of us, and I had a glob of a face, with straight blond hair, and was big and chunky. She had black curly hair, dimples, and was completely feminine. Me? I had nothing going for me.

My hands and feet were like a boy's—maybe I should have been one—I'd be more in touch with myself. And she fluttered around like a fragile daisy. Our mother kept a baby book, and I read that Jackie walked long before I did, talked earlier, had better grades throughout school, while I struggled to earn mediocre ..." She shrugged helplessly.

"Whoa, there! Those aren't fair comparisons. You should be judged on your own—"

Janine charged forward at an angry pace. Then just as quickly, she turned and walked back to face Liz. "Sure!" She almost snarled. "In another lifetime! I always loved Jackie – would do anything for her, but she wallowed in all the attention from everyone and I didn't even get scraps of left-overs. I was always judged second best – even our young cousins idolized her and were in awe – the girls tried to imitate her. I've always worked hard not to remain jealous of her, or envy her easy successes in love, friendship, and everything she attempted in life, while all those same things have been a struggle for me. My parents requested that we remain together in classes in elementary school, but the principal and all the teachers agreed, early on, that I was better off in a different classroom. I even insisted that I should attend a different middle-grade school, because she was a star athlete, made the cheerleading squad, and I was this klutzy, not too bright dweeb with huge glasses. I decided to live within my own shell to keep from being hurt."

"Sounds like you don't like yourself at all," Liz's heart ached for Janine. She tried not to sound sorry for her. "Were your parents supportive of you in any way? Did you go for counseling?"

"Hey!" Janine mood changed as she said, "From the time I was preteen, I've seen more shrinks than Barbra Streisand or Joan Rivers. Those head-doctors would listen to me, then call for a family conference and wham, I'd be on the back-burner again. I won't refer to myself as a black-sheep but I will say I was a misfit, a black duckling waddling among beautiful white swans. I didn't do anything wrong; I just wasn't right. Even when I finally met some jerk who was interested in me, he'd meet Jackie and I was out of sight again. I wanted to lead a secret life and hide all my friends from her. For a while there, I thought of her as a LSF."

"LSF?"

"Sorry, Life Sucking Force. She sucked the life outa me and anyone she came in contact with … I hated her but I still loved her. If that doesn't sound like a dichotomy, nothing does."

"So, that was in the past and would you like to talk about what's up now? Have you worked out some of the kinks in your relationship with her? You've told me about your pain, but you haven't told me how she related to you."

"Isn't that funny? My psychiatrists never approached it from that angle. Come to think of it, we were close and she watched over me when we were little kids. You might say we clung together as tight as the frost on a frozen martini glass. I like my vodka straight up. But as our interests broadened, and we became teenagers, we veered off in different directions. She gave up including me in her activities while I got tired of picking up after her escapades. Mom got her birth-control pills, but she obviously never asked me if I needed them. What does that tell you? I even covered for her when she stayed out late at night, breaking our curfew, or when she took money out of Mom's wallet. She began to use drugs when she got in with a fast crowd, and I tried, but I couldn't help her anymore; couldn't stand her life-style or the fact that she became narcissistic, so I headed out on my own when we graduated high school and she went off to college." Janine stopped for a moment, to catch her breath and to straighten her thoughts. She kicked a stone and looked away, "Of course, I've always had to ask for financial help from my folks, because I couldn't cut it, what with minimum wage jobs, but at least anyone I met could judge me for myself." She gave Liz a disarming look.

Her face lights up when she smiles, Liz thought. She's had a tough nut to crack. I'll bet her parents worry about her a lot. I wonder when they realized there was a serious sibling problem and why they didn't attend to it years ago. I'm not going to say something now, it'll be as if she's asked for a compliment. I think she just wants me to listen. Liz gave her a reassuring hug.

"But still, since we'd been separated in school, something positive happened. I found myself through my art. All through the years, the only thing my teachers always encouraged me to do, was to draw. That ability became my salvation – I'd lose myself in it – I felt like I was finding my way out of a horrible maze. Like George Bernard Shaw who wrote that life isn't about finding oneself, life is about creating yourself, I transformed myself. Recently, I updated my portfolio and that helped me find a decent job and get on my own, financially. So, after all that time, I'd forgiven her for using me in so many ways, and I tried to understand her. Jackie was so vain, so full of herself that as she walked, she'd watch herself in store windows – always primping. She wasn't satisfied with the size of her breasts and even had surgery to enlarge them. She'd gone through a dozen men, had broken their hearts; she was fickle and selfish. So, a couple of months ago, I asked her if we could take off on vacation together, just the two of us; try to get to know each other again after all those years. We began to spend time together, planning our trip, and that was fun. Most of it was adlib because we decided to keep everything easy and if we saw anything to change our itinerary, that would be fine, too. You know, just keep it flexible and loose. We traveled out to Chicago, did everything tourists do and then headed west."

Janine stopped walking as she hesitantly touched Liz's elbow. "Hey! I've been talking like a damned Energizer bunny. Are you tired? Should we turn around now?"

"Yes, I guess so. I've promised not to overdue this, it's only my second time out. Maybe we could stop and rest on this wall for a moment. Please go on."

"Well, we had a great time, renewing our friendship and touring the country and then it happened outside of Salt Lake City. We had a horrible car accident because I had just sketched something funny, like a political cartoon that you'd see in *The New Yorker* and when I stupidly showed it to Jackie, she only took her eyes off the road for a second…" Janine pulled a tissue from her jean pocket, continuing with a shaky voice. "she swerved and lost control. We hit a tree. She pulled me out of the van, then reached for her backpack in the back seat when the car exploded and went up in flames!"

Janine sobbed as Liz put her arms around her, not knowing what to say.

"Her face! Her beautiful face!" Janine doubled over with heart-wrenching sounds. Unspoken words thundered around them as Liz patted her back as if she were burping a baby.

After a while, Janine lifted her swollen red face from Liz's shoulder. "Why did this happen? Our lives are one glob of despair. My parents are taking turns to stay with Jackie in the hospital, and they won't even look at me. I'm just an appendage. They sense I'm to blame. So that's why I'm here – clearing my head, wondering if there is a God. What's he doing? Playing us like chessmen in this stupid game of life? The doctors say she'll need lots of plastic surgery and they can't guarantee what the results will be. She's also going to have skin grafts for her arms, will be hospitalized and in rehab for a year, if she's lucky. Her face will never be the same and she swore she'd rather be locked in a dark cell wearing a full Phantom's mask. That's not the worst of it – the medications can't help her a lot. Her body had absorbed and abused all those drugs for years, so stuff doesn't affect her as it should. She's in terrible pain and it's tough to watch her. Jackie has given up and just wants to die. I'd help her do that, if our parents would just leave us alone. I know she'd do the same for me if our roles were reversed."

"Are you talking about euthanasia? Is that what she's asking you to do?"

More sobs. "Yes. How do I live with this? I know I'm responsible for the accident."

"Think twice about all this."

For the first time in an hour, Janine smiled. "Are you saying that because I'm a twin?"

Liz tried to find some words to advise or to console the girl but couldn't speak. Silence was better than saying something inane. In those quiet moments, she thought of the novel and the movie, *My Sister's Keeper*. In that book, the young sisters worked out their own solutions, side-stepping their parents who were angry with the younger one for giving them a hard time. She refused to do what they demanded; all her young life, she'd undergone surgery to donate painful amounts of bone marrow to keep her dying sister alive. Their parents weren't listening to them so the girls finally chose to do what was better for each of them.

After a prolonged silence, Janine let go of Liz's hand. "There's no justice," Janine's voice was low and toneless. "It should have been me. Someday, I'll drive here with her, and we'll add the other charred boot."

Liz could only think about a quote she'd read recently, written by Mary McCarthy: "We all live in suspense from day to day, from hour to hour; in other words, we are the hero of our own story."

Chapter 24

The sharp ringing jolted Liz awake. She cleared her throat to answer the insistent noise of her cell phone. "Dwayne! Don't you realize it's only 6:30 here?" She listened. "Yes, honey, I'm fine, but why--?" Pause. "Wow, that's terrific! Good luck with this interview. Call me as soon as you know. I love you. I miss—"

Smiling, she turned off the phone. Simultaneously, Joan knocked on the door and entered without waiting. "I heard your phone. What's going on, kiddo? Is Dwayne---?"

"Oh, he's great! Just had to call to get a good-luck kiss before heading into his important interview. He hasn't sounded this excited in a long time. God, I miss him. Sorry about such an early call. He knew you'd be up."

"Don't worry about it. I was just leaving to get that kitchen humming. By the way, you've got an eight o'clock date for breakfast with a guy who came in last night after you'd gone to bed. He looked like an Adonis. See you soon." She left before Liz could ask her about the mysterious man.

He stood when Liz entered the restaurant.

Oh! She thought. What a gorgeous hunk!

Slim but muscular, he could have graced the larger-than-life Times Square electric billboard, advertising Calvin Klein underwear. He stood and shook her hand with a firm grip. "Hi, Liz. Thanks for joining me. I'm Philip Smith."

Flashing a dazzling toothsome grin, he helped her by pulling out a chair. She liked his after-shave lotion. Why is he turning on his charm for this bloated blimp, she thought? Maybe he wants top billing in my novel.

After they'd exchanged niceties with Joan, and ordered their breakfasts, Philip began. "I'm an artist. Read about your fascinating tree and decided to hot-foot it out here before you left the area. Let's see, you're going to want some background info; I'm from West Virginia but studied art in Tibet for about ten years."

Liz couldn't take her eyes off him. He seemed unaware of how remarkably handsome and spirited he was. He oozed élan, an eagerness for action. "You studied painting in Tibet? I'm impressed. What a great opportunity. I can't wait to hear more about your work. What's your medium? You must be good."

"Let's say, I've had some success. I live in Massachusetts and some of my paintings are permanently exhibited in several museums there. I've been lucky to have some fans, but I've never gotten financially independent or had a wealthy patron."

Liz's mind whirled like a gyroscope while she listened; she had to force herself to focus. She couldn't help but think that with his looks and talent, he'd find a lot of benefactors in Boston or in New York. *Maybe I'll suggest that he needs an agent to get him some one-man shows and advertise his work. His clothes are non-descript – I'd have pictured him in something wild—perhaps paint spattered and shabby.*

"My place is on the edge of a state park, where I grow my own veggies. I'm a vegan. My pride is an acre of really pretty open land planted with thousands of daffodils. I have a party each spring when all the daffodils open to one massive display of yellow flowers, as far as you can see."

"That sounds wonderful, like a Cezanne scene. What's your place like?"

"Oh, now that's an interesting subject. I live in a hay house – it's small but comfortable."

"A hay house? Real hay? Isn't that very flammable?"

"Of course, you've seen the rectangle bales that are harvested every year. My home is made up of those bales. I sealed the exterior walls with stucco, which I painted with whitewash, to prevent rain and snow from coming through, but I painted the interior straw just a natural color, as nature intended. It's just one open room; a couch, a small table and a chair, a low loft where I sleep. The walls are so thick, so well insulated, that it's cool in the summer, and my wood-burning stove keeps it toasty all winter."

A few customers had been seated and served, but Liz and Philip had been so busy talking that neither one of them had even noticed. Liz's eyes had been wide open in amazement. She had to concentrate to keep from sitting like a jerk with her mouth open. "How fascinating. What's the floor made of?"

"You'd probably have trouble living with the dusty hard-packed earth floor. I cover most of it with carpets because it does get damn cold in the winter. They also help to keep the place clean. I'd describe my place as minimalistic, it's actually bordering on bare necessity. I have a generator outside and some wiring brings in a little electricity, and there's a lead sink and a water pump."

"Wow! You almost live like a pioneer from the seventeenth century. A hand pump! I've used one once."

Joan came out with their order so that she could check up on Liz. The three of them chatted a few minutes until more customers arrived. "Sorry, I've got to go. Wish I could join you."

Liz waited until they'd eaten a little, then said, "It's probably not table talk, but I didn't hear you mention this – no bathroom?"

His laugh was infectious. She couldn't help but join him. "Of course, a hand pump just wouldn't give you that luxury of a toilet and shower. I know it's primitive, but I have an outhouse; of course it's a little removed, and it's a real chore getting through the snow or mud, fighting the wind and rain sometimes, even thinking about lurking animals. I carry a flashlight at night. And I'm sure you'll want to know there's a cold shower just behind my place. Believe me when I refer to it as my 'yelp' facility, because–"

"–you yelp from the cold water, especially in winter." Liz's eyes shone. "You're sure unusual, but I don't think I'd be very good living like that. Never wanted to travel in a covered wagon out west. On the other hand, you'd have fit right in." She realized she was completely mesmerized with their conversation and she hadn't been eating. She finished her cereal and leaned back.

"Your place must be semi-dark, so, where do you paint? I've read about the necessity for northern lighting and all."

"Aha," he said as he signaled Greg for more coffee. He looked around and noticed the breakfast crowd had grown. "I didn't get to tell you about the large old barn. It's got electricity like a modern edifice."

He laughed again and was unaware that he had completely charmed Liz into a becoming a lump of teenage idolatry. Not wanting to look like a smiling hyena, she worked on keeping a blank expression to hide her feelings. In between eating and drinking coffee, Philip elaborated about painting the enthralling scenes of 365 sunrises over the nearby river. "It was a labor of love. Believe me, it was damned cold out there, especially in the winter, exposed to snow and rain and all the various weather conditions. Sometimes I had to set up a lean-to for protection like a duck blind, but overall, I loved being in the elements with Mother Nature. I like the smaller scenes that I painted, but I've often copied them in larger sizes, showing only a couple of barges. Mostly, I tried to capture the moment, the brilliant color, or the subdued shades and patterns reflected from the unusual sky onto the water. And I paint those beautiful fields of daffodils over and over again. I also frame my paintings in a simple gold leaf."

"I'd love to see some of your paintings. Do you have any pictures of them on your cell phone?"

"Don't I wish I'd thought of that. Now I will. So, I'm living a simple monastic life almost like I did in Tibet. My work is signed with my Tibetan name. Everyone I met in that wonderful country took me in like a brother and now it's pay-back time. I've sponsored some of the men I met there and helped them find work and a place to live here. I'm proud to say that now there's a community here of over twenty-five Tibetan men, women and children."

"You're a fascinating man. That's a wonderful thing to do. How have they adjusted to such different lifestyles here? Tell me about them—"

154

He waved his hand. "They're hard-working people with simple demands. They're a tight community but after they got over their initial shyness, they began to assimilate. They're all learning to speak English, but I've encouraged them to teach their kids to be bi-lingual, not give up their heritage and their native tongue. Let me tell you what we did a couple of months ago, before the fire..."

Liz almost rose out of her seat. "What fire? Your..."

His physical body seemed to decimate. "No, wait. People come first. These Tibetans here are as good to me as I've been to them. They bring me all kinds of meals, and logs for my stove, and we're like family. They work hard, save their money, and keep bringing more of their relatives here. So, we had a birthday party for Buddha last May."

Liz took out a pen and a pad. "I have to confess that I'm ignorant. Don't know beans about Buddha. I hope you don't mind if I take a few notes. Please tell me all about him."

He seemed excited and eager to teach her. "Every May, the first day after the full moon, Buddhists celebrate the birth, enlightenment and death of Buddha over 2,500 years ago. It's called the holiday of Vesak or Visakah Puja. We sit in a circle and sing his praises, then dance, holding hands while we pray. Even the littlest children are participants. Then we feast on all the food everyone's brought to share."

"I wish I could have been there," she sighed. "What kind of food is served?"

"Healthy stuff. Some Buddhists are vegetarians. Others, the more modern people, eat mutton, yak, pork. Their staple is roasted or stir-fried barley, called Zanba; it's unhusked, mixed with ghee, which is yak's milk made like butter. These people mostly eat with their hands, using few utensils. They are shy, resourceful, and honest."

When Liz finished taking her notes, Philip said, "Now, the reason that I'm traveling is that I was offered a position as Artist in Residence at UCLA. I was lucky to get it, because I'm wiped out, financially, that is." He took a long, deep breath. When he hesitated, contemplating, his face became more heroically

Grecian. His green eyes turned a deeper color against his contrasting abundant blond curly hair.

"Wiped out? Did your hay house …?"

"My barn, my studio with all my work, was destroyed by fire. An electrical short-circuit. See what happens when you go modern? The paints and turpentine are all so combustible. The volunteer fire department saved my hay house, but I wish it had been the opposite. I've lost every damn painting and all my supplies. It's all gone. My friends, and even some strangers in town have rallied around me. They've had fundraisers and have done what they could, but I need to start from scratch." He pushed his fingers through his hair. "Maybe I'll begin with a totally new perspective. Buddha must have some kind of future for me in mind."

"I'm overwhelmed. I don't know what to say but offer platitudes. I'm so sorry."

"Hey!" He forced a wan smile, his body becoming bowed. "Pardon the double meaning. I don't usually say that word because of the similarity to my house, but what I mean is…" He spread his arms wide.

Liz was enthralled with his hands to which she hadn't paid any attention, she was so mesmerized, staring into his eyes as they spoke. The backs of his hands were slightly stained with various pigments, probably from his paints, but what finally caught her attention was that his palms were scarred. Without hesitation, she reached forward to take a closer look at one of his hands.

"You were hurt in the blaze? I didn't feel the scars when we shook hands."

He had anticipated her question. "Yes. I woke in the middle of the night and called the fire department on my cell phone. There's no fire hydrant near my place and they had to get a special water truck out to me. In the meantime, I tried to save some of my paintings but I was too late to get more than a few. So, that's the reason for my detouring here on my way across the country."

He raised his foot. The hand-made leather sandal was partially singed—what was visible was paint-spattered.

"I thought you'd like to know the story behind the burned sandals if someone should mention them to you some day. When I leave, I'm going to visit your tree."

Chapter 25

That evening, Liz had a quiet dinner and was delighted to get into bed early to work on her laptop. She couldn't get Philip and his unusual story out of her head. What a powerful personality! Her thoughts raced faster than she could type. She was interrupted by a soft knock on the door.

"Come in, Greg."

"How'd you know it was me?"

She laughed. "Your light staccato tap, like you're afraid to wake me, but it's only 9:30, the best time for me to write."

"I wouldn't bother you, but there's a lady out there, Carol Miller, who wants to speak with you. Says you know her from back home, and..."

"Carol! I want to see her! Are any other people in the restaurant? I'm in my PJ's and don't feel like dressing."

"We're closed for the night. You're O.K."

A minute later, Liz embraced her girlfriend. "Wow! You look fabulous for an old lady."

"And you look tremendous!"

"Tremendous is not what a pregnant woman wants to hear!" Liz laughed, to show she was only kidding. She waved a hand over her large belly. "Must be Joan's pastries."

They settled down with some tea in Joan's living room. Carol explained that her husband David was relaxing in the motel, and that they were just returning from driving across the country to help her cousin, Anne, relocate to LA. "While passing through New York, I thought we'd get to see you, but when I called, Dwayne explained why you were recuperating here. He told me everything about your time with his parents, the accident, and how many interviews he's planning. I just had to come to check up on you while we took some time to tootle around this marvelous country. Here I am, remembering to keep my promise."

While her friend talked animatedly, Liz listened patiently, nodding without comment. Then she said, "I'm sure happy to see you, here of all places. I'm still shocked by your visit. I've always liked Anne, she was sharp. But now tell me why she moved out to the West coast, and exactly why you're so involved with her move when she and Ron can afford–"

"Whoa! One question at a time! Anne's recovering from her husband Ron's death six months ago and has moved out west to be near her oldest daughter. I'm sorry I didn't contact you when he died, but you know how hectic things get with a sudden death, and the quick funeral and all that stuff. You haven't seen Anne in years. She's a trouper, has been all her life. I know you've met them at our home, at some of our parties. I always included her because we were so close, almost like sisters."

"I remember her well, and I was always impressed with her. She was married and had kids, worked in the primaries and for the elections, volunteered at her kids' schools, all while she was handicapped."

"Well, she wasn't always that way. She was active and was a cheer leader until her senior year in high school, when she came down with polio. They didn't have the Salk vaccine in those days and it was touch and go about her even surviving. Ron was a few years older, but they were deeply in love since childhood. When she was in an iron lung for a year, he wouldn't give up on her and proposed marriage to her before she'd taken a dozen steps with her braces, which she'd wear the rest of her life. He was studying law, attending college in town so he could be near her. She finally graduated from high school, but it wasn't easy in those days, with steps to climb, but she persevered. They married when he graduated and then she continued with her studies in college. We didn't have computers or college courses on the Internet and you'll remember, attending classes in those old buildings with stairs had to have been the pits. She climbed them with her legs in braces. Nowadays, there's ramps set up to make things easier for handicapped people in wheelchairs."

When Joan entered the room, Liz introduced her to Carol. "Stay as long as you like," Joan said. "I'm closing the kitchen and thought you might want something to go with your tea." She offered them a dish filled with goodies.

Liz laughed. "See why I'm never leaving here? Those chocolate covered peanut-butter squares are her trade-mark."

"M-m-m," Carol said, licking the chocolate topping off her fingers. I just might move in here, too."

Trying not to be bored with the topics and people she knew nothing about, Joan sat with them for a few minutes, finally announced that she was bushed and was heading off to bed. "Liz, would you mind locking the door and turning off the lights when Anne leaves?" she asked. "Because I sent Greg home already. He wanted to set the tables for breakfast, but I shooed him out."

"Of course. No need to worry. We're fine, here. I promise we won't disturb you. Good-night, Joan."

Carol stood up to hug Joan and say good-night. "You're very special, helping my friend this way."

Joan actually blushed. "She's the special one and I'm lucky I've had her company here. I'm going to miss her." She hugged Liz and walked away.

Liz waited until Joan was out of the room before she said, "Joan is responsible for my feeling so well, and for helping me save my baby. I'll never forget that."

Carol nodded. "I know, but don't forget that you're giving back to her by being here and making her feel that she's doing something so wonderful. How many people would extend themselves and take in a perfect stranger?"

When Liz's eyes began to tear, Carol decided to distract her by returning to her cousin's story. "Now, to get back to Anne. She wasn't able to maneuver without her braces, but she was fine, otherwise. One night, as they were driving home, Ron fell asleep at the wheel. He wasn't hurt in the crash, but Anne's back was injured. That's when she lost the total use of her legs and ended up permanently using braces and crutches or a wheelchair.

In those days they didn't have the powered ones they have now, so she built upper-body strength to push it."

Liz gasped. "I had no idea that's what happened. I thought the polio—"

"Well, we didn't want to talk about it. The guilt almost killed Ron, but he made up his mind that he'd take care of her the rest of his life. Besides, Anne had lots of spunk. That's what's carried her through all these years. That's the woman you know. She raised kids, car-pooled, got involved in community work, even became a great cook. I'd watch while she'd stand up from her wheelchair to reach dishes or food from the cabinets, and she'd refuse my help. Ron was making good money, and he had a house built for her, using the wheel chair as a measure for doors, counters, space around the dining room table, everything you'd think of. She drove a car that had hand pedals for the gas and brakes, lived as normal a life as she could. They socialized, went out to events, entertained a lot—"

"You know," Liz interrupted, "I remember when I was invited to a cocktail party at your home when they were visiting, and she was able to climb the front stairs with only a little help, then used her crutches to maneuver around the house. We were sitting in the living room, drinking and eating your hors d'oeuvres. She probably had one too many glasses of wine, and she slid forward, off the couch. Ron was furious and yelled at her. It was embarrassing. The men picked her up, but Ron's attitude bothered me."

"Now here's where you're all wrong, Liz. Ron and I had many discussions through the years, and I admired him for marrying her, for being her backbone. It was a daily yoke around his neck. He loved her so much, and was very proud of her, but he felt that she would wallow in her own sympathy unless he gave her the strength to go on leading as full a life as she could. He told me that it was difficult for him to see her struggling to maintain her dignity when she had to accept help. He figured that his tough love would challenge her to carry on and do a yeoman's job; becoming independent while raising a family, volunteering in the schools and getting involved with political organizations."

"I like that term 'tough love.'" Liz said, trying not to get too emotional. "It says so much. It's what she must have thrived on. I'm really sorry to hear that Ron passed away. I often hear about caregivers dying before the one they spend so much time helping."

Carol grimaced. "Oh, yes. He had the tremendous burden of worrying about her, working hard to keep them financially stable, but mostly, he suffered from the knowledge that he caused their accident. It never left him throughout their marriage, but he didn't share that with their children. His heart could take just so much, I guess. Anne took his sudden death badly. All the years of his propping her up suddenly stopped and she receded into a period of deep mourning." Carol shrugged. "I tried, but I lived out of town, and could only spend a certain amount of time with her. We did talk endlessly on the telephone. No matter what I said or did, nothing could get her out of her depression."

"I'm sure her friends were there for her. But what made her decide to move across the country at her age? Professionals usually warn the spouse not to make any major decisions for at least a year."

"I agree, but these circumstances are different. Their three beautiful kids are out of graduate school and on their own. She doesn't need to ramble around in that big house. One of their daughters lives in Los Angeles. It was a smart move for Anne to go out there and make a real change in her lifestyle. Her daughter's pregnant and there's nothing like a baby around to keep everyone smiling. Anne will feel useful again."

"What's her new apartment like? She's used to wide open spaces…"

Carol smiled. "Yep, it's in a new independent living facility that's built with wheelchairs in mind. She'll have her own quarters and her own small kitchen but can eat in the main dining room every evening, to socialize. She loves bridge, and there's always a game available. The place brings in entertainment or arranges tickets and transportation to various functions elsewhere. There's no need for her to drive to go shopping because they have shuttle buses equipped to handle those mechanized wheelchairs, to take her to a doctor, or whatever, but she's keeping her special car so that she can drive to see her grandchild whenever she pleases."

"Sounds like the perfect place for her, instead of staying alone in her large home. If I know her, she'll be organizing political meetings and rallies for the next campaign. I'd bet anything she becomes the next chairwoman of any committee there. Well, good for her."

"Yes, and good for her family, that they can share her company, yet keep an eye out for her." Carol began to cry. "I just wish I won't be living so far away. We've shared a lot all these years."

Liz handed her a tissue. "Hey! It's a win-win situation for them, so you should be happy for her. And you're in the position to fly out there whenever you please because I'm sure David won't object. I mean—"

"Object? Dave's already planning our visit there in two months to go to all the museums and sights, because it's a working visit. In the meantime, I've got to say good-night. He wants an early start so that we can visit your tree and drop off Ron's sneakers."

Chapter 26

In the morning, when Liz decided to take a walk before breakfast, she stopped to tell Joan her plans.

"Actually," Joan said, "I think that's a great idea – it's healthier than walking with a full stomach." She cringed.

Liz laughed as she pointed to her bulge. "I do that anyway, don't I?"

Joan chuckled. "Wish I'd thought of that. I mean, just be careful, O.K? No sense in tripping and getting that baby riled up."

Liz walked up the street without seeing anyone to speak to, but there were plenty of cars that slowed down, their drivers or passengers waving and yelling a greeting.

"This wouldn't happen in a billion years in New York," she said to the nearest tree. "Well, maybe when I walked the path next to the Hudson River, sometimes I'd recognize a jogger or so, but that wasn't often." She raised her hands as if to gesture at someone. "This is getting to be a habit, talking to myself. I must be getting–"

She stopped, thinking she heard someone running behind her. Did she hear her name being called? Within the time it took her to turn around, a middle-aged woman, breathing hard, caught up to her. It didn't occur to Liz that she should be worried that this person might harm her; especially since she called her by name. She waited.

Panting, the woman stopped to bend over to catch her breath. When she lifted her head, she reached out to shake Liz's hand. "Hi," she breathed deeply. "Guess I haven't run like this in a long time. Joan told me you'd appreciate some company. I'm Jeannie, recently of the light brown hair."

Jeannie had bright red hair, a bottle job gone awry, plastered down on one short side, with the other side styled longer, stiffly pointing to her cheek. The hair spray assured that the wind couldn't dislodge anything; it looked like a shiny helmet. But somehow, Jeannie carried it off. Anyone else would have looked like a clown. Liz smiled, acknowledging the woman's sense of humor.

The two women walked as they discussed their accents. Jeannie had a nasal Philadelphia high-pitched voice, in contrast to her square body, which Liz thought looked like a box on stilts. Liz had always worked hard to disguise her New York inflection, by keeping her voice well-modulated. She'd always winced when she heard a heavily accented New York voice speaking too loudly in a public place.

"So, now that I've caught my breath, are you ready to hear my reason for looking you up?" Jeanne asked. "It's all about getting rid of my excess baggage and getting my man ... but that second part will come later. My friends can't wait until I go home and bring them up to date with my busy social life in Nebraska. They're all married to the same guys, nice as they are, for 35 to 40 some-odd years. They think I'm really hot! But the story's not about me; it's my friend, Audrey. That woman's a pisser—she buried her fourth husband."

"Her fourth? My God! How old is she? What does this black-widow spider look like?"

"Well, let's see. That sixty-year-old woman is really nice looking in an all-American-wholesome way, with long straight brown hair and she wears no makeup. But what makes you take a second look is that she has a dramatic natural grey streak in the side of her bangs, which isn't a dyed, phony job. That, with a nice figure, is a super combination."

They'd walked several blocks and turned around when Liz said she'd had enough. "I try to pace myself so that I can get back before I'm totally exhausted."

"Good idea, since I'm already tired. I'm ashamed to admit it; I'm out of shape. Here I am, trying to keep pace with you and your baby. Now, on with my story. Audrey had two kids with her first husband, then divorced him when she met a married man, whom she claimed to be the great passionate love of her life. They moved in together. She behaved like a free spirit, a flower child, sewing her own clothes, cooking and baking and happy to be a housewife. Her kids got along with the new guy, and everything seemed wonderful. Two of our girlfriends talked both of us into taking a ladies' trip to London, and first night there, we stopped at a pub. Sure enough, Audrey has eye contact with a tall good-looking man across the room —"

"I know that song! *Some Enchanted Evening*."

"You've got it! I wish you could have heard this first hand from her, but I've got a fabulous memory for unimportant details. Audrey, a sure stand-in for Cleopatra, gives him the come-hither look, so he walks over, they talk, then he asks her to go to dinner with him."

They stopped in front of the restaurant. Liz grabbed Jeannie's hand. "NO! There's definitely something wrong here. She's in another country, on another continent, and she leaves her friends to go with a man who just picked her up in a pub!"

"YES! That's called 'chutzpah' in any language. Let's go in for breakfast and I'll continue this."

"You betcha! I can't wait!"

The two women ordered. Then Liz said, "You know, of course, that there's a term for a chemical reaction between strangers. It's something like pheromone." Liz tried to get the correct pronunciation but got impatient. "I'll think of it later. Go on."

"Well, Audrey told me that this man, Kenneth, had a polished British accent, earned a doctorate from Oxford, and actually lived in America with his wife and two kids. He returned to England every year to visit his mother, and to establish residency as a British citizen. He managed to spend a couple of evenings with Audrey when the old lady went to bed. Now, they were still married to others and lived in different states out West, yet after they returned to the states they met a few weekends—"

166

Liz interrupted, "This sounds like the play and movie, *Same Time Next Year.* Ellen Burstyn performed in both and won an Oscar and a Tony that year."

"Yes! And it might as well have been Audrey filling those roles. But she changed the script. You can guess—she left her second husband, the so-called love of her life, for Kenneth. Her kids were grown and gone, and just like that, he got divorced from his wife, so the loving, happy couple moved together in Nebraska, away from their families. And they married after a few years."

The two women talked as they ate their breakfasts, so absorbed in their conversation that when Greg stopped by to refresh their drinks or bus their table, they didn't miss a beat.

Liz didn't take notes. She knew she'd recall every word later that afternoon just as Jeannie spoke them, her eyes shining. She looked genuinely happy to be sharing her story. "My husband got a promotion and we relocated to Nebraska where Audrey and I reconnected. We saw each other a lot and it was great that the men got along so well. All that changed when Kenneth wasn't feeling well for a while and after procrastinating about seeing a doctor and undergoing many tests, was finally told that he had stage four cancer—it had metastasized rapidly before it was even diagnosed. He decided he didn't want to go through all the debilitating treatment that might help him live only a little longer, but with no dignity. Audrey became a fantastic caregiver, devoting all her time to be with him. She'd only leave the house for a few hours to shop or do her errands when he needed full-time aides to take care of him. We met for lunches because she needed that break and I became her mentor, helping to keep her spirits up. He became frail and lost his strength quickly. Audrey and Kenneth had always lived simple lives, despite the fact that they were multi-millionaires. Years before we arrived, while he was still healthy, she'd tried to talk him into buying a nicer home or a fancier car, but he watched the buck. When he died, she was left with more money than she'd ever dreamed of having. Kenneth's friends and former co-workers began to send condolences and one man who worked with him years ago

167

offered to help her to understand what she faced with her financial decisions and all the legal papers involved. They began to correspond daily via email and telephone, and eventually met at a motel somewhere between their towns. This went on for months. He claimed he loved Audrey and would leave his wife, but you know the usual story, he finally said the woman was sickly and his family was too young, and it wasn't the right time for him to forsake her."

"Forgive me for being critical, but your friend Audrey sounds like a home-wrecker to me. I can't wait to hear the next chapter."

"You'll love it! Despite the low-key way she and Kenneth had lived throughout the years, she immediately decided that he would have wanted her to enjoy her life, and not be lonely, so she sold the house, bought a jazzy car, and moved into a new top-drawer subdivision in a nearby community."

Jeannie stopped talking when Greg came over to fill their mugs and ask if they needed anything.

"Walking sure does give me an appetite," Liz said, pushing her empty plate towards him. "Please don't give me such a large portion again, because I'm the president of the Clean Plate Club."

Greg winked at Jeannie. "If you want to know the truth, it isn't like she says; it's my boss who cooks and fills her order, but don't tell Liz, because Joan's a health nut and really watches her. Wants her to eat properly for the baby too."

Liz pretended to scowl and leaned toward him to pinch him, but he dodged her fingers and slid away, smiling.

Liz turned to Jeannie, "Well! I can just imagine what you're going to tell me now."

"You'd never guess! Audrey attended her first singles club meeting at her up-scale new country club, where she spotted a good-looking man surrounded by half a dozen women. She pulled up a chair, and brazenly asked the woman sitting next to him to make room for her. She'd developed a new bold approach… no, I'll restate that. She'd always been forward with men; she'd made up her mind to meet someone immediately and saw the opportunity to change her lifestyle, no matter who she pushed away. During the evening, he mentioned that he had surgery scheduled that week and asked the ladies for suggestions about selecting a home-care service to aid him during his recuperation. When asked about his family, he stated that he didn't have any living relatives. So, guess what?"

"It doesn't take a genius to know –"

"Yessiree! The very next day, she calls him and offers to have him come to her house to recuperate. No obligation, of course. Says she has a large home, his room will be on the other end of her place, he'll have his private bath, yackety-yak. Well, needless to say, he never moves out. They got married and moved into a larger brand-new place, totally furnished by a highly paid interior designer. When I visited them in what we called her marble palace, what with all marble floors, kitchen, and baths, she showed me her expensive new wardrobe–no more home- sewed stuff for her. While I'm standing there. He kept telling Audrey to spend whatever she wanted on window treatments, built-in bookcases, and leaded glass doors. He goes, he had more money than they could use up." Jeannie stopped talking long enough to sip her coffee.

"Wait a second! I'm having trouble digesting the fact that all this money was floating around. I've never been in that position. I'm one step away from being homeless. I can't visualize–"

"Oh, that's just a tiny bit of their lives. Jewelry, travel, cruises, the best of everything. I remember seeing her feed him all this fried stuff and high cholesterol junk while he sat watching TV all day. She told me that she wanted to keep him happy, and if that did it, then it was fine. If I knew that my husband needed a special diet and had to become more active, you'd better believe I'd get him off his ass. To make this long story short, he ups and dies a few years later, and Audrey inherits another ton of money. She didn't mourn him too long. They had purchased tickets for a cruise on the Queen Mary across the Atlantic, and she decided to go on that trip – no sense in wasting it, right? She flew into Fort Lauderdale the night before, and in the morning, got on the bus to ride to the pier and…"

169

This was almost too much for Liz. "Are you kidding me? This story is like a fairy tale. She meets a prince."

Jeannie laughed. "Almost. A man sits next to her on the bus, he's a sucker for her 'come-hither look' and by the time they got to the ship..."

Liz held up her hand. "They only used one stateroom on that voyage, right?"

"What makes you so smart? That simple country gal must have taken lessons from the best. Cruise over, they spent a couple of days together in London, then he said he had to get back to his wife and family, but of course he claimed that their marriage had been on the rocks and he'd planned to get a divorce. Audrey went sightseeing alone but they met a couple of times and they were very much in love. Back in the states, she told me he planned to see his barrister about a legal separation and after a few months she'd fly to London to see him, but..."

Liz had to interrupt, "Shut up... the bubble burst. He'd had a change of heart and couldn't do that to his beloved wifey of so many years."

"That's why you're the writer, Liz. Audrey called me and sobbed like a teen-ager with a first love. She couldn't believe he was jilting her. I kinda felt sorry for her. She needed a man in her life, and really seemed scared of living alone. Her money sure didn't give her the happiness she sought. After that ordeal, she began to cultivate friendships with single women and did lots of things with them, but when we'd see each other, she often referred to her need of a companion. She turned to dating services on the internet and ran around with many different men. It was fun hearing about these short-lived affairs. It always sounded like she was in a serious relationship, had high expectations, but after a while it ended in a heartbreaking disaster. My hubby and I tried to include her in our lives, but we didn't see much of her. She'd be so busy with new activities and we didn't even talk as often as we had. Whenever she'd call, she sounded unhappy about one disappointment after another, said she had trouble sleeping and had been taking sleeping pills. I worried about her getting addicted to them, and also lectured her because she drank too much when we'd meet for dinner. She began to see a psychologist about her depression and took uppers and downers, lost weight, and the strain became too much. She died of an overdose."

For a minute, Liz stared in disbelief. "I'm flabbergasted–I didn't expect you to say that."

Jeannie nodded, her eyes filled with tears. "I loved her. Audrey really lived a full life; enough for five or six women. I miss her terribly. She was so full of hell and lived under her terms, so she didn't regret anything. Well, maybe she could have had a better relationship with her kids. But that's another story. As her executor, I had to take care of all her arrangements and when all's said and done, I kept a pair of her Jimmy Chow spikes which were never stepped on, to add some glamour to your famous shoe tree."

Chapter 27

It was almost eight o'clock that evening when Joan knocked on Liz's door. She grinned and applauded. "Well, look at you! You look glamorous! Where are you going tonight? Some hot date?"

Joan laughed as she whirled like a schoolgirl dressed for her first prom. "I guess you forgot that I'm a new member of the town council. You missed all the hoopla when I ran for election against pretty tough competition. Got voted in by a landslide. Tonight, for my first meeting, I wanted to make a statement and let them know I own a dress."

"This is the first time I'm seeing you with make-up and earrings. I'm impressed with your boots, too. You'll knock 'em dead."

"Hah! It don't take much to bedazzle them ole coots. Don't wait up for me."

"Hey, hold on. Let me take your picture. Dwayne will get a chuckle."

Joan beamed and curtsied. Just then, Greg came in to say goodnight. "Wow! Is that my boss-lady? I've never seen you all duded up. I approve. Some lucky guy will be happy."

"Now cut that out!" Obviously pleased with all the attention, Joan cuffed his shoulder. "You've never seen me dressed up for the likes of you before. Are you telling me to cook and serve like this every day and night?"

As she left the room, he called, "I'd say week-ends will do."

He turned and saluted Liz. "Anything you want? I've cleaned the kitchen and the dining room. Tonight's special; I have a date, so I'm ready to lock the door and leave."

He hesitated when he saw her mood change. "Are you feeling O.K.? You suddenly look sad."

"No, I'm all right. And I don't need anything, thanks. Everyone's deserting me tonight and I can't seem to reach Dwayne. Is this a conspiracy?"

"Yep, we planned it a long time ago. Stay in bed like a good mommy and I'll see you in the morning."

Liz used a whiny voice. "I'm getting moldy from inactivity, Greg. My body's going to be hanging in folds, like an accordion."

"You're a trouper and you're in great shape. I know you'll spring right back like a Native American squaw, giving birth in the fields. See ya!" He grinned and waved goodbye.

Unable to control herself after he left, Liz burst into tears. "I'm allowed to feel sorry for myself once in a while," she murmured. "I've got to face the fact that I'm scared I'm going to lose the baby, Dwayne's having trouble finding a job in New York, and here I am, forced to remain in bed like a sick old woman, dependent upon strangers to care for me."

The pent-up emotions became overwhelming. It was the first time she'd verbalized her fears. She'd kept all this away from Dwayne, who felt guilty enough about the accident and was struggling to find a job in the depressed market. She didn't want to burden Joan by confiding her fears about the future. Joan, who'd been so fantastic, taking them in and giving Dwayne some work when he was down and out. And what kind of a world am I bringing my baby into anyway? *My grandparents came here as a young couple to give their baby, my mother, a better life than they had in Europe. I'm afraid I can't do that for my child. And they actually believed every word they read in the newspaper and heard on the radio. I'm not sure that I can do that today.*

Minutes later, she finally stopped crying; she hugged herself, shook her head, and turned on her desktop. Talking aloud to keep herself company, she asked, "What's the matter with me? I'm so lucky that Joan has taken me in—where would I be if she hadn't? And now I've got this exciting new book that I'm working on, and all these new plots. I can't write fast enough to keep up with all these phenomenal stories."

Her mood changed dramatically as she typed out the last story she'd heard. At least she had a good chance of getting more tales the longer she remained here. Deeply immersed in her work, she jumped when her cell phone rang about an hour later.

"Hi, Dwayne, honey. I've been so damned anxious to hear from you. I guess you haven't had your cell phone on." Pause. "Yes, I'm fine and the baby's fine and I'm behaving myself." Pause. "I miss you too, honey. Now tell me about your interview today." She grimaced as she listened to his long explanation. "I know, I understand that it's this housing crisis and we'll just have to wait it out. Yes, no new shopping strips, either. Architects are expendable for now. Don't worry about me."

There was a long pause as she listened to his negative reports, then her face brightened as she heard the tone in his final remarks. "You know, Liz, I have to tell you about my new attitude; since I had to take over the responsibility of Joan's diner, I learned the lesson of multi-tasking which I'm now applying to job hunting. I've been too simplistic, too minimalistic in my field of vision and I've become more dramatic and creative. I'm going to pursue my dream and it's about time I've taken control and gotten more aggressive."

"I'm proud of you, Dwayne, and with your new perspective I know somethings gotta change."

"As Joan would say, 'Yessiree, Bob.' Whoever he is. Sleep tight, Liz. I love you."

"Love you too, Dwayne. Kisses. Bye."

She stared at the cell phone. Her upbeat mood broken, she lay back and closed her eyes, sorrow washing over her again, like the waves of low tide slowly pulling back from the shore. She fell asleep.

When Joan quietly opened the door, Liz woke with a start. "Oh, it's you. Come in. I'm sorry to admit that I'm the lightest sleeper in this whole world. How'd it go tonight?"

"I'm sorry. I didn't want to knock, in case you were sleeping. So, I woke you anyways, and now that you're up, brace yourself–I've got terrible news." With a heavy sigh, Joan sat down on the recliner.

Liz tried to focus. "Yes, that's what I wanted to hear—terrible news at this time. First, tell me how everyone reacted to how you looked tonight. You must have shocked the crowd."

"I've never so much as gotten a second look from anyone before, and tonight, everyone threw compliments at me. I'll have to follow up and wear some makeup again. Oh, and you'll be happy to know that lots of people asked how you are and wish you the best."

"Isn't that nice. Thanks. So, now, what happened at the town hall meeting?"

"I felt bored much of the time, nothing important happening, but I did get sworn in and that was a highlight. Then it happened. I became so upset, that I couldn't speak. Can you picture me with my mouth shut?"

"Hey, lady, come out with the news or I'll strangle you! What happened?"

"It's about the shoe tree. There's a negative group that brought it up at new business. They felt that the tree is getting too unsightly and they wanted to clear it off."

Liz's mouth and eyes opened wide. Now fully awake, she swallowed hard. "Our shoe tree? It's the best thing that's happened to your tiny sleepy town in ages. It's in the middle of nowhere on America's loneliest highway, yet that tree has captured everyone's imagination and has brought so many visitors here."

"Hey! Don't shoot the messenger, okay? You shoulda heard the hollering back'n forth. Those stupid people complained that some young kids from town are using the spot to hang out. Lately, there's been some drinking there, and obviously, some drug abuse. The stupid kids didn't think about cleaning up after themselves, so's it's gotten bad publicity. Tonight, there were two groups trying to get the upper hand—the people who hate it, and them that's made money out of the tourists. Of course, my business has done right well, and the gas station and motels are happy enough, but it's the old codgers who don't suppose that kids will do those things wherever they can. If not there, then they'll just find themselves a better place."

"I can't believe this," Liz said in a high-pitched voice. "What's the final decision?"

"There weren't none for this go 'round. We'll meet again to have a hearing on both sides…"

"Did you see any reporters there tonight?"

"Naw, not that I noticed. Why?"

"You might get someone there to write an editorial for the local newspaper. Maybe you should get some educators behind you to talk about the situation with the kids in school. Oh, I have an idea – perhaps the school should have the responsibility of various programs in the evenings, to give the students social wholesome outlets–movies, dancing, fund-raisers for the teams or the band–there's so much that could be done to give them a healthier outlet."

"What great ideas you have! Maybe you'll write them out and present them at the next meeting."

Liz lay back, her energy spent. "Well, I'll write them out, but you should get some of this started before the next meeting. I'm pretty sure Dr. Matthews won't let me attend that meeting, but you'll do this footwork beforehand. Maybe you'll talk with the high school principal. People have to get the facts and most importantly, some suggestions to fix the situation."

Clapping her hands, Joan enthusiastically hugged Liz. "You're wonderful! That's what we've needed here! Some new blood. We're so, so…"

When she hesitated, Liz spoke the words for her. "…so ingrained with status quo that it's almost incestuous."

Joan laughed, "I can't say that better. But don't think things here will change that quickly. The school board's gotta think about them extra costs, and who's going to be in charge of them programs? Things don't get decided that fast. It might take many meetings afore they vote on it."

Liz thought about it for a moment. "What a lousy situation. Do you think that any of those dissenters would take things in their own hands and go there to take everything down?"

"Naw, I doubt that. Although you never know. I'm going to drive out there with Greg after breakfast, see if we can clean it up a bit. Take some pictures, just in case."

"I wish I could to go with you. It really isn't your responsibility to clean anything. Why don't you ask him to get a group of his buddies out there and take control before it's lost? I'd love some pictures, though. They'd be important in my book. I'll give him my camera before he goes, okay?"

"Y' know, Liz, I've always been a cock-eyed Pollyanna. I'll swear that things don't just happen without some reason." She choked up. "You being here has changed so many things for me, especially."

"Hey! I feel the same way. I've been thinking how lucky I am that you took me in and have been such a good friend. So, don't lay any of that philosophical stuff on me. I also believe that things do have a way of working out in the long run, and if I can help you in any way, just shout it out." She paused and grinned. "By the way, Joan, I'm curious, did anyone make a pass at you tonight, or are they all blind as well as stupid?"

"Girl, you're so right! Nobody sidled up to me, but I felt good. It's like wearing pretty underwear and nobody knows it but me. I'm gonna get dressed up more often." She paused, "I've gotta tell you what I'm thinking—with you here, my life has some meaning. I have no kin. Most folks, for better or worse, have a family to call their own. So, Liz, you've become mine!"

Chapter 28

The air crackled with a carnival atmosphere. This evening's specially called town council meeting brought many extra patrons into the restaurant and Joan scrambled to leave on time. Greg had gotten some of his friends to pinch hit as waiters and busboys so he could help with the preparations. For the first time, Joan closed the doors early, and left Greg and his friends to clean up.

Since the news spread that the shoe tree would be discussed, and probably voted upon, Joan had the support of many of her customers, including Dr. Matthews, who finally allowed Liz to attend. She'd pleaded with him, because the fate of the shoe tree might be determined that evening. It was her first night out in more than a month. She preened, as excited as a school girl, and grabbed a notebook and her cell phone, hoping to record some of the proceedings.

The small hall reverberated with a pitched noise level. It was standing room only for the large, boisterous crowd. Because some of these townspeople had never attended a meeting before, they inadvertently disregarded the protocol; it took a while for the mayor, Ben, to get everyone settled. He had obviously learned his role by rote as he barked into the microphone, "In the interest of giving everyone an opportunity to have their say-so, we must be orderly." He hammered his gavel several times. When he'd gotten everyone's attention, he breathed a sigh of relief and turned to look at the seven council members seated at the long table with him.

"Madam Secretary, call the roll." Satisfied, he asked, "Will the secretary read the minutes of the last meeting?"

When the motion about the shoe tree in New Business was read, the crowd erupted into boos. Turning crimson, Ben pounded his gavel on the table so hard that Liz thought he might crack it. She covered her mouth to hide her smile.

"Now hear this," Ben shouted. "If you-all don't keep it down and let us go about our business, I'm duty-bound to throw the lot of you out!"

The crowd became subdued.

"Are there any corrections or omissions? O.K. All in favor of accepting these minutes as read, raise your hands." Satisfied that no one dissented, he said, "Seeing that most of you came here for the first time because of one special thing, I'll go to that first. Under Old Business, we'll have Calvin, here, repeat the motion he brought up in New Business last meeting, because we didn't have time to discuss it then."

An imposing man stood up. Liz had spotted him among the Council members because of his face looked like rutted leather beneath his large, sweat-stained Stetson hat. His narrowed eyes slowly moved about the room as his voice rose from his barrel-shaped chest. "I made a motion that we clear up that blasted tree of all the disgusting-looking shoes and boots on our new highway."

A scrawny-looking woman sitting next to him raised her hand and in a strained voice, seconded the motion. Someone in the rear booed. Liz turned quickly and got a high sign from Greg, standing with a large group of his friends.

"Now see here!" bellowed Ben, striking his gavel while maintaining a menacing look. "You guys cut that out! I'm determined that this here meeting will be run according to Robert's Rules and Regulations. If you want to stay, you'd best be **quiet**." He banged his gavel for emphasis and turned to the members of the Board. "We'll be open for discussion of the motion now."

Two members raised their hands. Ignoring Joan, the newest Councilman, Ben called upon Calvin.

"We-all spent a heap a money from our state highway funds, and with some help from Uncle Sam, to build that new extension and I'll be hanged before I let that monstrosity of the so-called shoe tree keep that place looking like a garbage dump."

Joan mumbled something under her breath. He gave her a dirty look and said, "I heerd ya say that, and it's what I think. My Mabel had nothing 't do with my arguin' this."

Joan raised her hand again. This time Ben acknowledged her. "We're not supposed to be arguing, Calvin, it's just that I never heard you say anything 'bout it all these months. That tree has many benefits for all of us. Firstly, I've heard lots of people say that they exchanged some of their old worn-out boots and sneakers for better ones that were left there, making it like an inexpensive swap shop. Secondly, that has become a legend hereabouts, so people from far and near are coming this way purposely to see that eighth wonder of the world."

The crowd roared and clapped, obviously looking for any excuse to be a part of the meeting.

Pounding the gavel, Ben shook a finger at the group. When they quieted down, Joan continued. "All this new traffic has been good for our town. Business is better–"

"Not for everyone!" a voice muttered, loud enough to be overheard. "Your restaurant, yeah, but not us cattlemen."

"Hey!" Joan responded, raising one hand for emphasis, "I'm buying more beef and vegetables from the locals; Joe's gas station is busier'n ever; Peggy's boarding house is full, so's our motel. Our neighbor, Sam, opened a souvenir shop where we'd had an empty store for too long. Lots of us are gaining from the tourists."

The little woman who'd seconded the motion stood to gain attention because Ben hadn't looked her way. "The way I sees it," she said, her head bobbing, "some of our young folk are carousing there. We've got to put a stop to all that."

The group laughed. She snapped her mouth tight, looking like a bird shutting its beak.

"Is that so?" asked Ben. "How'd ya know?"

"My niece, Beverly, told me so."

"She's a snitch!" yelled some kid in the rear. "That's 'cause we didn't include her."

Ben held up his hand, to silence the catcalls. "Well, tell us, Minnie, whadaya mean by 'carousing'?"

180

Minnie held her head up high, exposing more of her scrawny neck. "Heaven knows, besides drinkin' beer, but it could lead to much more…"

Someone whistled, making her clamp her mouth shut again.

"Are ya tryin' ta tell us we don't know how ta raise our kids, ya ole windbag?" A male voice yelled.

"You've got your dam nerve, judging everyone that way," a woman screamed. "You don't know what you're talking about!"

"We're not carrying on like that," a young girl said, waving her fist at Minnie.

Several people in the rear of the room got into a shouting match. There were fists flying and young people shoving each other. The noise of chairs falling over amid screams woke up Ben, who had frozen when the fracas began. He banged his gavel to no avail. Like an old schoolteacher had done in school years ago, he walked to the wall and quickly flashed the lights. Miraculously, the room became quiet. He composed himself and said in a soft voice, "This is your last chance. I'll have no more shenanigans or we'll have a closed meeting."

Safe from the melee in the front row, Liz had strained to see the disturbance. Every minute of this became imbedded in her mind. Somehow, she planned to include this in her book. The room was still silent. She raised her hand. Ben hesitated. He wasn't sure if he should open the discussion to the crowd but thought better of it. When Liz stood, someone handed her a microphone. For a moment, she became blinded by a flashbulb. Good, she thought, there's a reporter here from some newspaper.

"I've done quite a bit of research about shoe trees in the country, and this is hardly the only one. You can find all the details and even pictures of them on the Internet, for example, under RoadsideAmerica.com. Indiana has one and Michigan. By the way, there's a story that began there, but it was only shoes that a mass murderer—"

People groaned.

Liz brushed that thought aside. "In Beaver, Kansas, people use magic markers to leave messages. There's two shoe trees right in California; one on Highway 62, in Vidal. The other one, strangely enough, is in the famous Balboa Park, in San Diego."

"You stand to gain by keeping it goin'," yelled a woman on the side of the room. "You can't even vote here, so sit down and mind your own business."

Liz stood her ground. "That's beside the point. I could leave here tomorrow, and still write about the shoe tree right off the top of my head. What I'm trying to say is that this is a wholesome kind of American heritage you're able to perpetuate."

Several people broke into spontaneous applause.

When Ben acknowledged him, a portly gentleman came forward to take the microphone from her. "You-all know me – Hiram Scott – I'm your principal of the high school and I'd like to address Minnie's concerns. I've heard that some of our kids have had a rowdy party there and didn't clean up after themselves, but that's beside the point, the cleaning up, that is. And that's been taken care of, by **them**."

Laughter bubbled.

"It's been brought to our attention that we're not doing right by our kids, who need some place to hang out, doing what Minnie would call, wholesome things."

A titter, here and there.

"The school gym is a right good place that we could utilize without too much cost, if people would volunteer to chaperone and bring some nibbles. We could have game nights, dances, put on community theater, even raise some money for the band. Now, I don't know why we didn't think of all this before, but some good has come out of this resolution, or motion, or whatever you-all call it. I see this as a way of keeping our young folks happy, and keeping the shoe tree right there, accumulating whatever foot-wear we want to do without. I've been there, and left my old baseball shoes, size thirteen, if anyone wants them."

Some people clapped. Ben gave them some time. He looked at each person sitting with him, got their almost imperceptible nods, then stood up and held up both hands to silence the group. When it became quiet, he said, "Well, let's deal with all this, one thing at a time. Does someone up here want to bring the motion to vote?"

A man at the end of the table stood up quickly. "I move we call for a vote on the tree."

Ben said, "Will the secretary read the motion?" He nodded. "All those in favor of eliminating all the paraphernalia from the shoe tree, raise their hands."

Even Calvin, who'd made the motion, sat still.

"All those opposed to changing the shoe tree raise their hands."

After all the Council members voted by raising their hands, everyone in the room raised both their hands, cheering wildly.

"Well," Ben beamed, obviously relieved, "This motion is defeated by a unanimous vote. Without further ado, we'll now move to New Business.'

Minnie lifted both arms to get his attention. "I move that we hand over some money to the high school for some fun goings-on."

Before she sat down, she looked at the back of the room. Most of the young kids were stunned.

Grinning, she added, "And I'll bake some of my famous oatmeal raisin cookies and I'll even be a chaperone."

Whoops and stomping ended the meeting as her motion was seconded.

Chapter 29

That night, startled awake by severe cramps in her calf, Liz massaged her leg while fighting the tears that wouldn't stop flowing. She felt lonely. In the past, whenever she'd had these painful incidents in the middle of the night, Dwayne would knead the constricted muscle, and then force her to walk, leaning on him until the pain diminished. She lay awake for a few hours, trying to sort her ambivalent feelings about listening to Dr. Matthews, the most conservative doctor she'd ever encountered, who felt she'd jeopardize her health and the baby's safety if she didn't stay put. There wasn't even another doctor in the vicinity to verify his diagnosis or give another opinion.

She breathed deeply, as her thoughts sought an alternative answer to the present situation. Then she smiled. Or, why not just get on a plane to fly to New York? How wonderful it would be if Dwayne were there when she delivered. She finally fell asleep, still trying to decide where she wanted to give birth to her baby.

Liz woke up later than usual that morning, tenderly massaging the sore calf, aware that her body ached all over. She stretched in bed for twenty minutes, and breathing deeply lay still, in a gratefulness Yoga position. She had a lot to be thankful for, and almost fell asleep again, concentrating on her talk with God, then sat up to complete the last few minutes of her routine.

Timing what she thought would be the end of the morning breakfast rush, she walked into the restaurant.

"It's about time you got here, sleepy-head," said Joan, pouring a cup of green tea for her. "Wasn't that a super special meeting last night? Thanks for speaking up. I'm sure that helped. By the way, there's a lady near the door who's been asking about you, but Greg and I were too busy to call you. She said she wasn't in any hurry and we knew you'd be here eventually."

Liz thanked her and said she'd come into the kitchen to get her oatmeal with fruit.

"You will not!" Joan ordered. "I'm still the boss here and you just sit there and look grossly pregnant." She walked away as the woman approached Liz.

The thirtyish Oriental woman had a flawless complexion and jet-black hair tied in a long ponytail. She was petite and perky, almost bouncing on the balls of her feet as she walked. "Hi, Liz. I've been waiting for you. May I join you?" Her melodious voice seemed to sing.

"With a large smile, Liz waved her to a chair. "Of course. I'm always happy to have company."

The woman reached out her hand. "I'm Suzie Wong. I've heard all about your book and am planning to stop there this morning, but I wanted to meet with you before I went there."

"This is great! You're going to tell me your story before visiting the tree? I like that."

"Well, let me give you the background and tell you all about my hairy experience when I gave birth a couple of years ago."

Liz winced. She hated those old wives' tales and crazy stories about childbirth. Her stomach lurched at the thought of some scary details. "I don't know," she said hesitating, "I haven't eaten yet."

Suzie grinned. "Would I dare tell you a horror story? And you almost ready to pop? No siree, babe." She leaned back. "I'm from New York, near the Canadian border, and had to relocate to Boston, quite Assante, if you know what I mean." She made a large circle on her belly. "I loved my new OB-GYN, but I lived about an hour's drive from his office, out in the boonies, so to speak. About a month before my due date, my doctor advised me to drive to the hospital after I left his office, to get my bearings and feel comfortable about the place. So, I drove over to it, then took the highway to go home. Of course, babies have a way of arriving much earlier than expected, and at three a.m. only two days later. My husband and I were so excited, and so naïve, that we even stopped to get some coffee on the way. We're cruising along, when I see a sign on the highway for the hospital. We're coming from a different direction than the time I drove home from there, so I figured that we were lucky to find the sign. It turned out that it wasn't the right hospital, not even close. It couldn't be any smaller – converted from an old mansion, way out in no-wheres-ville. My husband, Jimmy, went in to get directions to the correct one, but it became too involved. They called the police in the next town to escort us there. When they arrived, they gave us the high sign to follow them, and sped up the hill. But Jimmy had left the lights on in our old car, so the battery had gone dead. The policemen realized we weren't behind them. They returned, bumped our car to push us until the motor kicked in, then we got off in style with the cruiser's lights flashing, and the sirens blasting."

Liz's eyes shone brightly. "Did you give birth in your car because of all that shaking up? This is really exciting, like a comedy in the movies."

Suzie's motion with her hand meant, be patient, it's my story. "It was a hairy ride on dark, curvy back roads to get to my correct hospital. The staff met me at emergency, then rushed me up to be prepped, telling my husband to sit tight until they called him. Before they could prep me, I certainly fooled them, because my baby decided otherwise and wanted out immediately. Instead, they wheeled me right into delivery, with the doctor rushing down the corridor right behind us, yelling for me to keep my legs together. My baby couldn't wait! He came bouncing out the moment they put me on the table, just like you hear about women years ago, giving birth on the floor or in the fields."

"What an exciting delivery! I'll bet the policemen were happy they didn't have to attend to you on the way there. That always warranted a headliner in the local newspaper. And the doctor had arrived when you did?"

"Right on! The hysterical part of the story is that my O.B. barely made it there to my delivery, because he'd just delivered a baby in that small hospital where we'd originally stopped!"

186

The two women laughed at the preposterous scene. Liz had gotten into the habit of holding her belly when she laughed hard. It had become a new protective move.

"So, you haven't told me the best part—what did you have?"

Grinning proudly as she produced a picture from her handbag, Suzie said, "Twins! One of each!"

"Twins! You never mentioned that!"

"Somehow, despite all the tests, the doctor never confirmed more than one fetus. He had predicted that I'd have a boy; even wrote it on my chart; said he had a 100% record. Well, I figured out how he hood-winked his patients. He probably wrote down the opposite of what he'd said, so he definitely won every bet."

They giggled like old friends.

"I'm thrilled for you, Suzie. Did you name the babies after the policemen who escorted you so dramatically to the hospital with all the bells and whistles, or did you name your daughter 'Serena' after the sirens?"

"Funny, we didn't think of that! She's Amy and he's Adam. As you can see, I carry pictures by the dozen. The babies are a handful and I've been feeling weary for two solid years, but I wouldn't give them up for anything!" She stopped and took a deep breath. "So, the reason that I'm here is that my neighbor is the guy who wrote that fabulous article about your shoe tree."

"That's a coincidence, isn't it?" Liz sighed, "I've gotten most of my story plots from people like you who've read his column. Please thank him again for me. I've kept in touch with him and I'm so grateful for the publicity."

"Yes, of course I will. My purpose in coming here is double – I've brought many of my babies' shoes to hang from the tree, but also…" Suzie stopped to reach into her tote bag. "I've knit some tiny socks for your baby. I wanted to be the first to bring you a gift."

Liz caught her breath. They were the softest, palest green. "They're gorgeous!" She leaned over to kiss Suzie on the cheek.

"Wait! I'm not finished." With a flourish, Suzie presented Liz with a matching hand-knit sweater and hat. Liz hugged all the clothing to her chest and cried. Every customer in the restaurant craned to view the items. They clapped when Liz stood and showed off the gifts. Joan and Greg came out of the kitchen when they heard the applause.

"Yes! They're the very first gift. Thank you! Thank you! The set is gorgeous. My baby will love these. Especially the booties. Booties are the most perfect gift in the world."

Before the luncheon crowd began drifting in, Joan took a break to check up on Liz. She found her talking on her cell phone and signaled that she'd be back, but Liz held up her hand to ask her to wait. In the meantime, Joan unwrapped the gift and examined each piece more carefully.

Liz's eyes shone; her face was flushed and she exuded happiness as she put down her phone.

"These are so delicate, Liz. Just look at the details in the pattern. You'll have to keep bibs on the baby so he won't drool on this masterpiece. Wasn't that woman terrific? She hadn't even met you."

Liz grabbed Joan's hand. "I'm going home!"

Joan staggered back. "What? You can't!"

"I just spoke with Dr. Matthews! He agrees that I'm strong enough to travel. I called the airport and I'm leaving tomorrow morning. Dwayne's beside himself. Said he'd spend the day getting our place ready. He's already painted the baby's room so there's no odor and I…" Liz stopped talking as she realized that Joan was crying.

"Oh, Joannie, you know how much you mean to me, but I want to be with Dwayne when I'm ready to have our baby. Suzie did more than give me a gift. She made me see that I've got to be in my own space, facing childbirth with Dwayne, and my own doctor, in my familiar hospital."

Joan opened her mouth to speak, but words failed her. The shock of the sudden decision and the quick departure the next day became too much for her to handle.

Moving quickly, Liz took her hand. "Joan, I owe you so much—my baby's life, even my own. Sure, I could have stayed at a motel, or a boarding house here, but we only met once, for an hour, and you literally adopted me. I haven't thought about anything else but what a dear, dear person you are in my life. In our lives, Dwayne and the baby too. Do you think I'm walking out of here the same as I was six weeks ago? Do you honestly think that's the end of our relationship?"

Numb, choked up, Joan couldn't respond. She simply hunched her shoulders a bit, as if they were twitching involuntarily. They sat down on the edge of the bed.

After a minute, Liz said, "I wish you were free to come open a place like this in New York. Wouldn't that be terrific?"

Joan had to giggle. "Oh, sure, just like that? And those sophisticated people in the Big Apple with all the gourmet chefs and world- class eateries abounding would just drop everything and come to knock down my doors. Fat chance! My life is here, and we both know that."

"I know. Just wishing, like Jiminy Cricket. I need that fairy to come to help make all things beautiful."

"Did you hoodwink Doc? Were you really honest or did you do some jivey-fast-talking rap to talk him into doing what you want? Are you sure this is the best thing for your baby?"

Liz winked, making her tears fall more quickly. "You caught me! Nope, everything's on the square; we talked about all the possibilities and he's given me his blessings. I hope my doctor there will be half as smart as our Dr. Matthews."

Liz stopped talking for a moment. "Oh! I didn't tell you Dwayne's great news today. He found a position with an outstanding architectural firm. Isn't that wonderful! What timing."

"That is good news!" Joan hugged Liz, tears streaming freely. "I'd planned to be with you here, had been studying all about the Lamaze…"

"I know! You've been too wonderful for me to ever know how to thank you, but–"

"But you belong with Dwayne and I'll just have to take off sometime soon to visit you in New York. Haven't been there yet, and it's about time I took a vacation."

Liz sobbed as she said, "You better!"

Chapter 30

That evening, with her suitcases all packed for her flight to New York, Liz had trouble falling asleep. She and Joan had talked for a couple of hours while Joan helped her pack the last carry-on. It was bittersweet when they hugged goodnight; their last night together for a while. Liz was so excited about her reunion with Dwayne that she lay there just staring at the clock.

Oh, well, she thought, when she realized that she'd been awake for an hour. I'll have plenty of time to sleep on the plane. I'll call him when I change my flight in Vegas to confirm my arrival time there, although he'd know enough to check before going to the airport.

She got up and checked the itinerary that she'd printed from her computer. She was talking out loud, as if there were another person in the room with her. "There's not a lot of time in between flights. Maybe I'll ask for a wheelchair so that I'm not running from one terminal to another in Vegas. Of course, if there isn't going to be any delay, I could take my time to walk it. No! A wheelchair is the better way to go. I'd better arrange that now."

As she began to open the internet to bring up the airline, Liz felt some sharp pains. She grabbed her stomach and felt the baby kicking more than usual. Oh, well, she thought, I'll have time to do this in the morning.

She lay down and holding her hand on her belly, closed her eyes and fell asleep.

Jolted awake by the shrill ringing, Dwayne reached for his telephone. The clock illuminated the time–3:15 am. He struggled to clear his throat, his heart pounding in a staccato rhythm. "Hello. Who is this?"

190

"It's Joan. Liz—"

"Is she all right? It's 12:15 there! Isn't Liz flying into JFK this afternoon?"

"Don't panic, Dwayne. Liz is fine but the baby wants out! We're leaving for the hospital now. You'd better get on the next plane."

"Wait! Don't hang up! Let me talk with her."

"She can't right now, and I've gotta go. Let me know when to pick you up at the airport."

"Tell her I love her—" The line went dead.

Dr. Matthews had just pulled out of his driveway when Joan's jalopy careened around the corner. She patted Liz's arm. "He's on his way, Liz. Try to take slow, deep breaths, O.K.?"

Liz nodded as she tried to stifle a moan. She'd never experienced such intense pain which emanated from every part of her body. They took her breath away. The searing jabs had pulled her out of a sound sleep. She called Dr. Matthews, but when he asked her to describe her symptoms, she could hardly speak. She managed to yell for Joan as she grabbed her bathrobe and slippers. They were out the door within minutes.

Dwayne called the airline. The next flight was at 5:00 am. He quickly dressed, packed a bag, and high-tailed it out of the apartment. Even at that hour, traffic seemed heavy. He remembered the trite expression, 'New York never sleeps.' Crisscrossing highways, he deftly maneuvered between heavy trucks and almost missed his exit. In the long-term parking lot, he had to circle around before finding a space, then barely caught the jitney to the terminal. Long lines made him worry that he'd miss the flight. His nerves were frazzled. He sweated profusely.

Praying didn't come easily to Dwayne, but he reverted to the frenzied words he'd uttered when facing rounds of mortar in the war. *We were so scared that all of us almost crapped our pants daily. I have that same dreadful feeling right now.* His lips moved in his silent message as he gazed upwards.

191

"Are you all right?" a man standing near him asked. "You look like you're gonna faint."

Dazed, Dwayne realized he hadn't kept up in line. He thanked the stranger. "Yeah, I'm O.K. My wife's having a baby and I…" He stopped talking as he thought, Am I spilling out my guts to a total stranger? Shaking his head like a puppy leaving the water, and squaring his shoulders helped him stand straighter.

After he paid for his ticket, an exorbitant price that almost made him choke, the next barrier awaited him–the long snaking maze for the baggage and body scans. He kept checking his watch, wondering if he might miss his flight. But suddenly, they opened another lane, and he breathed a deep, shuddering sigh of relief.

Luckily, they weren't boarding at his gate yet. He had a moment to catch his breath. He dialed Joan's cell phone, praying that she'd give him good news, but she didn't pick up. He left a frantic message, telling her which flight he was taking, begging her to give him some news about Liz before he boarded. This was going to be an unbearable morning, with a stopover in Las Vegas for an hour. He bought a large black coffee and spilled some of it when he sat down.

"Oh, fuck," he said aloud.

"I know what you mean, man," someone near him said, but he didn't respond as he tried to wipe it up.

In the next few minute, he checked his cell phone several times, thankful that the battery registered full.

His mind whirled like the rotors of a helicopter. *Why doesn't Joan call? I hope Liz is all right. It isn't time – six weeks is too early. Maybe the accident…* He wiped his tears. *I hope the baby's O.K. Please, God take care of them both.*

When the orderlies swept Liz away in the wheelchair, barely letting Joan kiss her cheek and wish her well, Dr. Matthews promised to let Joan stay with Liz after she was prepped. Without looking around the waiting room, Joan plopped down on a chair, closed her eyes, and concentrated on sending positive vibes to Liz. She looked as if she were sleeping when her cell phone began to vibrate in her pocketbook. A woman sitting near her hesitated about waking her and decided to let her sleep.

After meditating for several minutes, Joan opened her eyes, and looked around, surprised to see how many people there were in the waiting room in the middle of the night. The woman sitting opposite her smiled and said, "Lady, your bag moved a while ago. Either you've got a mouse in there, or your cell phone went crazy."

Joan jumped. "How stupid of me!" she said, nodding to the woman. "Dwayne must be trying to reach me." She saw a voice mail icon and listened to his message. He had called before leaving his apartment, promising to call again from the airport. She looked at her watch. Nope, she thought, he couldn't have gotten there yet, but I'll change my phone to a soft ring, then I'll hear when he calls again.

Impatient, Joan got up to find some coffee. The cafeteria hadn't opened yet in this small local hospital, but she found some coffee in the surgical waiting room at the end of the hallway. It must have been sitting there on the warmer for at least eight hours, she thought. *This is what they mean when people say it'll put hair on your chest.* But as acrid as it tasted, even with lots of sweetener, it was better than nothing.

She walked back to the emergency sitting room, anticipating good news from Dr. Matthews. She found a chair in a quiet corner, far away from inconsiderate loud conversations.

A nurse came running into the room, looking relieved when she spotted Joan. They were good friends. Joan's face drained of color as Pamela took her hand. "She's going to be fine. Dr. Matthews says she's going through premature labor, and she's in such pain, that he's giving her a caudle – you know, a spinal block. We're taking her to the delivery room, so why don't you go to that waiting room where you'll be more comfortable. I'll keep you–"

"Promise? You know what she means to me."

"Of course. Don't worry about her–she's a trouper. She has a positive attitude. The only thing is–"

"What?"

"She keeps saying she wants to wait for Dwayne."

"That's pretty stupid! Tell her to get the damns thing over with and I'll be there when she wants me."

Joan walked down the corridor, which seemed longer this time. Once in the waiting room, she couldn't get comfortable, but was relieved to be there alone. Unable to focus on the television screen, she tried to read one of the ubiquitous, outdated magazines, but wasn't able to concentrate. Finally, she sprawled across a couch and closed her eyes.

Within a moment, her cell phone rang, almost making her levitate. She brought Dwayne up to date. She repeated his flight number and his time of arrival in Vegas as she copied it on a slip of scrap paper. "Yes, call me when you get to Vegas and tell me about your connecting flight, so I can pick you up. I'm sure I'll have good news for you then."

She collapsed into tears. "I hope I do."

Pamela opened the door. "They're going to do a Caesarian Section because we're afraid of losing the baby. His heartbeat is too weak. Another surgeon's going to assist Dr. Matthews. Liz is O.K. We'll let you know as soon as we can."

Chapter 31

The plane shook in sudden violent waves, throwing drinks and food onto the passengers' laps. The intercom squawked for a moment and bleeped. "This is Captain Tremont. We're encountering heavy winds, so all passengers must return to their seats. Fasten your seat belts for the remainder of the flight."

In a pensive mood, Dwayne had been staring out the window at the dark clouds surrounding them. He blinked at the sudden lightning strikes in the distance, realizing that several were coming closer to the plane.

Yeah, he thought, that's all I need right now to add to my other problems. Isn't it funny how the weather reflects my mood? Or is it vise-versa? Am I down because I'm worried about Liz? Yes, actually. He closed his eyes. *No, I'm going to admit it. I'm also scared because of this storm. I've read about accidents involving wind shear, when a plane drops to earth on its belly from the strong force of downward winds.* He realized his knuckles were white from gripping the armrests so tightly. He'd always hated flying. Even as a kid, when his father called him a wuss because he threw up from air sickness. Whoa, he derided himself, *stop thinking about all your negative experiences with your old man. You've come a long way from those early years of self-doubt and self-recrimination about taking all his shit. You couldn't stomach the farm and you hated working with him in the store, where nothing you did ever pleased him. Years of therapy have paid off. You're beyond being jerked around by him. It's good that we spent that month with my folks and got things cleared up. I'm glad we left on such a good note and I know they'll come to see us now that he's retiring.*

The plane rolled. The turbulence made Dwayne's stomach flip-flop. The pilot attempted to maneuver above the storm. Dwayne checked the pocket in front of his seat for the barf bag. Waves of nausea made him feel as if he were in a tailspin. He took deep breaths, forcing himself not to panic. He began to hyperventilate. After a few moments, he remembered the routine. He opened the bag, inhaling large gulps of air, then exhaled back into it, trying not to throw up.

That helped. He shook his head, forcing himself to focus on Liz. *Think about how much you love her and want her to come through this safe and strong. Think about your baby being born, maybe at this very minute. Think that your baby will be healthy. Think about all the things you'll do to keep that child happy, no matter what sex it is. Think about getting that great job you interviewed for yesterday...*

"We'll be landing in Las Vegas in twenty minutes," the captain announced, jolting Dwayne out of a nap filled with strange dreams. He felt lucky that he couldn't recall them.

The plane was flying steady. Dwayne felt confident that he'd be able to walk to the lav without feeling queasy. He made it! Once there, he washed his face and combed his hair. He ran cold water over his wrists to cool down his temperature and his nerves.

Ah! He had anticipated the bump of the safe landing. He realized how lucky he was that he'll make the next flight without a problem. *My plane is leaving on time and Joan will be there to pick me up. She'll have great news for me. I can't wait to see Liz and the baby. Please, please,* he said, raising his eyes, *make everything in our lives good.*

Within a minute of the plane touching down, Dwayne turned on his cell phone. Yes! There was a message from Joan. His eyes opened wide while he listened to her wonderful news. Liz is good. He closed his eyes for a moment. "Thank You," he whispered.

"Hey," he yelled to the passengers, "I'm a daddy! His name is Jonas!"

Strangers nearby cheered and congratulated him. The man next to him, with whom he'd only spoken a few words in the trip, clapped him on his shoulder.

Joan ran to him with her arms outstretched.

"Tell me everything you know," he pleaded as they left the airport. "Don't leave anything out."

"Liz came through this like a trouper. You'll probably have to wait to see her because she might still be in Recovery," she said. "But what I didn't tell you is that they almost lost the baby because the umbilical cord wrapped around his neck. When they momentarily lost his heart beat, they performed a Caesarian, but he's great. A little small, only four pounds, so he'll be in the neonatal section. We can go see him right away."

Dwayne stood there, crying. He couldn't speak. Joan waited until he composed himself, then they hurried out to the parking lot. She insisted on driving. "It's my car, and I'm the designated driver. Here, I brought you a drink and a turkey breast sandwich from the cafeteria, so you relax and eat whenever you want."

Exhausted and grateful, he wolfed it down.

"Let's see," Joan said, "Liz has probably told you everything that's been going on right along, but–" She sneaked a peak at Dwayne and smiled. He was sound asleep.

Chapter 32

Dr. Matthews had just entered the hallway on the maternity floor when Dwayne and Joan left the elevator. "Congratulations, Dwayne," he said, pumping Dwayne's hand with a firm grip. "You've got a boy! But I'm sure Joan, here, already told you that!"

Dwayne hugged him. "Thanks for taking care of Liz, Dr. Matthews. How is she?"

"I've just left her a short while ago. She's being monitored in Recovery, and she's still very groggy. I had to operate on her to save the baby. It's more invasive surgery than a normal delivery. That means her recuperation will take weeks longer. She's going to be mad at me."

"She'll do whatever you say." Dwayne patted his shoulder. "The most important thing is that she and the baby are both O.K. And if she gives you a hard time, just call me. Hey, did she tell you that his name is Jonas? Sounds like Joan, his Godmother, don't you agree?"

Joan gasped. "In my wildest dreams! Oh, I'm thrilled!" She hugged and kissed both men.

"That's terrific, Joan. I couldn't be happier for all four of you. Well, I'm on my way out. I know you can't wait to see your son. He's in the neonatal unit down the hallway, to the left. You might as well go there first."

"When will we be able to see Liz?" Dwayne asked.

"I'd wait another hour if I were you because she wouldn't even remember you were here. It'll be best if you wait 'til they take her to her room."

When Dwayne and Joan knocked on the locked door of the neonatal area, a nurse took them to a small receptacle where they put on paper wraps, hats, masks and booties. The few babies they saw in small plastic baskets were scrawny, attached to all kinds of tubes. It broke their hearts. The nurse guided them towards a baby lying in a blue blanket, wearing a blue hat and crying with gusto. He also had tubes attached to monitors.

Dwayne stared in awe. "Isn't he something? So tiny. I can't tell who he looks like. He's all mouth, but he's got a strong pair of lungs." He looked at the nurse. "May I touch him?"

"Of course," she said with a broad grin. "Here, he wants to be held."

"Welcome, my little Jonas. We're going to have such a wonderful life together, I promise you." The moment Jonas heard his father's voice and felt his love, he stopped crying and seemed to search Dwayne's face with large eyes. He stopped pumping his scrawny feet.

"Don't they look as thin as spider's legs?" Dwayne whispered as he uncovered them for a moment. When the baby's wrinkled tiny hand circled one of Dwayne's fingers, tears splashed down his face into his mask. He finally said, "Jonas has Liz's eyes, but I think he's got my chin."

As the nurse walked away to tend to another baby, Joan said, "You look so natural there, Daddy."

"Betcha he weighs less than my jacket. I'm afraid I'll hurt him."

Joan laughed. "Naw, you're great. Look. He fell asleep. He knows who you are."

"I'm glad he looks a little larger than those preemies. Poor babies, I hope they improve rapidly. They look like chickens." Dwayne lightly moved his index finger across Jonas's cheek. His nail moved the tiny hat. "See that? He even has some fuzzy blond hair."

"Yep. And I counted the right amount of fingers and toes. He's a good size, compared to the others in here. He'll come home when he weighs in at five pounds."

"Maybe that's best – it'll give Liz a chance to gain her strength." He shook his head. "That is, if we're able to talk her out of running here to see him every day once she gets home."

"Do you think I'd let her? I'm gonna hide the keys to my car." Joan whipped out her cell phone. "Quick! Let me take a picture of you and Jonas, my namesake, so's I can show Liz when she wakes up."

Dwayne looked at his baby with pride. "I'm glad you thought of that, Joan." He gulped. "I don't know what would have happened to us if you hadn't taken us in. Whatever thanks I've given you doesn't even touch–"

"Hey! None of that! And under that mask, you have to smile for the camera." She took several pictures. "Please stop thanking me for doing something that's made my life so damned wonderful these past two months. You've both gotten into my heart, more'n I ever dreamed. So," she wiped away some tears, "stop making me blubber like a jack-ass."

"I'll do more than that," Dwayne said, standing to put Jonas into her arms while taking her cell phone. "Now, sit comfortably and smile like you mean it."

Although her mouth was covered with the mask, Joan's eyes shone so brightly that the pictures showed how thrilled she felt.

A short while later, Dwayne hugged Liz. Overcome with emotion they clung to each other, unable to speak, as if they'd been separated for years. After a few moments, she assured him that she was fine. They talked about her surgery and their hopes for Jonas' future. He told her about his new position and outlined his upcoming project. When she fell asleep, he went looking for Joan and found her dozing in the waiting room. He sent her home to rest before her customers arrived.

Returning to Liz, he was thrilled to find her awake. He scooped her up and settled her in a wheelchair. "C'mon, I can't wait to show you our son." As he carefully picked him up to hand him to Liz, Dwayne spoke softly. "Hey, Jonas, Welcome into our wonderful family. I wish you a beautiful life filled with great dreams that come true. I'm thrilled to share my fabulous wife with you. I know you'll adore her as much as I do. She's going to be famous; she has simultaneously given birth to her first child and to her first novel."

The following is a list of real shoe trees across the United States, courtesy of **RoadsideAmerica.com**:

Shoe Trees

- Shoe Tree: Cherokee, Alabama

- Sardis Shoe Tree: Sardis, Arkansas

- Sardis Shoe Tree No. 2: Sardis, Arkansas

- Bra Tree: Flagstaff, Arizona

- Shoe Tree: Sunflower, Arizona

- Shoe Tree: Tonto Basin, Arizona

- Shoe Tree Unloved by the Elderly: Big Bear Lake, California

- Underwear Tree: Blythe, California

- Shoe Tree: Hallelujah Junction, California

- Shoe Tree: Long Barn, California

- Ono Shoe Tree: Ono, California

- Shoe Tree: Ravendale, California

- Shoe Tree: St. Simons Island, Georgia

- Hawaiian Shoe Tree: Flip Flops: Honaunau-Napoopoo, Big Island, Hawaii

- Shoe Tree - Only 3 pairs: Kuna, Idaho
- Shoe Tree: Highland Park, Illinois
- Shoe Tree: Ottawa, Illinois
- Shoe Tree: Woodstock, Illinois
- Shoe Tree: Albany, Indiana
- Shoe Tree: Milltown, Indiana
- Shoe Tree: Troy, Indiana
- Shoe Tree: Murray, Kentucky
- Shoe Tree: Atlanta, Michigan
- Shoe Tree - Cursed!: Belding, Michigan
- Shoe Trees: Comins, Michigan
- Shoe Tree: Kalkaska, Michigan
- Shoe Tree: Salem, Michigan
- Shoe Tree: Strongs, Michigan
- Urban Shoe Tree: Minneapolis, Minnesota
- Shoe Tree, High Heel Variant: Albuquerque, New Mexico
- Shoe Tree: Beatty, Nevada
- Shoe Tree: Virginia City, Nevada
- Sneaker Tree - Shoe Trees: Lyndonville, New York
- Shoe Tree: Bainbridge, Ohio
- Shoe Tree in a Cemetery: Cleveland, Ohio

- Shoe Tree: Worthington, Ohio

- Route 66 Shoe Tree: Stroud, Oklahoma

- Shoe Tree: Alfalfa, Oregon

- Shoe Tree in a Lovely Park: Beaverton, Oregon

- Shoe Tree: Bend, Oregon

- Shoe Tree Formerly in Redmond: Bend, Oregon

- Shoe Tree: Juntura, Oregon

- Shoe Tree: Mitchell, Oregon

- Shoe Tree: Tumalo, Oregon

- Dot's Mini Museum - Cowboy Boot Tree: Vega, Texas

- Shoe Tree: Emery County, Utah

- Shoe Tree: Hinckley, Utah

- Shoe Trees: Park City, Utah

- Shoe Tree: Green Bay, Wisconsin

- Shoe Tree Junior: Sundance, Wyoming

Acknowledgements

I wouldn't have persevered and published this novel if my daughter Sharon Sklar hadn't always encouraged me and actively edited my writing.

I am grateful to my editor, Martha Moffett who recognized the unique quality of my subject.

Thanks, Barbara Weitzner, and Leila Alson for your timely comments and corrections.

I am indebted to Kristina Miranda for her invaluable aid.

Thanks to my tough critique groups – I still hear their voices in my head.

Many thanks to my relatives and friends who have supported me in my endeavors.

Thank you, Bernard Baskin, for your two magnificent poems.

About the Author

Doris Oberstein is the author of the novel, *Riptide,* and is a member of WNBA, the *Women's National Book Association,* and SCBWI, the *Society of Children's Book Writers and Illustrators.* She has written three novels and two plays. Doris taught elementary education for twenty-six years while earning two Masters of Education degrees and training student teachers for four universities in Connecticut. She was listed in the 1975 edition of *Outstanding Elementary Teachers of America.*

As a retiree, Doris became an adjunct professor for the University of Nevada Las Vegas College of Education and also facilitated literature for EXCELL, the Learning in Retirement Group in the UNLV College of Continuing Education.

Currently, Doris gives fascinating lectures on Greek Mythology and is completing a book for Young Adults: *Amusing Tales in Greek Mythology.* What does she do in her spare time? A 'high-end' octogenarian, she plays tennis and bridge.

You can contact Doris at dodiewrites@att.net.

Made in the USA
Middletown, DE
03 January 2019